"I DON'T UNDERSTAND,"
SHE PLEADED,
TRYING TO MOVE CLOSER . . .

"I know you don't," he said. "That's why one of us has to act grown up. I ain't the sort of man you're looking for, Captain."

"Don't you think I'd be the best judge of that, Longarm?"

"Nope. You're packing too many stars in your eyes, honey. I *like* you, Captain Gloria Grimes. You got guts and brains and life's already stomped your pretty toes enough. I could promise you the moon, but Permanent is one thing I don't carry in my possibles bag."

He thought he had it settled, so he let go of her shoulders. She wrapped her arms around his neck and kissed him full on the mouth . . .

Also in the **LONGARM** series
from Jove

TABOR EVANS

LONGARM

ON THE BIG MUDDY

A JOVE BOOK

First Jove edition published February 1981

10 9 8 7 6 5 4 3 2 1

Printed in the United States of America

Jove books are published by Jove Publications, Inc., 200
Madison Avenue, New York, NY 10016

Chapter 1

It was early in the morning on the Fourth of July when Longarm saved the orphans from Vice-President Schuyler Colfax of these United States.

Old Schuyler wasn't really the vice-president anymore, and he had no way of knowing a streetcar full of orphans was on its way to a picnic in Cheeseman Park that morning. But while he'd been in office he'd managed to get one of Denver's main thoroughfares named after himself, and that was where the trouble started.

Colfax Avenue ran east and west, and because Schuyler Colfax had been the most crooked vice-president in U.S. history, his admirers in Denver had tried to make up for it by laying out the avenue they named after him as straight as possible. So when it got to the steepest hill in Denver, Colfax Avenue just went straight up the slope and to hell with the horses. Denver didn't have cable cars like San Francisco; when the horsedrawn streetcars came to Capitol Hill, they just had to do their best. When they were headed east with a heavy load, the passengers got out and walked up the long grade. On the way west, everybody just hung on and prayed that the brakes would hold.

Longarm wasn't thinking about any of this as he turned the corner of Lincoln and Colfax to walk downhill that morning. He was too close to the office to ride a streetcar and too mad at his boss, Billy Vail, to consider the past crimes of higher public officials. Here it was, a public holiday, and because the infernal U.S.

Marshal he worked for had decreed that the office would be open until noon, he'd had to leave the bed of a friendly schoolmarm who had the whole damned summer off.

Longarm legged it down Colfax slow and moody, looking for something to kick. It was shady under the cottonwood trees along the high red sandstone walk, but it was shaping up to be a hot day, and it was already too damned noisy. Folks in Denver didn't shirk the celebration of the Glorious Fourth; they'd been shooting off firecrackers and worse since about the middle of June. As he headed down toward the Federal Building, it sounded sort of like he was marching to Shiloh again. The small stuff crackled like small arms all around, and every few minutes some idiot lit a quarter-stick of dynamite that rattled windows for blocks. Folks were still talking about that cowhand who'd blown his head off the other night in front of the Silver Dollar. So, as Longarm approached the corner of Colfax and Broadway at the bottom of the slope, he didn't pay any mind to the flurry of minor explosions out of sight around the corner.

At the same time, a streetcar filled with kids passed him going the other way. He wouldn't have paid that any mind either, had not some little son of a bitch thrown a well-aimed torpedo at him.

Longarm cursed and sidestepped as the torpedo went off right where he'd been about to put his booted foot. He turned to glower at the kids on the streetcar as one of the little bastards threw another tiny bomb at the only handy target and a sweet little girl stuck her tongue out at him. He figured it was likely against the law to shoot back at them. The twin blasts had spooked the team of dapple grays pulling the streetcar, so it moved up the slope too fast for them to toss anything else his way. He grimaced and turned away to resume his lackluster stroll to the office. At that moment a trio of men wearing trail riders' outfits tore around the corner, running like hell. Longarm frowned but got out of their

6

way as he saw that they seemed to be chasing the streetcar. After he had taken a few more steps, a man in the blue uniform of the Denver Police Department staggered around the corner, a billy club in one hand and a revolver in the other. Longarm just had time to notice that the blue uniform was glistening darkly all down one side when a shot rang out from behind him and the copper went down with a bullet in the chest.

Longarm crabbed sideways as he drew his own double-action .44 and got a cottonwood trunk between himself and the streetcar the three men had boarded on the fly. He knew he'd made the right move when a bullet thudded into the far side of the tree at the level of his own heart.

He risked a quick peek around the trunk, saw that he couldn't fire at the cloud of gunsmoke hanging between him and a streetcar filled with kids, and pulled his face back just as another round spanged into the trunk to tear a divot of bark out and scream its way off in the general direction of the Rocky Mountains. He glanced at the gunned-down policeman and saw that trying to aid him would be pointless as well as suicidal. Either the copper was dead or he liked staring up at the sun with his eyes wide open.

Longarm saw that there were buildings to his left and the open grounds of the terraced state house park to his right. On the far side of the Capitol grounds he spotted some other blue uniforms running up the hill to try and head the streetcar off on the far side. Longarm performed some swift eyeball calculation and decided they were just going to miss their connection. The outlaws had obviously commandeered the streetcar, and once they made the top of the slope, they'd be able to whip the team into a run.

Two more coppers came around the corner. One ran to the fallen man. The other pointed his revolver thoughtfully at Longarm, who yelled, "Hold your fire! I'm a U.S. marshal!"

He saw that the cop who was bending over the dead

7

man was still alive, so he figured the streetcar had to be beyond pistol range by now. He shot a look up the slope, saw that he was right, and asked the copper who joined him behind the tree what in thunder was going on, besides the obvious.

"Telegraph office robbery, around the corner on Broadway," the Denver lawman informed him, adding disgustedly, "Damn small potatoes to kill a man over."

"I'll say," Longarm replied. "But, Jesus Christ, how do they figure to escape by streetcar?"

"Oh, they had horses," the cop said, "but some kid with a Roman candle spooked 'em while those jaspers was inside the telegraph office. We've been having a right interesting running fight, up to now. The goddamned fireworks going off all around sort of complicates things. Most times, when folks hear gunfire they get out of the way, but—"

"Say no more, I get the picture. Cover me while I catch a streetcar, will you?"

"You're crazy! I can't fire into all them passengers!"

"Aim high, damn it!" Longarm growled as, not waiting for an answer, he broke cover. The angle of the curbside trees concealed him for the first few yards. He knew, as he tore back up the slope the way he'd just come, that if he couldn't see the ass end of the streetcar, those on board couldn't see him, so he ran as fast as he was able in his low-heeled cavalry boots. The team drawing the heavy load up the hill couldn't move nearly as fast, so he started to gain. As he closed the gap, the end of the car began to appear on and off between the stout tree trunks, and some rascal began to toss lead at him as he dashed from tree to tree. The copper down the slope was sending fire over the arched roof of the streetcar, and that helped throw the gunman's aim off. The kids screaming all around him might have made the shooter nervous, too. Longarm would have started tossing kids off about now, had he been in the other's shoes, but this son of a bitch knew no decent cuss was about to fire at a target surrounded by kids.

As he broke cover, Longarm saw that the roughly dressed outlaw had picked up a little girl and was shielding his worthless hide behind her ribbons and bows as he took turns winging shots at the policemen down the slope and as much as Longarm as he could see.

Longarm dashed across the walk to the front steps of a brownstone as he saw that it was a standoff for the moment. He didn't dare move in closer. He gauged the range and made it to another tree, farther up, as the gunman missed him again. They were almost to the top of the slope. Capitol Hill wasn't a true hill; it was the edge of a flat-topped mesa that ran way the hell east beyond the city limits. Any minute he could expect the commandeered streetcar to take off at a greater speed than any man on foot could manage. It was annoying as hell, but Longarm was stuck for a better play, even though he knew he wasn't getting anywhere with this one.

Then the outlaws made a series of stupid moves.

The first one was that the man on the rear platform dropped the little girl and elbowed his way deeper into the crowd of passengers. Longarm ran like hell, ignoring the stitch in his side as he gained on the streetcar, grabbed the rear guardrail with his free hand, and got both feet on the car's sloping rear bumper. As he started to haul himself up and over, the heavy car came to a halt, paused for the space of a deep breath, and started rolling back down the hill.

Longarm cursed, holstered his .44, and grabbed for the brake crank at his end of the car. He'd watched them work these things up and down the hill often enough to know that one crewman walked behind the car on the downslope, braking the wheels with this son-of-a-bitch crank, which usually seemed to work when the brakeman did it, but wasn't doing a thing for Longarm.

But then the car began to slow down a mite, as the handle got painfully hot in his palm and the brakes squealed like a sow having a litter of broken beer bottles. But while it might have run away faster without him on the brake, it was still headed down Colfax a hell of a lot faster than the Good Lord—and the turn at the bottom—had ever intended!

A red-headed kid stuck his head over the edge to yell, "Those rascals shot the driver and unhitched the team! They've lit out bareback!"

There wasn't a damned thing Longarm could do about it, as far as he could see.

Then, as they screamed across Lincoln and started down the steeper slope beyond, he saw that there was. The improvising outlaws had apparently run into other lawmen to the east. The three of them were tear-assing off across the terraced lawn of the state house. Two men were aboard one draft horse and the other was on the one remaining. Both brutes were still harnessed together and making for a little trouble for the riders.

It wasn't too clear where the outlaws wanted to go, if they'd planned that far ahead. The erstwhile street-car horses were running downhill, almost parallel to the runaway car. Longarm could see that his attempts with the brake had done some good; the runaway team was gaining. So he let go of the hot and likely useless brake handle, drew his gun again, and started firing.

He aimed at the rear horse, of course, but his round carried a trifle high and knocked the rider on the off-horse from his mount. This seemed to discourage the two who were left. They rolled off, and after they'd slid and tumbled a spell in the grass, Longarm saw that they were rising with their hands up, and that the two coppers he'd left at the bottom of the slope were moving in to take them.

By this time the streetcar had almost made the bottom of the hill, and it was still moving far too fast. As it approached the intersection of Colfax and Broadway, Longarm hauled himself up into the car and yelled, "Everybody *down*!" as he dropped behind the bulkhead.

Nobody paid him much mind. They were all screaming and staring wide-eyed as the streetcar slammed into
the big brewery wagon that Longarm had seen they
were going to hit.

The runaway streetcar came to a halt, still upright
on the tracks, as the brewery wagon absorbed its mo-
mentum with a horrendous wet explosion that sent suds
and barrel staves four stories high and a half-block in
every direction!

Longarm peered gingerly over the edge of the platform, beer running off the brim of his Stetson and
everything else in sight, to see that the brewery teamster
was war-dancing in the middle of a very sudsy street
while his Percherons loped off toward Wyoming.

Longarm turned to see if any other passengers were
still alive. The noisy kids had been stunned to mo-
mentary silence, and it was hard to tell the girls from
the boys, with everyone covered with foam.

The commotion had attracted folks from near and
far. A man in business dress and a derby ran over to the
outraged brewery driver, slipped in the suds, grabbed
the already soaked driver, and they went down together, cussing fit to bust. Longarm saw more police
coming from the direction of City Hall, across Broadway. They were smart enough to circle wide of the
beer slick as they headed his way. Longarm rose and
made his way forward through the kids to where two
beer-soaked women knelt over a foam- and blood-
covered man lying in the suds between the seats. Longarm's pants were already soaked through, so he
dropped to one knee and placed a wet hand against the
streetcar driver's wet throat. "I'm alive, damn your
eyes," the man said. "Where the hell is Wabash?"

"Don't know. Where are you hit, and who's Wabash?"

"I'm creased under the floating ribs, but I don't
suspicion I'm hulled. Bullet knocked all the wind outta
me and I felt like I was dead for a spell, but it's starting

to smart, so I'm likely going to get up mad as hell in a minute. Wabash is supposed to be my brakeman."

Longarm looked around. The suds were sort of thick in places, but he didn't see enough foam anywhere to cover a body. The kid who'd been tossing torpedoes at innocent pedestrians chimed in, "I saw a man in street-car duds jump off and run like hell when them jaspers come aboard with guns."

One of the two women said, "Roscoe, you mustn't use such language!"

Longarm looked at her. She and the fatter gal with her were wearing outfits like the Harvey Girls who served vittles for the Atchison, Topeka & Santa Fe, but he doubted that they were waitresses. The woman who'd corrected Roscoe sighed through the foam on her face and explained, "Roscoe and these other children are from the Arvada Orphan Asylum. This is Miss Hewitt, and I am Morgana Floyd."

The fat one said, "I don't know how we'll ever be able to thank you for saving us, sir."

"Just doing my job, ma'am. My handle is Custis Long and I'm a deputy U.S. Marshal."

"Hot damn!" Roscoe said, awestruck. "You're the one they call Longarm! I seen you on Larimer Street the other day, talkin' to one of them fancy ladies from the Silver Dollar!"

Morgana Floyd gasped and said, "Roscoe! I've a good mind to wash your sassy mouth out with soap and water!"

"I'd start by taking away his fireworks before they dry out again, ma'am," Longarm interjected. "He's already foamed up enough."

The fat gal laughed, but Morgana moaned, "Oh, Lord, we are all messed up. What on earth *is* this foamy goo?"

Longarm frowned as he inhaled more malt and hops, but she seemed serious. As the bubbles began to burst, he could see that she was a right pretty little thing, and the soaking-wet, black bodice of her matron's uniform promised some fortunate man in the future a mighty nice honeymoon. He doubted that there was any other way to undress a grown-up woman who didn't know what beer smelled like. He smiled at her as charmingly as he could. "We hit a brewery wagon, ma'am. I'd say it was mostly lager with a little ale."

"Oh, no, we *can't* be drenched with Demon Rum!"

"No, ma'am, it's only beer, and as you can see, it's going flat and drying fast. It's a warm day and we're a mile above sea level, so—"

"Oh, heavens," Morgana Floyd cut in, "we're going to have to take these children back to the orphanage and get them out of these ruined clothes."

"Aw, hell, what about our picnic?" Roscoe pouted.

Miss Hewitt turned to Morgana and said, "I'm sure we'll be dried out long before we can get all the way back across town, dear heart."

"There you go, ladies," Longarm laughed. "It don't matter whether you head home or go on to the picnic grounds. You'll all be dried out in about an hour anyway." Then, frowning fiercely, he told the recalcitrant Roscoe, "Empty your pockets, outlaw. I'm disarming you in the name of the law."

"Aw, shoot," the kid protested, "I've only got one torpedo and some durned old ladyfingers."

Longarm relented slightly. "Well, I'll let you keep the ladyfingers if you promise to shoot 'em off after you get to the park. But I'm going to have to take that torpedo off you. Those things are dangerous even when a kid has sense."

Grudgingly, Roscoe handed over the almost dry torpedo as a copper came aboard to investigate the situation. Longarm identified himself and asked the cop to get a doctor for the wounded man.

The policeman smiled. "I might've known that was you under all them suds, Longarm. Mighty fancy shooting you just did. I'd have aimed for one of the horses, but I must say you took all the fight out of them

13

robbers when they saw you could nail a man in the ear at that range."

Longarm shrugged modestly. He saw no need to correct a fellow peace officer with ladies present.

More police and some civilians were gathering around the stranded streetcar now, so Longarm turned back to Morgana, who was getting better and better looking as she dried out, and said, "They'll have the tracks cleared pretty soon and they're bringing around another car. I was on my way to my office, but if you want, I'd be proud to see you all out safely to the picnic grounds. I mean, it's my duty to protect women and children and—"

"Don't be absurd!" the matron snapped. "I said we had to change all our clothes. Dry or not, I'm not about to be seen in public smelling of an alcoholic beverage!"

The fat girl met Longarm's eyes and sighed, "She's probably right, and she is in charge."

Longarm tipped his hat politely and got off the streetcar while he was still ahead.

Life was like that, he told himself as he headed officeward through the gathering crowd. The pretty one had been too prissy for a grown man to tarry with, and the good sport hadn't been too good looking. But what the hell, the short adventure had given him a good excuse for checking in late, and how many papers could Billy Vail make him fill out between now and noon?

He got to the corner near the Federal Building and took out his watch. He was still unreasonably early, and it was only fair that a hero ought to be allowed to steady his nerves and dry out a mite more before he slipped into harness. So Longarm headed for the nearest saloon as he pondered just where he'd most enjoy tossing the torpedo in his pocket after he'd dried it out and wet his whistle.

"You're over an hour late," said U.S. Marshal Billy Vail as Longarm came into his office, damp and sheep-

14

ish. Vail indicated a seat in the red leather chair across the desk from him, but Longarm said, "I'd best stand for now, Billy. My socks and longjohns are still sort of soggy. I got an excuse you're likely going to disbelieve, but this time I have the whole Denver P.D. as witnesses to the improbable."

"I heard the tale of your derring-do an hour ago," Vail snorted. "I repeat, an hour ago. Your heroic foiling of that telegraph office robbery will doubtless be recorded in the Denver *Post,* but it took place less than a quarter-mile away and, Christ, how much beer can one man drink in only an hour? I can smell your breath from here!"

"That ain't my breath you're sniffing at, Billy. I inhaled pure Maryland rye while steadying my nerves. I only meant to have one, but this police captain came in, and since he bought me one, I had to buy him one, and you know how time flies. Don't you want to hear how I got soaked from head to foot in beer?"

"No. Fortunately for you, your train leaves at one this afternoon. The clerk out front has your travel orders, vouchers, and such typed up already."

"You take a tardy arrival kind of serious, don't you, boss? I had local plans for this weekend."

Vail smiled crookedly and leaned back to fold his hands across his ample paunch. "I know about that schoolmarm up on Lincoln, old son. I ain't sending you out of town to save her reputation. I had you aboard the eastbound flyer even before you came in here late and oozing lager. We've been asked to give the Post Office a helping hand again."

Longarm perched one damp buttock gingerly on the arm of the chair and took out a smoke as he sighed deeply. "Aw, hell, Billy, I'm tired of the way those mailmen have been using and abusing the Justice Department. Can't they deliver their own durned mail?"

Vail saw that his tall, morose-looking deputy was starting to show interest despite his protests, so he rummaged through the papers on his blotter as he said,

15

"It's a job that's gotten too big for the postal inspectors, old son. As a matter of fact, a couple of them have gotten shot and the rest are sort of nervous. It's generally agreed that it's a job for a gent with your peculiar talents. You'll be working undercover, and this time the taxpayers won't fret too much if you have to gun the sons of bitches who've been interfering with the U.S. Mail."

"What have the owlhoots been taking from the mail cars this time, bullion or cash?" Longarm asked with an elaborate show of weariness.

Vail shook his bald dome and answered, "Neither. They've just been tearing up folks' letters and tossing them in the Missouri River. Post Office can't decide if they're Indians or just crazy. They haven't left any witnesses. The main clues we have to go on are undelivered letters, mail-order catalogues, and such, soggy in the waters all the way from Great Falls to St. Louis."

"That sounds more ornery than profitable. What about the postal clerks they robbed?"

"*They* tend to float down the river a lot, too. The ones whose bodies have been recovered, at any rate. We're missing mailmen, postal agents, and some innocent bystanders."

Vail watched Longarm from under his own bushy eyebrows as the tall deputy struck a sulfur match and lit his cheroot. Longarm had a pretty good poker face, but Billy Vail had worked with him for a long time and was one of the few people who could read his seemingly expressionless face. He knew that Longarm tended to look off into nowhere in particular as his gunmetal gray eyes went *click-click-click*. Vail kenw that schoolmarm on Lincoln faced the next few nights alone, no matter what Longarm said between now and the next train east. The towering lawman was a born hunter. Hunting women was his hobby; hunting men was his vocation.

Longarm grimaced as he took a drag on the beer-soaked cheroot. It tasted weird. He blew a thoughtful smoke ring and said, "I'm listening now, boss."

16

Vail nodded. "Here's the picture. A private contractor has the mail franchise between Milk River and Kimaho, near Great Falls. Like I said, the mail ain't getting through, so—"

"Hold on, Billy Vail," Longarm cut in with a frown. "I know it's hard to get good help these days, and I've no doubt that young jasper you have playing the typewriter out in the front office thinks the eastbound flyer runs north to Montana Territory, but *you* ought to know better, damn it!"

"Don't get your bowels in an uproar," Vail said mildly. "I told you I wanted you to move in sort of sneaky. I'm sending you east to board the steamboat at K.C. You'll travel north as a passenger, playing cards, flirting with the ladies, and acting your usual shiftless self. Post Office will most likely have some of their own agents on the case, but *you'll* work solo, and anybody watching them might miss watching you."

"That sure is a long way 'round," Longarm observed, "but I can see the sense in it, if I don't identify myself to the Post Office dicks. Who do I contact when I get off at Milk River?"

"You *don't* get off. You stay on. The steamboat line has the mail franchise. They pick up the mail from the railroad at Milk River, then carry it to the settlements along the upper Missouri, Lord willing and they don't get robbed and burned to the waterline again."

"This mail-hauling is by *steamboat,* Billy? It's my understanding that the upper Big Muddy ain't navigable."

Vail shrugged and said, "It ain't according to the Army Engineers. But the steamboat men ain't figured that out yet. We ain't talking about the Robert E. Lee. You've likely seen them little sternwheel pufferbillies they horse over the sandbars in the shadow of the Shining Mountains."

"Hell, those shallow-draft sternwheelers were a touch-and-go operation when I first came out here after

17

the War. I thought the stage lines and railroads had put most of 'em out of business years ago."

"They have, most places. The NP is planning a spur line up the Big Muddy's headwaters, and of course the stage lines would like the business too. But this one dinky steamboat line still stays afloat, barely, thanks to its mail franchise and the fact that the country they service is still a mite uncivilized."

Longarm stared at the tip of his cheroot and mused, "That's for damn sure," as he drew a mental map of the country they were talking about.

"By now you have a handle on why we picked you for the job," Vail said. "You've worked up there before. You know the country and, more important, you know the Indians. Both the army and the BIA agree, for once, that the Blackfoot, Sioux, and North Cheyenne have been behaving reasonable this summer. On the other hand, you're one of the few white men who seem to be able to get straight answers from the red rascals. Both the Sioux and Blackfoot owe you for recent favors, right?"

"Maybe. I'm on speaking terms with a few of the more reasonable chiefs, and of course the Indian police are supposed to be on our side. But I doubt like hell that any Indian I know is likely to tell a white man all that much about a blood-brother burning steamboats. I reckon I'll pass on questioning Indians, if it can be avoided."

"You think they'd lie to you?" Vail asked.

"I just said I don't know about that part. You ain't awake yet this morning, boss. How in thunder am I to pass as an innocent whatever if I go storming into Indian camps asking all sorts of fool questions? I can't ask the army for a mount like I usually do, either. If the jaspers we're after are watching for government agents, and spotting them, they have to have some confederate or at least a blabbermouthed fool working for Post Office, Army, or BIA."

Billy Vail looked a little sheepish. "You're right. I

admire a man who can think on his feet before noon. That's why I'm sending you. But won't you have to identify yourself to somebody working for the government, sooner or later? I suggested you move in and do some snooping. I don't expect you to take the rascals alone!"

Longarm rose, pulling the tobacco-brown tweed of his pants away from his wet crotch. "I'll figure that out when I find out who they are and how many."

He glanced at the banjo clock on the wall before he added, "Give me the files on this case and I'll study them on the way. You say my travel vouchers and such are ready for me out front?"

Vail nodded, but asked, "What's your hurry? Your train won't leave for almost two hours. I thought we'd jaw a spell about your plans once you reach K.C."

"I hardly ever cross a bridge before I get within a good five hundred miles of it, Billy. I've never seen this steamboat I'm supposed to catch in K.C., and I face a long, tedious climb up the Big Muddy on the same before I'm anywhere near the scene of the crimes. I'll memorize the files on the train, then get rid of them. I'll listen to the paddlewheel and other passengers until something interesting is said. I'd admire jawing with you here in Denver, but let's face it, we don't know enough to mention. Somebody is sending mail up the Big Muddy on a steamboat and somebody else has been stopping it from getting through. You and the taxpayers of these United States want me to find out who it is and make 'em stop. Is there anything else about the case that you haven't told me?"

"Well, not exactly, but—"

"But me no buts, Billy Vail. I thought this beer would just dry out and we'd say no more about it, but my unmentionables are starting to itch like hell. So I'm going over to my digs and I'm going to change. I figure this suit will make it. It'd take forever to have her dry-cleaned, but I'm not going to K.C. or anywhere else before I've had me a bath and put on fresh socks and such."

"Make it snappy, then," Vail said. "I can see you making it to your hired room on the far side of Cherry Creek in plenty of time, but if you soak too long, you'll wind up running for the flyer."

Longarm shot him a disgusted look and asked, "Did you really expect me to board that train in Union Depot like a big-ass bird, Billy Vail?"

Vail stared at him blankly. "Well, sure I did. Where the hell else would a man catch the train to K.C., old son?"

"Aurora, of course. Hardly anybody knows me out that way. I just had a sassy twelve-year-old tell a whole streetcar full of folks who I was. I seem to get pointed out a lot on the streets of Denver. How long do you reckon it would take for word to get around that your top hand was seen boarding the UP flyer in the middle of town?"

Vail nodded. "That's true, and boarding the train out in that dinky settlement to the east would be slick as hell, save for one thing you seem to have missed in your infinite wisdom. The UP flyer doesn't stop in Aurora, Longarm!"

"Hell, I know that. So does everybody else. That's why nobody's likely to notice a federal agent boarding a train out there amidst the sodbusters."

"You aim to flag down the flyer? That don't sound like such a slick disguise, old son."

Longarm grimaced disgustedly. "You've been riding that desk too long, Billy. You're starting to think with pins in a map and a filing cabinet in your head, in place of the brains you must have used in your Ranger days. It was *your* notion I was to sneak in on these folks in the first damned place. If you were on the other side, would you be watching for federal agents to come at you sudden by express, or would you expect them to sort of mosey along like they weren't going anywhere in a hurry?"

Without waiting for the obvious answer, Longarm explained, "There's a local train on the UP line between here and K.C. Nobody going from Denver to K.C. *ever* takes the local, so nobody seeing a gent get off at the other end will suspicion him of having come too far. Should anybody ask me when I board the steamboat, I'll say I'm from Topeka, Kansas. Should anybody check with friends in Topeka, they'll never connect me with the law there. I reckon I'll say I'm a cattle feeder. Nobody is interested in a cattle feeder, and it's reasonable for one to be taking a look at the new rangelands opening up to the north, now that the Sioux are out of business."

Vail leaned back in his chair and grinned broadly. "I like it. I *told* 'em you were sneaky. Your UP through-fare will be good on the local. But ain't it going to take you forever to get there?"

"Not really. There's a couple of hour's difference, which is why anyone from Denver will be on the flyer. I don't mind watching them throw mail sacks off and on all that much, if it means I'm less likely to be bushwhacked before I get anywhere important."

So his boss agreed and Longarm left, trying not to grin like a stoat in a hen house. He hadn't told a single lie. He really did intend to go home and freshen up. Then he'd go pick up the schoolmarm on Lincoln Avenue and take her out to the Fourth of July picnic as he'd promised. Old Billy hadn't asked, so Longarm hadn't told him that the train he meant to board in Aurora stopped there at twenty minutes after midnight.

He figured the fireworks display would be over at about nine-thirty, then she'd want a little foreplay . . .

He'd just about make it, both ways.

Chapter 2

The attempted train robbery between Topeka and Kansas City upset the hell out of everyone aboard the UP local. Women screamed and at least one grown man fainted when the two masked men stormed into Longarm's coach, waving guns and saying all sorts of dumb things as the train braked to a halt in a stretch of timber. Longarm doubted that anyone on either side was more upset than himself as he rose politely, with his hands raised shoulder-high, and braced a knee on the seat he'd just vacated. He could see that the two kids who were trying to look so scary were scared themselves. Their faces were pale and clammy above the bandanna masks they wore. Neither one of them had sense enough to aim their guns at the ceiling, ready to throw down on anyone in the coach. They just yelled too fast to be understood, and waved the fool guns enough to make the women beg for mercy, loud. A fat man holding a gold watch out to them sobbed, "Oh, God, it must be the James gang!"

Longarm tended to doubt that as he sized things up. He'd positioned himself so that the cross-draw holster on his left hip was screened by the back of the seat in front of his. By holding still and staying quiet, he'd avoided drawing particular interest to himself. They gave him one chance after another as they moved down the car, yelling dire threats as they made folks empty their pockets into the flour sack one of them was holding. Flour Sack was in the lead, his gun gripped awkwardly as he held one side of the sack with the hand

22

holding the gun. Of course he kept looking down to see what the passengers were putting in the pot. The other young idiot was on the far side, and kept moving his gun behind his own partner. Longarm knew he or any other gun hand worth his salt could draw and gun them both whenever there wasn't a passenger in the line of fire. But that wasn't his problem. He'd spent a long, boring time, sitting aboard this infernally slow train in order to arrive quietly in the river city just down the line. How in hell was he going to gun or even just arrest two half-assed train robbers without having to talk to the reporters who'd be meeting the train in Kansas City? He'd have to identify himself to the local county law, and they'd naturally put the story on the trackside wire. The goddamned passengers would point him out as some sort of hero, too.

All in all, it might be best to let the kids get away with it this time. They hadn't gunned anybody, and it was obvious they wouldn't be in business long.

But if he waited until they got to him, he knew they'd take his guns, and he'd grown fond of his specially fitted .44 sidearm and the little derringer on the other end of the watch chain draped across his vest. He knew they'd spot his badge and ID too, if they searched him. Punks were unpredictable when they found themselves with a helpless lawman on the wrong end of their guns, too. Above all, like it or not, Longarm knew he was law, damn it. He couldn't afford to jeopardize a more important case; but he couldn't just stand there and watch a whole trainload of taxpayers getting robbed, either.

He cursed silently and braced himself to make his move. He'd wait until somebody else threw something in the bag. That would lower the close one's eyes. The one on the far side was about to frame his fool head against a window, so he'd blow that one away and nail the one holding the bag as the muzzle swung back from the recoil.

But just as Longarm's hands started down, three

shots rang out from somewhere behind him. Without waiting around to see where they were coming from or going, he threw himself down between the seats and got his own gun out. As he twisted around on one knee, a man ran past him and fired again, toward the floor. Longarm saw that the shooter didn't seem to be interested in him, so he took a peek around the edge of the seat backs.

The man who'd fired stood with his back to Longarm, clad in a dark gray suit. But he had on a tengallon Texas hat and wore border boots with three-inch heels. As Longarm holstered his own gun, Gray Suit bellowed loudly, "It's all right, folks! I'm a federal agent!"

Longarm had figured he was law as soon as he'd spotted the two shot-up owlhoots stretched out in the aisle and noticed that the man who'd gunned them was still covering them for some reason. Anyone could see they were both stone dead. That last shot he'd fired into Flour Sack after he was on the floor had made hash out of his head. The other kid had lost the top of his face too.

Fair was fair, Longarm decided as he rose. The jasper dressed and acted sort of overdramatic to Longarm's taste, but he'd fired high and true down the aisle, and hadn't hit anyone else with anything but blood and brains. From the sound, Longarm knew the other lawman favored a .45. From the damage, he knew it was loaded with mushroom slugs.

A conductor came warily into the car, and the man in the gray suit said, or rather announced, "Postal Inspector Donovan, here. Topeka office. What's the tale up forward?"

The conductor said, "There was five or six covering the engine crew and trying to get into the mail car. They took off like spit on a hot stove when they heard the shooting, Inspector!"

Donovan looked frustrated. "Damn—sorry, ladies—

I was hoping they'd stand and fight. You say they didn't get into the mail car this time?"

"Not hardly. They hammered on the door some and said mean things, but the boys inside just set tight. You reckon they was the James Boys?"

Donovan shrugged, and again Longarm had to give him a point for knowing his trade. "I doubt it. They weren't very professional."

Then he turned, as if to receive applause, and Longarm could see that he was a big, good-looking Black Irishman, as he asked, "Are all of you folks all right?"

A woman said, "I feel faint, but praise the Lord, you saved us all."

Donovan grinned boyishly and indicated the sack at his feet to the conductor. "Be good enough to restore their belongings to these folks, would you?" he requested.

Then, as the conductor bent to obey, Donovan met Longarm's glance and something clicked. Donovan's Kerry-blue eyes bothered Longarm too. He could see that the postal inspector was quick-witted and sharp looking. He'd just made all the right moves. But there was something in those big blue eyes that spooked Longarm. Donovan nodded slowly as he looked Longarm over for a long, silent moment. Then he said, "I see you're packing a double-action in a serious-looking rig, stranger. Would I be far off if I read you as a man who's seen the elephant?"

Longarm said, "I rode in the War. You can call me Lansford. I feed cows for a living."

"That's a Colorado crush to your Stetson, ain't it?"

"I reckon so. My feedlot's just this side of the Kansas line, though."

Donovan was *good*! There went the idea of saying he was from Topeka. If this nosy lawman worked out of the Federal Building in Topeka, he'd be able to check with a single wire, and he looked like the kind who would. Longarm made a mental note about his own hat. Most savvy Westerners could read the general

25

region a rider hailed from by the crush of his hat, but not even Longarm could pin it down to a single state. Either it had been a lucky guess, or there was some microscopic difference between the way Colorado and Kansas hands telescoped the crowns of their hats.

"Why didn't you throw down on them, just now?" Donovan asked. "I can see your gun was screened by your seat, and you don't look like a sissy."

"The War was a long time ago, and I ain't packing all that much gold," Longarm replied easily.

He detected the faint look of dismissal and milked it further by adding, "Besides, I ain't the law aboard this infernal train. You are, and you sure just proved you didn't need much help."

Donovan nodded and said, "Well, all's well that ends well. We'll drag these rascals up to the baggage car and be on our way. I don't know about the rest of you folks, but I've got a steamboat to catch."

Longarm sat back down in his seat as he digested that. There had to be more than one damned steamboat leaving a river port, didn't there?

He pretended to stare out the window as the officious postal dick took the sack of booty from the conductor and ordered him forward to start the train. Longarm could see that Donovan enjoyed handing out goodies, even though he'd avoided stooping to pick them up. He probably felt like a combination of Sir Galahad and Santa Claus.

Longarm had met jovial bullies like Donovan before. He didn't like them much, and they were usually on the other side. He'd never understood the breed. He couldn't see what they got out of being in charge of everything and everybody. But that wasn't what bothered him about men like Donovan. Longarm knew that, for some reason, he bothered them a lot more than they bothered him.

It had been like that since he'd been a schoolboy. There'd been a kid like Donovan at his little red schoolhouse in West-by-God-Virginia, and nothing he'd

26

been able to do or say had prevented the knock-down-drag-out they'd had at least once every season. The bully hadn't made it back from the War, but Longarm had met him, over and over, ever since. They'd always recognized one another on sight, and no matter how he tried, Longarm knew that once he'd locked eyes with a man like that, they were headed for Showdown City.

Billy Vail and Longarm's other friends could have explained it to him, had he ever asked. Longarm didn't see himself as others saw him. The tall deputy wasn't prey to false humility. He thought he saw the same thing that others did when he saw himself in a mirror. But he was wrong.

Longarm could plainly see that he stood a head taller than most men, and while he looked sort of ordinary to himself, he didn't see fit to argue with the ladies who'd said he was sort of nice looking. He knew he could get most folks to do what he wanted them to, if he really tried. He'd been told more than once that he scared the shit out of folks he was really mad at. But he considered himself a live-and-let-live cuss who didn't much care what other folks did, as long as they weren't violating the law beyond reason or hurting somebody. He saw no need to prove his manhood by beating up drunks and sissies, and he seldom whipped a horse, as long as it was trying. He didn't understand why some old boys had to push folks around. He knew *he* didn't like to be pushed around.

This, of course, was the key to Longarm's problem with natural bullies. The Irresistible Force just can't relax when it meets the Immovable Object. Anybody dedicated to dominating everyone he possibly could had to test the quietly self-assured Custis Long. It was spooky, to a bully, to meet up with someone who neither asked nor gave an inch. Everybody knew that if a man was tougher than you, you had to kiss his ass. Everybody knew that if you were tougher than he was, *he* had to kiss *your* ass. It was discomforting to meet a

27

man who just didn't *care* whose ass got kissed! So, like a kid probing at a cavity with his tongue, the average bully had to probe at Longarm until it hurt.

Longarm had that last part figured out. He knew Donovan would try a few tentative jests to see what happened. Then, when nothing did, he'd push a little harder, and a little harder, until Longarm told him to stop.

If they were both lucky, Donovan *would* stop. Longarm had once faced down the Thompson Brothers in Dodge, and they'd all come out alive when Ben Thompson detected death in a stranger's eyes in time to back off gracefully. The Post Office dick looked smarter than both Thompson Boys put together. Being a lawman made him feel important already and likely took some of the pressure out of whatever drove his kind. If push came to shove, Longarm knew he could avoid an outright fight with the other lawman just by showing his own cards. But he didn't think he'd better. Donovan was a one-man band if Longarm had ever heard one. He wouldn't gun another lawman, but he wouldn't work well with him, either. Longarm had met gents like that in the army. They'd scared him worse than the enemy had.

The train started up with a jerk, and Longarm put Donovan out of his mind as he saw that the train crew had carted the owlhoots out, put sawdust on the floor, and handed out wet towels to those who needed them. Cold water with a little lemon juice in it was good for bloodstains.

A trackside sign said Kansas City was only twenty miles down the track, so they'd be there in less than an hour, and the pushy lawman had gone off somewhere. With luck, they'd never see one another again.

Longarm reached in his jacket and took out the tickets and timetable they'd issued him in Denver. He'd guessed right on the time. The K.C. & Kimaho Steamboat Line ran north from Kansas City as a night boat, and claimed to take a week to reach the head of navigation near the Great Falls of the Missouri. Longarm doubted that, but he knew he'd make the night boat with hours to spare. It was too bad he didn't know any gals in Kansas City. The timetable said the boat he'd be catching was the *Minnitipi,* piloted by one Captain Grimes. Longarm knew he'd have no trouble remembeing that, so he put the tickets away, tore up the timetable, and dropped it in the cuspidor near his seat. He was still studying where he aimed to hide his badge and ID. The last time he'd worked undercover, he'd sewn them in the lining of his vest. It hadn't worked out so well. It was hard to whip a badge out quickly when you had to cut open a seam, and that gal he'd been hugging that time had asked all sorts of fool questions about the bulge between their bellies.

Longarm turned his head as somebody sat down in the seat next to him. It was Donovan. The Post Office dick said, "Well, it's all settled. The law is meeting us at the depot to haul those dead rascals away. They'll want a statement from both of us, of course."

Longarm shrugged and replied, "I'll tell them what I saw, or, if you want to brag some, I'll back you up within reason."

Donovan didn't smile. He said, "I'd like to ask a favor from you. I've already cleared it with the conductor."

"Do tell? Ask away, then."

"I've already told you I work for the Post Office. I'm on an important case involving the U.S. Mail. There's no telling how many questions the coroner in K.C. is likely to ask about those two bandits you had to gun, but I'm sure there's a reward out on them, so—"

"Hold on," Longarm interrupted. "I disremember gunning any bandits. *You* were the one who terminated their budding careers, as I recall."

"Let's not get technical, Lansford. Most of the passengers were looking the other way when I threw down on them. By the time anyone had time to turn

29

around, we were both standing there with guns, remember?"

"Mine was in its holster. Yours was out and smoking."

"All right, you put yours away. I might have fired a shot, backing your play. The important thing is that *you're* going to take the credit and any reward that's due you, and I'm going to catch the steamboat *Minnitipi*, see?"

Longarm saw. He saw that Donovan was bullshitting a stranger too. But he couldn't give a professional opinion on mythical rewards without giving himself away. He'd have to refuse the kind offer the hard way. He said, "I feel for you, old son, but I just can't reach you. I'm booked aboard the same night boat, and I don't aim to miss her, either."

Donovan's eyes narrowed as he said flatly, "You don't seem to understand my words, pard. I'm not *asking* you. I'm *telling* you."

Longarm met his unfriendly stare with a thin smile as he replied, "Tell a mailman, then. I don't work for the Post Office. I haven't taken orders much since I got out of the cavalry, and that was a long time ago."

"That's something else about you that bothers me," Donovan said. "I rode for the New York Seventh, wearing blue. What color were *your* riding britches, Lansford?"

Longarm remained unruffled. "It's hard to say. The battle flags and uniforms have faded some since we were all so young and foolish. I'd have taken you for a Texican, from the hat you wear these days. But every man to his own taste."

Donovan made a sound deep in his barrel chest that might have been either a chuckle or a growl. "For a man who was afraid to draw when he had the drop, you sure do push your luck around grown men. I've told you what I want you to do as a public-spirited citizen. I've asked you a direct question or two, and you've as much as told me to go to hell."

Longarm sighed and turned his gunmetal eyes on the other man in a gaze that had been known to spook horses and make most sensible men thoughtful. "Get off my toes, Donovan."

The obnoxious lawman blinked as though he'd been slapped across the face with a wet fish, and then he said, "Would you care to repeat that, friend?"

"I asked you to get off my toes. You're right about me being a citizen, and as a public servant, you are way the hell out of line."

"Now, see here—"

"No, *you* see here, Inspector. I'm aboard this train legal, with a bought-and-paid-for ticket. I've been sitting here in this seat, minding my own business. I don't work for you. Unless you aim to charge me with a federal crime and put me under arrest, I don't have to answer any fool questions about a dead and buried past, and I sure as hell don't have to lie to any other public servant for you! When we get to K.C., I'll tell the truth as the Good Lord shall direct me to call it. If that ain't enough for you, *do* something about it."

Donovan studied Longarm in dawning wonder. "By God, I don't think you're afraid of me. Most gents are, you know."

Longarm nodded. His smile was quite pleasant as he said, "I know. I used to be afraid of gents like you, too, when I was a very small boy."

Donovan tried narrowing his eyes some more. Longarm suspected that he practiced that a lot in the mirror when he was shaving. The Post Office dick nodded thoughtfully and said, "You're a gunslick, all right. I've met *your* kind before, too."

Longarm didn't answer.

Donovan's voice went sort of purry as he added, "You know, many a lawman might downright wonder about a stand-up gunfighter who held back when two punk kids were about to rob him."

"They hadn't robbed me yet. I noticed you sort of went out of your way to finish that last one off, considering we both agree they were just punks. I reckon you could make some trouble for me in K.C. if you carried out that veiled threat about the possibility that I was in on the robbery with them. But then they'd likely make us both hang about for days, to answer questions. So now *I'll* tell *you* what we're going to do and say. We've got half the afternoon to make a simple statement to the K.C. coroner. Then we're both going to catch the night boat north and say no more about it."

Donovan suddenly brightened as he said, "That's right. We'll be traveling together out on the river for quite a spell, won't we?"

As Longarm turned his head to gaze out the window, he said, "Yeah. I can swim. Can you?"

Chapter 3

By the light of day, the Big Muddy ran the color of stale coffee with a lot of cream. As the *Minnitipi* steamed upstream from Kansas City in the sunset, the river looked more like molten lava running between banks of bronze and purple. The little steamboat looked like a smokehouse on a raft.

The *Minnitipi* drew less than three feet of water under her keel—if she'd had a keel. The hull was flat-bottomed, with the lines of a scow and, seen from above, the dimensions of a brick. The squared-off bow turned up enough to let the water and most floating debris slide under. At the other end, a wide sternwheel churned the muddy water like a thresher rolling across a wheatfield. The boiler room occupied the aft third of the lower deck. The forward two-thirds carried freight, lightly shielded from the elements by the sort of sidewalls you'd see on a cattle car. The front end of the cargo deck was wide open, and a movable gangplank hung out ahead from a kingpost. At most stops, the *Minnitipi* just ran her blunt bow as close to the bank as it would go and cargo was rolled off and on as well as could be managed. Leaving K.C., she carried manufactured goods for the settlements upstream. Longarm hadn't asked about the cargo. He knew there was no mail aboard yet.

Above the cargo deck, the passenger accommodations, such as they were, consisted of what looked like a big soapbox with a veranda wrapped around it. The promenade deck, forward, crossed above the open cargo deck about ten feet back from the bow, leaving an open workspace around the gangplank. A flight of steps ran down on either side. Aft, the promenade extended out over the paddlewheel and a sign said not to lean over or try to fish. Longarm could see that that was reasonable. He'd have known better, but he could see how a greenhorn might be fool enough to cast a catfish line over the stern, and what the results would be when the wheel grabbed it. The rear end of the upper cabinwork was blank planking. A door on the port corner said GENTLEMEN, and a door on the starboard said LADIES. It was a logical place to put the shithouse.

The staterooms, as they were laughingly called, opened onto the promenade and were wrapped in a horseshoe configuration around the main interior "salon," which was a grand name for a barnlike, open space in the middle of everything that served as a lounge, mess hall, or saloon, depending on the time of day. The forward end of the main salon was provided with large windows and a central set of double doors. A counter or bar ran across the aft bulkhead. Longarm doubted that they cooked in the shithouse, so they probably brought food up from the galley, down by the boiler. The single smokestack ran up like a pillar through the salon, and a sign said not to lean against it. Everything that wasn't whitewashed was painted oxblood. It was likely real oxblood, since the steamboat put in at Omaha, and barn paint was expensive this far west. Most packing houses set aside hogsheads of fresh blood that served as a tolerable weather-resistant paint if you admired the color and didn't mind the flies until it dried some.

There were narrow steps fore and aft, leading up to the Texas deck and the little bandstand wheelhouse. But Longarm knew, before he'd read the signs, that any passenger trying to go topside to the sacred precincts of the pilot would be lashed below with curses that could put an army mule skinner to shame. River pilots had been known to throw solid objects too, on occasion. They were a moody breed who had enough on their minds up there when the river was acting ornery.

The unseen pilot kept sounding the whistle long after the trip commenced, and as the lights of Kansas City winked out downstream, Longarm knew the echoes from the high banks on either side were likely to make for a sleepless night. As he lounged against the rail near the stern, it seemed to him they had plenty of open water all to themselves, and he knew the river ran nine or ten feet deep, this far downstream. He hoped the pilot was just getting the feel of the echoes from the bank as he prepared for darkness; if he was one of those silly sons of bitches who just liked to hear himself toot, it figured to be a tedious night. Longarm was stiff and physically tired from his long, jolting train ride, but he knew he was a mite keyed up to sleep through a tinny steam blast every couple of minutes.

Donovan, the Post Office dick, had apparently holed up in his own stateroom. Longarm hadn't seen him since they'd boarded together after leaving the K.C. coroner's office. The inquest had taken longer than Longarm had figured it would. For a gent who liked to shoot folks, Donovan had certainly prolonged the proceedings with his long brag and a lot of dumb talk about Jesse James. Longarm had thought everyone had agreed that the punk kids who'd tried to stick up a local couldn't possibly know the James Boys or anyone else who'd ever done it right. But Donovan had gotten interested in that angle when it turned out that nobody could identify the young cadavers. They hadn't been known to anyone important in Kansas, after all, so Donovan had insisted on sending wires all over, at the taxpayers' expense, and then they'd had to wait forever at the courthouse for the answers. Longarm, of course, had had to keep his own opinions to himself as he chewed an unlit cheroot and listened to all that foolish talk. Longarm had no more notion than any other lawman as to where Frank and Jesse James were hiding out these days. Since the James-Younger Gang had messed itself up in that bungled Northfield bank job, Longarm had been sent on a dozen or more wild-goose chases after the survivors. It was his personal opinion that the gang was finished. They'd ridden out of Northfield in a hail of lead, leaving most of their sidekicks on the ground or on the way to prison with old Cole Younger. The surprisingly tough townspeople of Northfield were still bragging that they'd put at least ten rounds in every damned one of the rascals who'd tried to rob their bank, and since all the robbers had worn the same kind of slickers, nobody could say which of the scared-skinny owlhoots had been Frank and Jesse, but they had both probably been wounded on the way out of town. The Youngers had been bleeding like stuck pigs when the posse came upon them down in the woods. It was even money that both Frank and Jesse had just died a mite farther down the trail. If they hadn't, both of them seemed to be trying to go straight. They were still getting blamed for robberies all over creation, but the ones Longarm had investigated had all turned out to be someone else's work. He'd asked Billy Vail not to send him out on any more dumb leads. If either of them were still alive, somebody who knew them was bound to turn them in or bushwhack them for the awesome reward on them, dead or otherwise. That was the trouble with stealing for a living. No matter how discouraged an owlhoot got, it was hard to take up another line of work.

Longarm noticed that someone else was moving aft along the promenade, and as he saw that it was three skirts, he straightened up, took the cheroot from his mouth and his hat from his head, and waited politely. It was bad manners for a gent to speak to a lady until she'd spoken to him.

The three ladies nodded to him, but kept going as they took their stroll around the deck. To be accurate, the trio had been two girls and an older lady walking between them. All three were wearing picture hats with veils and identical tan poplin travel dusters. But even in the ruby light of sunset, Longarm had noticed that the two younger ones were pretty and their chaperone hadn't been bad, a few years back. The young gals looked like twins. They had identical rear ends and walked the same nice way. The older woman was out of step between them. She was broader in the beam, but hourglassed attractively amidships. He knew all three were wearing corsets. No human being had ever reached maturity with a fourteen-inch waist. Make it twenty-four for the older one. Longarm put his hat back on and turned back to stare morosely at the muddy water as the steamboat whistle blew. It sounded sort of lewd. He chuckled and murmured, "Yep, I thought so too. But forget it. Two is company, three can be interesting as hell, but four in a bed just don't happen!"

He wondered who they were and where they were headed. The purser could tell him, if he asked with two bits in sight. But Longarm didn't mean to ask. If the older gal wasn't the twins' mother, she was playing a mother's part. The only way a man could hope to move in on a convoy like that would be if they were fancy ladies traveling with a madam, and Longarm didn't pay.

It was getting darker as the sun dropped behind the trees on the western bank. Stars were winking on, and the river was a stream of blood winding between black lace banks. He spied what looked like a shaggy sea serpent bobbing its head in and out of the current off to the starboard. He knew there weren't many sea serpents in the Big Muddy, so it had to be a sawyer.

Longarm watched it thoughtfully, and forgave the pilot above for all that whistle tooting. A sawyer this far downriver meant more up ahead. The long drought that had added so much distress to the Depression of the seventies had ended that spring. Oldtimers said the climate on the High Plains ran in seven-year cycles, so the recent cattle boom figured to hold until the next dry spell, and the river was high between its banks for midsummer. But the sudden change in the weather had apparently played hell with the banks, and a lot of drought-killed cottonwoods were on their way to the Gulf of Mexico. Floating timber wasn't bad, unless it rafted on a sandbar. Even waterlogged timber on the bottom didn't cause much trouble, in deep channel. But a sawyer was a tree that hadn't made up its mind.

It was usually the muddy root end that dragged along the bottom as the busted-up branch end sawed up and down in the current. Savvy passengers worried about sawyers as much as the pilot did, because they were steamboat killers. Depending on the length of the soggy tree and the speed of the current, a sawyer surfaced and submerged at intervals, often smack in the middle of a channel. A boat could steam right over one when it was down. If it decided to come up, it could drive a couple of sharp stubs through your bottom. The boat's motion made it worse as the hull impaled itself against the angle of the submerged tree. If it speared the hull alone, most folks who knew how to swim had a chance. If it knifed up into the pressurized boilers, too bad.

Longarm saw that the pilot had avoided the sawyer by swerving over a stretch of slick, swirling "shallow-boil" that betrayed a hidden sandbar just covered with enough water to matter. Captain Grimes was good. He knew his ass from a hole in the river. Longarm decided to leave the navigating to the pilot as he headed for the main salon to see what else was going on.

They'd boarded too late for supper, so the salon was now a saloon, albeit sedate enough for lady passengers. The three gals in veils and dusters were seated in a row in cane chairs near the forward windows. A gal in a fancier hat and a sort of flashy maroon satin dress sat fanning herself in another chair near the smokestack, facing four gents seated at a round table between the whitewashed pillar and the bar. Three of them looked like cattlemen or maybe homesteaders, despite their summer suits. The one in the lavender Prince Albert and the big white sombrero was a professional gambler if Longarm had ever seen one. They were playing five-card stud.

It was none of Longarm's business how grown men threw their money away, so he moved past them and ordered Maryland rye from the Negro barkeep. He was pleasantly surprised when he tasted what he was served. It really was Maryland rye, and it hadn't been watered past common sense. Longarm made a mental note to congratulate Captain Grimes on the way he ran his vessel when they met. He knew the master would spend most of the night in the pilot house, but a mate could handle the wheel during daylight hours, this far downriver. So he'd likely meet the captain at one meal or another.

Longarm turned and braced his back against the bar as he eyed the other passengers casually and got the feel of the big salon. A man never knew when he'd be ducking for cover, and it helped to know a room's layout before the need arose.

Like the rest of the vessel, the barnlike main room was shipshape in a thrifty, no-frills way. The walls and ceiling had been whitewashed recently, and the floorboards were sprinkled with fresh sawdust. The brass spittoons near each chair had been polished to a shine that would stand an army inspection, and the hanging oil lamps had clean glass chimneys and trimmed wicks. They burned brightly enough to show him they'd been filled with coal oil instead of the buffalo oil some folks used to save on pennies at the cost of their vision. Billy Vail had said the steamboat line was fighting for its life. Longarm figured folks who didn't pass their troubles on to paying passengers deserved to stay in business.

As a passenger, he couldn't fault the layout. As an experienced gunfighter, he didn't like a couple of things he saw.

Save for the hatchway behind the bar, there was only one way in or out: the forward end, with its large windows and doorway opening onto the forward promenade. There wasn't enough cover should some-one start shooting in at them over the bow as they put in to some landing up ahead. There was no way at all to fire astern or to either side. All three were blind. He knew the crapper behind the bar and the staterooms on the far sides of the blank sidewalls offered some protection to the passengers in here from gunfire from the riverbanks, but there was simply no way to fire back. If the two boats that had been burned, up near the headwaters, had been built this same way, Longarm could see how easily they'd been ambushed in the narrow channels near the mountains. A volley through the wheelhouse would mean the sudden end of the only folks aboard who had any view of the banks.

The engine-room crew could be popped off as they popped out. Passengers inside a room like this would have been ducks in a shooting gallery for any rascal pumping lead from one direction. That told him one thing to look out for. The river pirates hadn't attacked from another vessel in the treacherous, braided chan-nels of the upper river. They'd been land-based and had simply waited at some point where they knew a steamboat would put in. The pilot would have spotted them on open prairie, and the mail clerks who'd wound up floating toward New Orleans had been armed and—on the last boat, at least—on the prod for trouble. That meant a landing where folks could lie in wait behind cover and then pour a hot and heavy volley into the vulnerable open end as the steamboat dropped her gangplank on the mud. They'd nail the deck crew and pilot with the first shots, and anybody left would have gone down as they raked the thin-walled vessel from stem to paddlewheel.

The case sheets Billy Vail had given him in Denver had said the burned-out hulks had been found on sand-bars, with nothing interesting near enough to matter. That was easy to figure. After gunning everyone and setting the boats afire, the killers had simply shoved them out into midstream and let them drift, burning, until the bottom grabbed what was left. He narrowed his eyes as he reconsidered his mental map. A burning steamboat was hardly likely to drift upstream, so the apparently senseless killings had taken place above the places where they'd been discovered.

That left him the senseless part to mull over. An individual lunatic who just hated steamboats was one thing, but you hardly ever found more than three or four lunatics running in a pack. Given armed guards and at least half of the passengers packing hardware in rough frontier country, Longarm couldn't see less than a dozen men ambushing a steamboat so easily.

A dozen Indians traipsing about off the reservation, that close in time and space to the Little Big Horn, ought to have drawn at least some curious comment. The headwaters of the Big Muddy were sparsely settled, but they weren't *that* empty. So the army and BIA were likely right about the Indians being innocent. Even a dozen white men riding together should have occasioned more comment than either the Post Office or the Justice Department had been able to find out about—unless, of course, they were riders who belonged up there and would be inconspicuous to the casual eyes of cowhands, hunters, and such that they'd have had to pass.

Longarm put that notion on a back burner for now. If he didn't luck onto a lead, working undercover, he faced some tedious riding and questioning with his badge pinned on. Few folks remembered just when and where they'd spotted someone they knew at a distance.

As he was pondering the variables of disguise and motive, Inspector Donovan came in, or rather made an entrance, like an actor, through the doorway at the front of the salon. Donovan stood there until he saw that nobody figured to applaud, then he spotted Longarm and came over to the bar. Longarm hadn't asked him to join him, but he offered to buy him a drink anyway.

Donovan sniffed and said, "I reckon I'll drink alone

41

until I know you better, Lansford." When the barkeep moved over to him, he called the Negro his good man and said he was drinking steam beer. Then he sniffed at Longarm again and continued, "I don't order strong drink in the presence of ladies."

Longarm shrugged and replied, "I'm sure they'll think you ordered a sarsaparilla. I thought you were drinking alone."

"I am. But it's a free country and I say what I've a mind to, reb."

Longarm grinned incredulously and asked, "Is that what's making you so broody, for Pete's sake? Hell, if you're going to fight the War over again at this late date, let's say I rode with the Seventh Union Cav."

Donovan ignored the beer the barkeep slid across the mahogany to him. "I think you're a liar," he said flatly.

They were just within earshot of the men at the nearby poker table. The tinhorn in the lavender coat stiffened, but didn't turn to look their way. One of the others got up, desperately casual, as he said, "I've had enough, gents. I reckon I'll just go see if my bunk's made up."

Longarm felt his neck redden as he became aware that even the three gals sitting at the far end of the room had sensed the sudden chill in the air and were looking his way, while the fancy lady with her back to the smokestack pillar was looking down at the floor, fanning herself fit to bust. Longarm turned and stared at the gals near the door as he said softly, "I saw this tombstone up near Creed, one time. The inscription read, 'He Called Bill Smith a Liar.'"

"Bill Smith must have took it personal," Donovan purred. "How do *you* aim to take it, Lansford?"

"I don't. It was you who just mentioned there was ladies present."

"I don't think you rode with the Seventh. I don't think you rode with any decent Confederate outfit. If you rode at all, it was with Quantrill or some other

42

cowardly guerrilla band. That Kansas hat has 'jay-hawker' writ all over it."

"I thought you said my hat looked Colorado, old son."

"I've changed my mind, reb. And don't call me your son again, unless you aim to fill your fist. Unlike your own, my mother was married when she gave birth to me."

Finishing his drink, Longarm left the change on the bar and turned his back on the bully as he stepped over to the vacant seat at the table and sat down, saying, "I'm in, if it's all the same to you gents."

The man in the lavender coat nodded silently, as Donovan laughed sneeringly behind him. Longarm took out his wallet and asked what the stakes were. The tinhorn replied, "Sign over yonder says no gambling for cash is allowed on board, sir. We're just playing for matchsticks."

Longarm nodded down at the pile of matchsticks near the gambler's elbow. "That sounds reasonable. How much do matchsticks cost these days?"

"Dollar a stick. How many do you want?"

"Oh, I'll take twenty off you, for now."

The other two men at the table exchanged thoughtful glances. One of the two, who looked sort of prissy, licked his lips and said, "I understood this to be a friendly game, gents. It's only fair to warn you all that I drop out when the table stakes get serious."

The dealer handed Longarm a fistful of matchsticks, palming the silver certificate Longarm gave him in return, before he said, "Nobody's pointing a gun at you, sir. You just raise or pass as you see fit. Are you still in?"

The man who had just spoken shrugged and nodded. The other one, with his back to the fancy gal holding the fan, looked bigger and meaner as he growled, "We're all in. Deal, Mr. Canfield."

Longarm doubted that the tinhorn's right name was Canfield as he watched him shuffle and cut. The man in the lavender coat wasn't nearly as good as he thought he was. Aside from giving himself away with the funny coat and frilly shirt front, the man who called himself Canfield dealt too pretty for a real pro. Longarm knew he'd never get any of the old boys in the Long Branch or the Silver Dollar to play against him, once they'd seen his shark's hands in motion. He was sort of young looking, despite his mustache. Longarm was tempted to ask him why he'd been run off the bigger steamboats down the river. But Longarm had paid for his own education, so it was only right that Canfield should pay for his.

Longarm picked up his hand. As he'd assumed, Canfield had dealt him a couple of pairs. Longarm put a couple of matchsticks in the pot to see what would happen.

The prissy man matched his bet, so Longarm knew he'd been dealt a nice hand indeed. The burly man, whose necktie was open around his sweaty neck, didn't give anything away as he put his own bet in the pot. Canfield said, "I'll pass," and the heavyset man shot him a curious look. It was up to Longarm now, so he put another stick forward and said, "I'll raise."

Prissy passed. Heavyset hesitated. Then he turned in his chair and asked the gal seated behind him, "Would you mind moving your chair, ma'am?"

The fancy lady looked startled and replied, "I beg your pardon, sir?"

Canfield said, "That's not very polite of you, Mr. Dobbs."

Dobbs, if that was in fact the heavyset man's name, said, "I ain't trying to be polite. I'm trying to play cards, and it makes me nervous to have folks reading over my shoulder."

The gal with the fan stared openmouthed at him. Then, as if she'd been given a signal, she rose with a head-tossing sniff and marched grandly over to another chair near the wall, where she plunked herself down and spat, "Of all the nerve!"

Dobbs threw his cards down and said, "I want a new deal," as he took his stakes back.

Longarm left his matchsticks in the pot as he tossed in his hand. He sure had fallen among a lot of crazy-talking folks this evening. It was a good thing this was a steamboat instead of a cowtown card house. Canfield was either yellow or sensible. Shooting folks in the middle of a river could lead to all sorts of fuss afterwards, even when they had it coming.

Canfield reshuffled and dealt again. Longarm drew aces and eights. He wondered if Canfield was trying to tell him something, or if he just had a grotesque sense of humor. The gal with the fan might be with him, but he didn't need her to signal with her fan. Longarm had spotted the way he was dealing. Fortunately for Canfield, nobody else had.

This time Dobbs raised ten sticks, so Longarm knew he had at least ladies and jacks. Surely Canfield knew better than to deal himself a winning hand right after a man had as much as accused him of being a mechanic?

He did. He folded, and when neither Longarm nor the other man across the table raised, the burly Dobbs drew in the pot with a satisfied sigh.

He asked Longarm, "Can I see what you had?"

Longarm said, "Not without paying me. Let's see how we do the next time."

The prissy little man shoved his chair back. "I'm out, gents. This is getting too rich for a farm boy's blood."

As he vacated the chair, Donovan came over and took his place at the table, saying, "I'm in. Any objections?"

Longarm smiled crookedly at him and said, "Not from me. I can see you're feeling lucky tonight."

Canfield glanced at Dobbs, who just shrugged, so the gambler started to deal again. But Donovan shoved his facedown cards back and said flatly, "I like a game where the deal moves around the table, friend."

Canfield's voice was quiet as he asked, "Are you accusing me of anything, mister?"

"Would you do anything about it if I was, sonny?" Donovan replied.

Canfield hesitated, then slid the deck toward Longarm.

Longarm said, "Smart move. He's a lawman, and it's gone to his head. Is it all right with you if *I* deal, Donovan, or am I a cardshark as well as an unreconstructed reb?"

"Deal the cards, Lansford. You sure make a lot of funny jokes for a man who sits down to pee."

Naturally, the fancy lady by the wall heard, so naturally she got up again and moved over by the three gals near the door. They eyed her warily, but held their ground.

Longarm had had just about enough of Donovan's big mouth. So, though he knew he shouldn't do it, he dealt the cards the way a friendly gal he'd spent some time with in his Dodge City days had taught him.

He dealt Canfield the low hand, to get him off the hook. The surly Dobbs couldn't be greedy enough to expect to win every hand, so what the hell, he decided to teach Donovan a lesson. He knew, by now, that the badge he packed made the bully cautious about drawing first, and he knew he was immune to the loudmouth's verbal goading. He dealt Donovan a good hand, and gave himself the hand it would take to beat it.

As Longarm expected, Donovan raised. Dobbs folded. He expected Canfield to do the same, but the tinhorn surprised him by staying in. So he shrugged, raised, and the other two matched his bet.

This was getting interesting. Longarm knew what everyone else had, so he just kept piling matchsticks, and when he had all twenty in the pot, he asked Canfield to sell him some more. The gambler took his money, but said, "I reckon we'd best set the limit at a hundred, gents. The purser tells me Captain Grimes don't allow high table stakes aboard this boat."

46

Donovan took out a fistful of bills, placed them in the pot, and stated, "I am the U.S. government, and I'll tell you when there's enough in the pot for *me!* You boys can see me or fold. I don't play cards like a sissy, either."

Longarm grinned wolfishly, took out his wallet again, and matched the Post Office dick with cold cash. He figured this would be where Canfield folded. But the dapper gambled shrugged, took a roll of bills from his pocket, and started peeling it like an artichoke as Donovan said, "Now, that's more like it."

Donovan resweetened the pot. The other two saw him. He studied his hand and shrugged. "I ain't greedy. I'll call." Then he spread his cards faceup and added, "Read 'em and weep."

Spreading his winning hand, Longarm said, "Weep no more, my ladies." He knew Canfield had a dog's hand, but it was polite to wait until he said so before he raked in the pot. As Longarm did, Donovan glared and said, "You deal from the bottom too, eh?"

Longarm smiled across at him and replied benignly, "If you want to say so, it's a free country. You had your chance to call a crooked deal before you bet, pard. So unless you aim to welsh, it's a mite late for tears and recriminations."

"Goddamnit, man, I just accused you of cheating."

"I know. You do have tedious manners. I ain't about to stop a grown man with a .45 from picking up his marbles and going home, if you don't like the way I play."

"You're yellow, Lansford."

Longarm went on smiling as the burly Dobbs slid his chair like a crawfish backing into a hidey-hole. Then Longarm said, "You've said *that* before, too. Take your money back and welsh if you aim to. You know damned well I'm too smart to draw on a lawman in front of witnesses in the middle of a river. You ain't about to explain an unprovoked gunfight over cards to the U.S. government, either. So, since I see you've left

47

your stakes on the table, I reckon I'll just help myself to the pot."

He would have, too, if Canfield hadn't stopped him. "Not so fast. Look what you dealt *me,* Mr. Lansford."

Then, to Longarm's surprise, he spread a full house and raked the pot over to his side of the table!

If Longarm, who'd dealt him no such hand, was surprised, Donovan was too upset to think straight. He roared, "You son of a bitch! The two of you were working together!"

Donovan started to shove his chair back. He might have meant it seriously, or it might have been more show-off dramatics. Nobody would ever rightly be able to ask him. Longarm stiffened and went for his own gun as an unseen weapon roared under the table, and the women near the door screamed and headed elsewhere. Nobody moved for a couple of heartbeats. Then, as gunsmoke curled up all around the edge of the table, Inspector Donovan gave a little sigh and fell forward to lay his face, very still, on the table.

"I hope you gents will remember what he called me just now," Canfield said.

"They were killing words, all right," Longarm agreed. "But are you sure you thought things out? I told you he was law."

The gambler shrugged with a defeated little smile. "I know. But nobody has ever called me a son of a bitch and lived."

Longarm turned his head as a loud, high voice shouted from the doorway, forward, "All right, who's the fool who fired a gun aboard my steamboat?"

The source of the question was a boyishly built lady in a black dress, with a pilot's cap perched atop her auburn hair. She would have been prettier if she hadn't been scowling so. She bore down on them, still looking mean as hell as she announced, "I am Captain Grimes and I don't allow no silly guff aboard the *Minnitipi!"*

Longarm stood up as he removed his hat and said, "It wasn't silly, ma'am. It was serious. The gent with

48

his head on the table just passed a remark I dasn't repeat to your female ears. And now, as you can see, he's dead."

Captain Grimes stared morosely down at Donovan. "Oh, damn. He was supposed to be guarding us from river pirates for the Post Office, and now he's gone and got his fool self shot. Which one of you done it?"

Longarm didn't answer as Canfield rose gravely, removed his own hat, and answered, "I did, ma'am. Post Office or whatever, he had it coming."

"Coming or no, you are under arrest to quarters until we get to the next landing, Mr. Canfield," the female skipper said.

"I assure you, these other gents will bear witness it was self-defense."

"I don't care what anybody says. I'm a river pilot, not a judge. You go to your stateroom and stay there. We'll let the coroner at Willow Bend decide the rights and wrongs of it. I'll thank you to hand over your arms too."

Canfield smiled sheepishly and took the derringer from his pocket to place it respectfully in her outstretched hand. Captain Grimes seemed satisfied it was his only weapon, but she'd never seen him produce a full house from wherever the hell he'd had it stashed.

"It's a good thing for you that you gunned him this far down the river, Mr. Canfield," she said. "We'll have other lawmen coming aboard with the mail at Milk River, and if I didn't know who and what you was, I'd likely suspicion you of being a river pirate myself."

She looked at Longarm again as she put Canfield's gun in a skirt pocket and said, "You'd be Lansford, right? You're booked through to Kimaho Landing at the end of the line. I hope you'll keep it short and simple for the law at Willow Bend, for I don't mean to tarry there longer than it takes to shift some freight and firewood."

She caught the eye of the colored bartender and asked, "Just how much of it did you see, Mr. Blue?"

The barkeep said, "All of it, Captain. It was like these gentlemens said. The dead man was just plain asking for a fight with ever'one. He hoo-rahed Mista Lansford, there, and I was sure I'd see a killing right at the bar. But Mista Lansford tried to git away from him by joining the card game. Then that trashy dead man followed him and started up with Mista Canfield, too. *I* can't tell a lady what he said, neither, but I'd of *cut* him, had he said it to *me!*"

The female skipper nodded and exhaled heavily. "All right. I know you have kin in Willow Bend to stay with, Mr. Blue, so you'd best go ashore and act as this gambling man's witness. You other through-passengers didn't see all that much, if you mean to stay aboard. I don't mean to stop a full hour there."

"Are you saying you mean to leave me ashore at the next landing, Captain Grimes?" Canfield asked.

"You're damned right. I told you other lawmen working out of this one's office would be boarding us further upstream. How many gunfights do you think I'll tolerate aboard this vessel?"

"I, ah, have business up near Kimaho, ma'am."

"That's just too bad. You'll have to get there another way, won't you?"

"Miss Grimes, there ain't no other steamboat that goes that far."

"I know. I said you'd have to find another way. Take the Black Star as far as Milk River and grab a stage or train west. You'll likely have some complicated transferring to do, but you'll reach Kimaho alive, sooner or later, unless you can get folks aboard a stage to play cards with you. I've said all I've a mind to, Mr. Canfield. You just go to your stateroom and behave yourself until I send for you, hear?"

She pointed out the corpse to two crewmen who'd just come in and told them, "Put that under a tarp near the gangplank, and make sure you lay more sawdust. I've got to get back up to the Texas before the mate runs us aground."

As she started to leave, Longarm fell in at her side, saying, "I didn't know this was a mail boat, ma'am."

"Well, you know it now. Where do you think you're going?"

"I, uh, thought we might jaw some about what you want me to tell the law, up at the next landing."

"You tell 'em you were reading the *Police Gazette,* if you aim to stay aboard tonight. I'm headed for officer's country, mister. Are you a licensed river pilot?"

"No, not exactly."

"Then you ain't going nowhere with me, jawing or no. This is a steamboat I'm running, mister, not a public auditorium. I give you credit for common sense, now that Blue says you ain't as wild as you look. And since I can mount these stairs and you can't, I'll say good night to you."

Longarm stared after her for a moment, then turned back to see if the bar was still open. It was, but everyone else had left the salon to himself, the barkeep, and the men cleaning up the mess.

Longarm went to the bar and ordered another drink. Blue poured him one and said, "This one's on the house. I admire big men with sense enough to live and let live."

Longarm smiled broadly. "Yeah. Your boss is sort of tough for a lady, ain't she?"

Blue said, "She calls me 'mister' and I calls her 'captain,' and you won't like what I puts in your next drink if you go mean-mouthing her, hear?"

Longarm laughed and held up a hand, palm forward. "Hey, flag of truce, Blue. I never said I didn't *like* her. I was just sort of surprised to see anybody called Captain Grimes wearing skirts."

Mollified, Blue said, "She's young and handsome, but she's the best pilot on the upper river, now that they've kilt her daddy and her man. I've known Miss Gloria since she was in pigtails, mister. Her daddy was Big Bill Grimes, and we paddled up a lot of water together since I run off before the War. *He* called me 'mister,' too."

"I can see they was gentlefolk. You say she's lost *two* men, recent?"

Blue nodded. "Big Bill was piloting the first boat they stopped and burned. Miss Gloria's husband, Johnny Bishop, was in command of the second one they burned. Nobody never found his body. Or maybe they did and just couldn't say. The folks they fished outta the river was sort of messed up, between the scalding and the crawfish in the shallows. This here *Minnitipi* is the only boat the line has left. Miss Gloria's had a time hiring help, what with crazy folks in wait up the river!" He wiped the mahogany with a rag and added, "But it don't matter. Like I said, she's about the best pilot there is. Her daddy used to let her take the wheel while she was growing up. If there's a sandbar on the river she ain't met by now, it's a new one. When they bought the *Minnitipi* off another line that was going out of business, it was only right that they should give her the command. She talks sort of tough 'cause a lot of folks feel funny about a lady pilot. But like I said, she treats us old friends, who *know* her, *right!*"

"I understand, Mr. Blue," Longarm said. "This may strike you as a nosy question, but how come Miss Gloria is still sailing under her maiden name, if she's the widow Bishop?"

Blue shot him a suspicious look and replied, "I might answer that, if you'll tell me *why* you're so nosy. If you've got country thoughts about Miss Gloria, I'll tell you right up front that *I* may be going ashore, but there ain't a man in the crew who wouldn't cut your heart out with a rusty can opener if he thought you meant to trifle with her!"

Longarm shook his head. "You got me wrong, pard." Then, since he really wanted to know, and since Blue was not only leaving the vessel but seemed to be a savvy old cuss, Longarm took out his ID and spread it on the bar between them as he warned, "I'll take it

52

personal if word of this gets about. I'm trusting you because I feel you are a loyal-hearted man who'd like to see Miss Gloria and the family line stay in business."

Blue nodded thoughtfully and said, "I thought you acted a mite cool, for a man your size who was being bullied by a fool he had a couple of inches on. I'm feeling a lot better about that free drink, and I'm fixing to serve you another. The reason Miss Gloria uses her maiden name is because it's famous in every river port, and you can see how hard it is for a gal to command respect if she acts human. She wears them widow's weeds for her Johnny. She bears the name Grimes because it's an old and proud one on the river."

"That sounds reasonable. You say they never found Johnny Bishop's body? How long had he been on the river, and what sort of a rep did he have?"

Blue looked away as he rubbed at some microscopic imperfection in the polished mahogany. "I didn't like him. He called me 'boy.' But fair is fair. Big Bill never would have let him pilot one of his boats if he'd only been a son-in-law. Bishop served a summer as mate before he got his own command. That's how he met Miss Gloria, of course. As to who he was or what he was afore he come to the river, I can't say. He always said he'd fought in the Michigan Volunteers but . . . never mind."

"Come on, you can do better than *that*, Mr. Blue!"

"Well, you might have noticed I'm a gentleman of color."

"I never took you for a Shoshone. Get to the point about Bishop."

Blue hesitated again before he said, "We notice you folks, too. Some of you are all right. Others sort of look *through* us, like they wished we wasn't there. There's another kind of white man, with another kind of look in his eyes when you pass him on the street. We call it the 'hate look.' You'd have to be colored to know what I means."

"Are you saying this Johnny Bishop bullied you?"

53

"No. Miss Gloria wouldn't have stood for it. As a matter of fact, he smiled too hard at colored folks, and joshed too much for a man who was comfortable around us. He pretended to call me 'boy,' friendly. But ever' once in a while I'd catch him looking at me— well, like I was a snake and he was wishing he had a big stick."

Longarm pondered this for a moment before observing, "Some white folks are mixed up about their feelings toward your kind. The War was only fifteen years ago, and let's face it, there's been ugly doings in the North. A man could march with the Michigan Volunteers without being overly fond of colored folk."

"I know," Blue said. "Some of *us* ain't sure how to act, neither. But, well, I told you I was a runaway slave. I'll tell you something else, since we is sharing secrets. I never run off because some mean old overseer was hitting me with a whip. I *never* got whipped. I just didn't like being a slave. I've never said this too much, but the folks I worked for back in Georgia were quality. I reckon I'd have liked them, if they hadn't *owned* me."

"I can understand that. But we were talking about Miss Gloria's late husband."

"I know. I'm trying to put into words how I know he wasn't never no Yankee. It wasn't 'cause he looked down on me. Lots of Northerners do. It wasn't 'cause he was shifty-eyed and hateful. I see that all the time, on this side of the bar. You see, Deputy Long, he *knew* I was from the South!"

"I follow your drift. Can you really tell a Northerner from a Southron, Mr. Blue?"

"No, not if they try hard. But I don't think old Johnny Bishop knew that. Not for sure. I means, if he was what I think he was, he'd been raised around colored folks. He'd growed up knowing how he was *s'posed* to act about colored folks. As a Southron, I mean."

"Right. But a Southron who'd never been a boy up

North might be sort of confused about the exact form. He'd know there were Northerners who had colored help. But he wouldn't know exactly how a Northerner treated a free Negro. A man who'd changed sides, either during or after the War, would be more comfortable without any around him at all, if he was hiding his past. But what in thunder could he have been working so hard to hide, Mr. Blue? The fact that he'd been in the Confederate Army? That makes no sense. Lots of men who fought on both sides are out here now, getting along right well. Were the Grimeses fanatic Abolitionists or something?"

Blue shook his head emphatically. "No. Big Bill was too old to take part in any war, and Miss Gloria was jest a little girl. I come to work for them before the fighting started, so I know they never lost anybody important. Big Bill was agin' slavery, as my working for him would show you. But I was up and down the river with him all through them years and, while he said it was an awful thing, he never seemed to get too excited about what was going on back East. I know he's hired more than one white crewman who rode for the South, too. But I still say Johnny Bishop was hiding *something* about the War."

Longarm fished out a cheroot and groped in his pocket for a match. "Well, in the first place, he's likely dead. In the second, I can see a dozen fairly innocent reasons why a man might come out West with a new name and a new past. More than one could have no connection at all with the War. A boy might have owed money or been in a fix with some gal he didn't want to marry."

"Then why would he lie about being in the Union Army?" Blue pressed.

"Hell, I know men who *were* in the Union Army who lie about it all the time. In any war, there's ten men behind the lines for every one that ever makes it to the front. But who wants to brag about being a quartermaster or a clerk? Many a man who never heard a shot fired in anger or wore any uniform at all can tell a thundering great tale about the time he helped U. S. Grant or Robert E. Lee, depending. We could be doing a disservice to a plain old fibber who died at the wheel of his steamboat, Mr. Blue. I mean to send a few telegrams anyway. The army keeps records, and Bishop ain't as common a name as Smith. But we'd best let the dead lay, whether we liked 'em or not."

"If you say so," Blue replied. "But it was your notion to ask me why I suspicioned him."

Longarm took the second drink and bolted it before he lit his cheroot and said good night to the barkeep. He walked out to the forward deck to smoke and watch for Willow Bend. The gambler, Canfield, had done him a greater service than he'd known in getting rid of that pushy postal inspector, even if it had been rougher than Longarm might have played it. Now that he had a less cramped hand aboard the boat, he felt suddenly sleepy. He hadn't realized how tensed up he'd been about poor old Donovan. But it would all be over in a little while. Or would it?

Canfield wouldn't serve time for the killing. Even the Post Office would have to put it down as one of those foolish things that happen to a man who gets into a card game with strangers. Donovan had started up with the tinhorn. There was no way Canfield could have been lying in wait for a federal agent, was there?

Sure, there was. Anybody who'd known Donovan would have known he was a swaggering loudmouth just begging for a fight. Sooner or later, he'd have hoorahed every grown man aboard. A man who meant to kill him only had to be aboard and wait for a chance to make it look good.

Longarm made another mental note to check out Canfield by wire, once he had a chance. Canfield might have a record as a gambler. Or he might have killed someone like that before. A flashy tinhorn front made a neat disguise for a hired assassin meaning to plead an honest showdown. And what could Blue's suspicions mean—if they meant anything?

Longarm took them out and marched them up and down the deck in step with the lavender-clad gambling man. They marched sneaky as hell. Canfield had gone out of his way to get into a stranger's fight with a man he knew was the law. He'd been primed and ready when he spread that flagrant full house, instead of just sitting tight like a sensible survivor when Donovan started his war dance. And a dead river pilot who'd been hiding something and then wasn't there for certain when they went to bury him could lead a man down all sorts of garden paths. But nary a one made any sense.

Longarm took a long drag on his smoke and started counting them off on the fingers of his free hand. One: Bishop was in cahoots with somebody who was out to steal his father-in-law's business. No, that wouldn't work. Why help them sink two out of three steamboats, when you were likely to inherit the business sooner or later? Two: Bishop had been in on the ambushing of Big Bill Grimes, and the second burning had been to make everyone think he was dead, to throw suspicion off him. That was even dumber. Nobody but the quiet barkeep had been suspicious of Bishop, and as a certified corpse, a man couldn't wind up owning a thing. Three: There'd been something of great and portable value aboard Bishop's second steamboat, and he'd faked his own death to light out with it. But that left the first attack up in the middle of the air, and what in thunder could have been so stealable aboard number two? The mail had been scattered on the river. That could mean someone had torn open the mail sacks, searching for one single item. But it still didn't implicate Bishop; who was going to question the skipper and god of a riverboat if he poked through the mail or cargo at leisure?

Longarm snapped his fingers and exclaimed to no one in particular, "The postal inspectors who got killed!"

A man alone couldn't wipe out a whole boatload of armed men, but a pilot in cahoots with owlhoots on the bank *could*.

The whistle blasted above him, and a necklace of shore lights appeared as the *Minnitipi* rounded a bend. Other passengers joined him at the forward rail as the steamboat backed its paddlewheel to slow them, and the pilot swung her helm to put in. The folks nearest him were the apparent twins and their older chaperone. She'd placed herself protectively between the gals and Longarm, so he didn't say howdy. But she stared down at the lumpy canvas just visible on the foredeck below them and asked in a soft, sad voice, "Is that the man who was killed?"

Longarm nodded. "I fear it is, ma'am. They'll carry him ashore well before you ladies have to go down the steps, though."

"The girls and I didn't really see what happened," she said. "Do you think they'll want to question us?"

Her voice was carefully casual, but Longarm detected the worry in it, so he replied softly, "Not if you don't want them to, ma'am. As I remember, you ladies had just left the salon when the shooting at the table started, right?"

She gave a pleased gasp. "Oh, I *took* you for a gentleman, but it's so nice to see I was right. My name is Lavinia Lee, and these young ladies are the Gilmore twins, Mary Jo and Cindy Lou."

Longarm touched the brim of his Stetson to the three of them as they all sort of dimpled at him. He couldn't tell which was Mary Jo or Cindy Lou, but it hardly mattered, since they were dead ringers for one another, and it wasn't likely he'd get to kiss either one, in any case.

The *Minnitipi* tooted some more and some crewmen ran forward down below to throw the lines ashore as they moved in to the landing. Like most on the Big Muddy, the one at Willow Bend was not a regular dock. It was a sort of otter slide, gouged out of the steeper

58

banks on either side. The water level rose and fell with the seasons, so that flat-bottomed boats just slid their bows ashore like turtles meaning to lay eggs. A couple of shore men waded out ankle-deep to grab the thrown lines and haul them to snubbing posts set on higher ground. Longarm couldn't see much more of the town than its lights, but it seemed that everyone who lived there was down by the shoreline, waving. They likely didn't have a library or opera house, so a steamboat putting in must have been entertaining.

The *Minnitipi* grated her bows to a shuddering standstill, and the crewmen swung the gangplank around and dropped it in the mud. Captain Grimes came down the steps from the Texas and joined her crewmen in the bows as she cupped her hands around her mouth and called ashore, "Is the constable about? We had us a shootout, downstream!"

A short, fat man with a tin star on his faded blue shirt came up the gangplank, removing his hat, as Gloria Grimes pointed at the canvas. Then she looked closer, strode over to it, and lifted a corner.

Longarm could see from his vantage point above her that there was nothing under the tarp but a few sticks of cordwood. Gloria turned around, put her hands on her hips, and shouted, "All right, who's the joker who thinks he's being funny?"

The Willow Bend constable joined her on deck and asked, "You say you had a shootout, Miss Gloria? Who got shot?"

"A lawman sent by the Post Office to guard the mails. He was right here under this durned old tarp!"

She stared up at the passengers above and called, "Did any of you folks see that dead man get up and jump overboard?"

Longarm excused himself to the ladies and went down the steps to join the folks around the tarp. He said, "I've been smoking up there for maybe fifteen minutes, Captain. I didn't see anybody on the foredeck."

"Are you sure the dead man was under this tarp when you came out on deck?"

Longarm thought, then shook his head. "No. From up there you can just see the canvas as a square shape in the dark. To save you your next question, I went into the bar right after leaving yourself up yonder. I was talking to Blue until a few minutes ago. I won't take it personal if you want to ask him if that's true."

Gloria turned back to the town law and said, "This is Mr. Lansford. He saw the shooting, but he didn't do it. It was that gambling man, Canfield. He and the lawman had words over cards, and he claims it was a fair fight. I've got him in his stateroom whenever you say the word."

The constable said, "We'd best hear his tale, then," and the lady pilot ordered one of her crewmen to fetch Canfield. While they were waiting, the town law asked for Longarm's version. So Longarm called it as he'd seen it, adding, "It looked reasonable to me, constable. The late Inspector Donovan was a proddy cuss who'd been shoving everybody around. He passed a remark about Canfield's mother with ladies listening."

The town law stared down at the empty space between them on the deck and said, "Nobody has a right to do that, packing a badge or no. But as I see this problem, we have to have us a corpse before the proceedings can go much further. Are you sure this Donovan jasper was dead when they laid him out here?"

Longarm started to say yes, but something struck him. "I sure *thought* he was dead. But I'm no doctor. I never tried to take his pulse. Canfield fired a derringer into him under the table, and if he wasn't hit anywhere important, he sure lay quiet for a man with a wound below the vest."

The town law gauged the distance from the turned-over tarp to the nearest freeboard and scratched his stubby chin with a thumbnail as he opined, "A gent with all the wind knocked out of him and maybe bleed-

60

ing bad inside could mayhap come to and start thrashing about in pain, don't you reckon?"

"It's possible. But he sure suffered sneaky." He turned to Gloria Grimes and asked her, "You can see the bows from up there in your wheelhouse, can't you, ma'am?"

She nodded. "I follow your drift. I might have missed someone sliding over the side like a 'gator, though. We'll search the vessel, and if he ain't anywhere aboard . . . well, how do *you* see that, constable?"

The town law said, "I ain't sure. We've never had a killing without a corpse in Willow Bend before. I reckon we'd best hold Canfield polite, and see if the coroner wants to drag the river some."

The crewman that Gloria had sent aft returned, sounding out of breath as he reported, "He ain't there, Miss Gloria. His carpetbag is missing from his stateroom, too."

She stamped her foot and said, "Durn it, this is really starting to vex me! He must be hiding somewhere."

"If he is, we'll find him, ma'am," the crewman said. "I told Smitty and Al to search for the rascal and, no offense, the *Minnitipi* ain't that big."

Gloria pushed her cap back on her head. "Well, meanwhile we're wasting time, and I've a timetable to keep. Let's shift some cargo and load some wood, and we'll be on our way."

The constable cleared his throat and said, "Ma'am, you said you'd had a killing aboard this vessel."

"I know that, durn it! It was me who reported it to you just now. But as you can plainly see, we don't have a cadaver for your coroner, and we don't seem to have a shooter for you to arrest. You can search my vessel for both, if you want to. I'm leaving in twenty minutes come hell or high water."

She meant it too. Longarm went up to the passenger deck and smoked another cheroot as he watched them manhandle cargo and cordwood. His Ingersoll watch made it a minute less than twenty when the paddles

61

started churning them back out to midstream. Nobody had found hide or hair of either Donovan or the gambler who'd shot him—*if* he'd shot him.

Longarm went back inside and moved the table they'd been sitting at. He kicked the sawdust away and stared down at the floor. How in thunder was a man to spot a bloodstain on planks that had been painted in the first place with oxblood? He shook his head wearily and murmured, "I sure wish dead folks would stay *put* on this infernal river!"

Chapter 4

Longarm lay in his longjohns on the bunk in his state-room, smoking in the dark. He knew the dangers of smoking in bed, but he knew he wasn't about to fall asleep. That fool girl in the wheelhouse kept tooting her damned whistle every few minutes, and while Long-arm was used to sleeping in strange beds, he had a lot on his mind.

He had to pee too. He'd been putting that off as long as possible. There was a chamber pot under the bunk, of course, but he didn't like to smell his own piss if it could be avoided. The men's latrine was just a few doors down. The problem was his state of undress. It seemed sort of formal to get fully dressed just to take a leak.

The whistle tooted again and something scraped the length of the hull. Then the whole vessel shuddered like a coffee grinder as the object got chewed up by the paddlewheel. It had sounded like a floating tree. He'd noticed that the *Minnitipi*'s paddles were clad in sheet iron, so they only had to miss the big stuff. The whistle's echoes doubtless kept Miss Gloria informed about the high banks, but of course she couldn't bounce sound off floating debris in the ink-black current.

He swung his bare feet to the floor and debated the pros and cons of using the pisspot, pulling on his pants, or waiting until his molars floated. He shrugged and cursed himself into his tweed pants, then he stood in his bare feet and slipped on his hickory shirt, leaving the tails out. It seemed formal enough for a shithouse run at midnight. It was dark outside anyway.

He hesitated again as he considered the gunbelt draped over a chair's back near the bunk. That seemed formal too, but a man who lived by the gun couldn't afford to get into sloppy habits, so he strapped it on.

He cracked the door open and had a look-see. There wasn't much to see. They were moving through a bank of river fog and, except for the glow of a lantern down the deck, it was black as a bitch outside. He forgave Miss Gloria for leaning on her whistle so much. He had no idea how in thunder she could steer through fog on a moonless night, but she seemed good at it.

The deck felt clammy under his bare feet as he went down to the latrine and stepped inside. When he closed the door it was totally dark, so he lit a match. He was sorry he'd gone to so much trouble just to get out of using a chamber pot. The facilities consisted of the usual bench with holes cut in it. As he urinated down one of them he held the match over the hole and saw that he'd been right about the noise down there. He was pissing on the inboard curve of the paddle wheel. The rising paddles looked like they'd seriously threaten the genitals of a well-hung gent if he sat down to shit.

Naturally, that reminded him that he hadn't taken a crap since he'd come aboard. What the hell, he was already back there, so he dropped his britches and perched gingerly on the hole. It felt sort of spooky as the dripping paddles fanned his bare behind, but they'd likely measured the fit, and the spray seemed to just miss wetting his tail while he moved his bowels. The whole mission only took three matches, and they'd been good enough to hang a mail-order catalogue for the comfort of the passengers.

He buttoned up and went back outside. His eyes were getting used to the dark now, so he could see out into the fog maybe ten feet. The running lights up on the Texas made the fog glow sort of mustard yellow. The diffuse glow lit the deck just enough so he could see where he was going. He came to what he thought was the door of his stateroom and gave the knob a turn, but it wouldn't budge, and he knew he hadn't locked it behind him. He'd picked the wrong door.

Longarm let go of the cold brass knob and listened, but if he'd disturbed anyone on the other side they weren't making a fuss about it. He stared aft to count doors, but he couldn't see all the way to the end of the corridor in this light. He stood there feeling foolish and fished for another match in his pants pocket. There weren't any. He had a box of them in his coat, but he'd used up the ones he'd taken to the privy with him.

He was about to try reading the carved number in the door panel with his fingertips when he caught movement out of the corner of his eye and dropped his hand guiltily. A female wrapped in a sort of dressing gown was moving toward him like a wraith. She'd gone out on deck barefoot, too. Longarm was too polite to ask why or where as she stopped awkwardly, then said, "Oh, it's you, Mr. Lansford. I seem to have lost my way."

"That makes two of us, ma'am. What's your stateroom number?"

"Starboard, E," she replied, and he said, "You're on the wrong side, ma'am. I'll be blamed if I can figure out which of these doors is mine, but I know this is the port side of the boat."

"Oh, dear," she fretted. "I must have circled the deck some way. Would you be willing to show me the way?"

"I'd be proud to, ma'am," he answered as he offered her his elbow. They headed forward together. Forward was the long way around, but he was in no hurry and it might be embarrassing for both of them to pass the latrines back there so soon after. He wondered if she was thinking about the fact that they'd been sitting back to back with their bare bottoms exposed. Then he wondered why he found that idea so interesting. He had no notion who she was or what she looked like, but she'd unbound her hair and it smelled nice as she walked beside him, barefoot and likely not wearing much under her robe.

She'd apparently expected them to head the other way, for she'd taken the outboard position as they strode the deck. He knew a gent was supposed to walk on the outside, but it seemed sort of silly to mention it. He doubted any wagon would pass by to spray mud on her skirts from the street.

As they passed the front of the main salon, Longarm saw that it was closed for the night, but Blue had left a lamp lit over the bar. The woman he was escorting to her stateroom said something, and he glanced down at her. Now he could see that she was the fancy gal who'd been accused of signaling Canfield with her fan. He didn't comment on it. It hardly seemed likely, now, that she'd been in cahoots with Canfield after all.

They rounded the corner and started aft as the whistle above them hollered. Longarm heard what sounded like someone breaking up kindling behind them. He turned his head just as the jagged branches of a sawyer slammed into them and tried to haul them overboard!

The woman screamed as Longarm hung onto her and dropped below the level of the rail. A wet branch bounced off the top of his head and he'd have lost his Stetson for sure, if he'd been wearing it. The gal, closer to the rail, was having more trouble. A branch had caught in her loose robe and was trying to tear her away from Longarm as the steamboat continued up the river and the sawyer kept going downstream.

"I got you, ma'am," he told her calmly as the gal screamed and the twigs and branches contested his possession of her. He dug his bare heels in and dropped his rump to the slick wet deck as he hung onto her arm with both hands. Then something gave and she collapsed on top of him, sobbing, "Oh, my God! What was that?"

"Sawyer, ma'am. Big dead tree in the water. We're all right now. It didn't scratch you, did it?"

Then, as he started to help her to her feet, he discovered that she was stark naked, save for the one sleeve he'd saved along with the rest of her.

She became aware of it too, now that the horror of being snatched overboard by some unknown monster had passed. She gasped and would have run blindly off, had he not steadied her and said quickly, "Easy, easy, I can't see all that much. Here, I'll wrap my shirt about you."

She turned her back to him, her unbound hair spilling down her ivory skin, and sobbed, "Oh, God, how do I get into things like this?"

Unbuttoning his shirt and draping it around her shoulders, he soothed her, "There, now you're decent. Nobody's seen your undignified, and we'll get get you safe inside before they can."

She held the shirt closed with her free hand and protested, "It's too short! My knees are still exposed!" as he moved her down the deck. He'd kept count of the doors this time, and as they reached hers, he opened it for her and said, "There you go. I'll stay out here and you can just hand out my shirt and we'll say no more about it. I never looked at your knees."

She suddenly laughed as she stepped inside her dark stateroom and turned to take off the shirt. She likely didn't realize how visible she was in the dim illumination from the vessel's running lights, but Longarm didn't see fit to mention it as he enjoyed the view. She handed him the shirt and he started to say good night as he slipped it on. But before he could begin his tactful retreat, she restrained him with a touch on his arm. "I can't believe what just happened. It was all so sudden. If I'd been alone on deck when that awful thing grabbed me . . . Come in and close the door, Mr. Lansford. The very least I can offer you is a nightcap."

"My friends call me Custis," he told her as he entered and closed the door, plunging them into darkness. It was hard enough to remember the family name he'd made up, without contriving a new first name. Not many folks knew his real given name anyway. He expected her to strike a light once she'd slipped on some more duds, but she didn't. He heard the tinkle of glass as she introduced herself. "I'm Sylvia. Last names aren't important in my business. That sawyer thing snatched away my only robe and it would take forever to dress properly, but we can manage by feel, don't you think?"

"It's your stateroom, ma'am," he replied as he stayed put so as to keep from tripping over anything or anybody.

She groped her way to him and handed him a tin cup. "There, have you got it?"

As her cool hand left him standing there with only the drink, he heard her say, "Cheers," and he raised the cup to his own lips. It was brandy. Expensive brandy too. He'd already had enough Maryland rye for a prudent man, so he decided he'd nurse it a spell.

He heard the creak of bedsprings as Sylvia asked, "Would you like to sit down?" He started groping his way over to her, holding the cup close to his chest. His outstretched hand encountered soft, warm flesh in the dark and she giggled as they both flinched, and then she said suspiciously, "Are you sure you can't see me? You couldn't have aimed that well by accident!"

He sat down on the bunk beside her, leaving a polite distance between them, and didn't answer. For a gal who'd just had her bare tit grabbed, Sylvia was taking it like a sport. With one bare heel he felt the cold curve of the chamber pot under her bunk. As he moved it away, he heard it slosh just loudly enough for his keen ears to detect. If she heard it too, she didn't mention it. Victorians were used to not hearing or seeing things that might seem improper in their very proper world. Not a man in a hundred would wonder why a lady had used a chamber pot, since that was what they were for. But if she'd peed in her thunder mug earlier, why had she been out to the latrines at all?

She started to say something more about his saving her life, as he heard her pouring herself another drink in the dark. He took advantage of the distraction to lean forward, pull the chamber pot out a bit, and empty his own cup quietly. As he straightened up, she asked, "Are you ready for another, Custis?"

"No, thanks, I've got a head start on you, and I'll have enough trouble finding my own bunk as it is."

"You sound like you're in a hurry. You, ah . . . don't have anyone waiting for you over there, do you?"

He chuckled. "Not hardly. But it's late and I was trying to be polite."

"Don't you think I can trust you, Custis?"

"I'll have to study on that before I answer. According to the timetable, we'll be putting into another landing about two in the morning, and it's after midnight now."

"Surely you're not getting off at the next stop?"

"Nope. I'm aboard all the way to the end of the line. But how does it figure to look if someone sees me leaving your door, half dressed, as they get set for the landing?"

She laughed deep in her throat. "You're right. That would cause a scandal. Maybe you'd better just stay here and . . . well, keep me company until the boat moves on up the river. Nobody would see you if you left . . . well, just before sunrise, would they?"

"I don't reckon they would," he said, fiddling with the empty cup in his hand. "But I'm a mite confused about the rules of the house here. I was raised to treat gals with respect, but setting here three to four hours with a naked lady strains my properness some. Don't it worry you?"

She put a hand on his wrist and purred, "If I was worried, I wouldn't have invited you in. What on earth do you need, an engraved invitation?"

Gently he placed the tin cup on the floor and took her in his arms. She responded warmly to his kiss, and didn't resist a second feel of that same rounded breast, but she stiffened as he slid his hand down her bare

69

belly. She turned her face and gasped, "Stop that! I never told you you could go *that* far!"

He stopped since she'd asked him to, but his voice was puzzled as he asked, "Why are we having such a foolish conversation, ma'am? I didn't invite myself in here, and I've said I'd leave!"

"I know. You took me by surprise, I guess. Can't you just, well, hold me?"

He leaned her back and kissed her again. "Sure, we can take our time. But you sure dress funny for schoolgirl kissing games."

She smothered his comments with hungry kisses, and this time, as he ran his palm over her after what was perhaps a politer interval, she let him get it between her thighs. But as he cupped her groin and began to gently stroke it like the nervous kitty it seemed to be, she went rigid again. "No. I can't. Please don't force me, Custis."

He left his hand in place quietly, and said, "There you go talking funny again. What do you call this game we're playing?"

"I don't know. I want to respond to you, but I'm frightened. I know it was my idea to start this, but I suddenly realized we're total strangers and it makes me feel . . . well, *low*."

"I ain't married up and the law ain't after me. Did I misunderstand your meaning when you said you were, uh, in business?"

"Oh, for God's sake, are you suggesting that I'm holding out for money?"

"Don't know what you're holding out for, but it's getting sort of tedious. We're in your quarters and in your bed, so it's dealer's choice, but let's make up our minds, pronto. We'll be coming to that landing soon, and I ain't about to be trapped inside with a gal who can't decide whether she's Lola Montez or Queen Victoria."

"My, you *do* have a smooth line with the ladies,

don't you? Do many girls respond to that direct approach?"

"Not all that many, but some. I generally only bother with grownups. I'm sorry you don't like my style, but it's the only style I have. So we'll just part friendly. It's been interesting talking to you, ma'am."

As he released her and started to rise, Sylvia clutched at him and sobbed. "No, I can't let you go. Please don't leave angry."

"I ain't angry. Confused would be more like it. I suspicion I understand what's going on here better than you do, Sylvia. You got all mixed up when I saved you from that sawyer, and that brandy you bolted down didn't help. Everybody knows the fair maid is supposed to kiss the hero after he rescues her, so you just acted natural, forgetting you were naked until *I* started acting natural too. There ain't no right or wrong here. We both made a mistake, is all. I ain't sore. I ain't going to say a thing about this to anyone else. I'll just leave while there's still time, and we'll go back to being what we were, fellow passengers."

He rose, and this time he made it almost to the door before Sylvia leaped up and wrapped herself around him, pleading, "No, I won't let you go! I'll do anything. Anything you want."

His common sense told him to get the hell out while he could, but his glands didn't seem to care much for the notion. He moved her back to the bunk and laid her down gently across the covers. Then he said, "I'm taking off my clothes. Then I aim to mount you proper and go all the way. All I want to hear from you is yes or no."

"Custis, I'm all mixed up and—"

"Yes or no, goddamnit! I already know you're mixed up. The question before the house is yes or no. I'll go or I'll stay, but I don't mean to palaver about it any more!"

She laughed a trifle hysterically, and then murmured more calmly under her breath, "Yes, take me, darling."

71

So he did. He thought he was in for another round of crazy talk as he mounted her more gently than his words might have led her to expect. She stiffened in his arms and hissed throatily as he entered her. But as he started moving, she suddenly relaxed in total surrender as she sighed, "My, there certainly is a lot of you, isn't there?"

Some gals were like that, he knew. He didn't know why, any more than any other man could hope to. But once she'd stopped turning herself off and on, Sylvia settled down to a long, enjoyable ride. He was sort of surprised when she acted so surprised about having her first orgasm. He'd thought that was what everyone wanted, if they got around to it at all. But it seemed to drive her even crazier. He went sort of crazy too, since he hadn't had any since he'd had to leave the schoolmarm back in Denver, when he'd left to catch the midnight local. He had no idea just how they'd wound up on the floor with himself on the bottom and Sylvia bouncing up and down with her bare heels against the floor. But if she didn't mind his hitting bottom with every stroke, he wasn't about to argue.

They took a breather while the boat stopped, at around two. Then, as it churned out into the main channel again and folks stopped passing the locked door, Sylvia was at him again like a wooly bear in heat.

He sort of wondered about that, between times. She acted almost as though the unimportant stop back there had freed her of some worry. He couldn't see what it could have been. Neither of them had planned on getting off there. When he asked, she said it had been in the back of her mind that somebody was likely to pass the door just as she was coming, and that she tended to be a trifle loud. Sure enough, she yelled like the *Minnitipi*'s steam whistle the next time, while he pounded her over the hill to glory.

Along about sunup he allowed that it was time for him to sneak back to his own bunk. She asked him if he wanted another round, but he declined politely. It was a good thing he did. As he slipped around the afterdeck to his own side, he met another male passenger headed for the shithouse. Longarm nodded and passed by, knowing the gent would assume that was where he'd just been.

He got to his own door, and this time, when he tried the knob, it opened. So he'd been right about having picked the wrong door a million years ago, near midnight. He ducked inside and stripped again to fall face up on his own bunk with a contented sigh. "Thank you, Lord," he told the heavens above the room's low ceiling. "You were considerate as hell last night. Had I found my own door before Sylvia came along, she might have been snatched overboard and I might have woke up with a hard-on." And then he was asleep.

Longarm had no idea what time it was when he woke up again and found himself staring at the ceiling, wondering what had awakened him. The steamboat was motionless and silent around him. That was it. They'd put in at another landing. The silence of the paddlewheel and the absence of that infernal whistle had told him the world had changed, for better or worse.

He lay quietly looking up at the sunlight reflected from the river as it danced on the whitewashed planks above him. It had to be near noon, and here he was, slugabed and likely missing dinner as well as breakfast. He sat up and rolled out to stagger to the washstand and splash water on his face. In the small mirror on the wall he saw that he needed a shave, so he rummaged through his bag for his razor. He unfolded it, stropped it on the thick wool of his trousers, and went back to the stand to shave. Then he frowned and went back for another look in the bag. He was missing a box of .44-40 cartridges.

Cursing, he quickly went through the pockets of the coat he'd left unguarded like a fool. But his wallet was still in the inside pocket—money, badge, ID, and all. He reached for his vest. His watch and derringer were safe and sound too. Could he have lost the box of ammo somewhere along the way? He hadn't fired either of his guns, so he hadn't reloaded since leaving Denver.

He shrugged and studied on the matter while he shaved and dressed. Somebody could have searched his stateroom easily enough, since it obviously hadn't been locked after all. But anyone not after his money would have settled for just reading his ID. Why give the show away by snitching a cheap box of ammo like a kid?

There weren't any kids aboard. Who the hell might need some .44-40s bad enough to take such a fool chance? The person or persons unknown would have had to know he packed that caliber. Then they'd have had to know he wasn't likely to pop in the door at them as they dug through his possibles.

He was putting on his hat when he suddenly sighed and said to no one, "Canfield, of course. That was a .44 derringer he was packing."

He locked the door this time, and slipped the key in the side pocket of his frock coat before moving forward to the salon. As he'd feared, it was one in the afternoon and they were taking the dirty dishes and linen away. He didn't go in. Folks were still getting off the steamboat, so he lit a smoke and leaned on the rail as he watched.

A familiar, a *very* familiar figure in a maroon dress was already ashore and moving away at a fast pace, not looking back. Longarm shook his head wearily as he considered his own brains with considerable contempt. Then he brightened and told himself, *It could have been worse, old son. You might have drunk that brandy! She must have wondered why you were taking so long to pass out from whatever she'd put in it. It's no wonder she acted so crazy! She had to hold you there while her husband, lover, or whatever, used your cabin for a hideout. They both knew some smart crewman might have tumbled to the fact that they were together. Like Dobbs did during that card game. It would have been embarrassing, but not fatal, if they'd*

74

decided to look for him in her stateroom whilst you were there, passed out like a lamb. So Sylvia gave her all to hold you there while Canfield just waited in the other stateroom and slipped ashore when they put in at two. Having time on his hands, he likely searched your possibles and, needing ammo, he helped himself. Longarm chuckled again as he considered how the gambler must have blanched when he spotted the federal badge.

They'd spend a lot of time jawing about that as they compared notes over there on the shore. She'd likely wait here until Canfield joined her. They were just a drifing gambler and his moll. It wasn't likely they knew anything about the business upriver, and of course Sylvia would make it up to her lover boy by screwing him silly as she assured him that the fool had gone right to sleep like he was supposed to. Longarm sort of envied Canfield. There were a couple of things he hadn't gotten around to with old Sylvia. *That*'d teach him to hold off for a second night.

He went inside and saw that Blue hadn't left after all. That made sense, since there'd been no need for his testimony. He ordered an eye-opener and Blue said, "You just missed the captain. Miss Gloria was asking about you at dinner."

"I missed breakfast too," Longarm said. "Must be this sea air."

"I could get you a sandwich, Mr. Lansford."

"Thank you, Mr. Blue. That's neighborly as hell of you. Uh, what did Miss Gloria want with me? Maybe I'd better have a word with her."

Blue shook his head. "You can't. She's in bed. The mate has the wheel right now, and Miss Gloria won't be awake until suppertime."

"She don't sleep much, does she?"

"Nobody sleeps much on the river. Not if they're crew, that is. She never said she wanted you for anything, Mr. Lansford. She just wondered where you was."

Blue went below to fix the sandwich. As Longarm

nursed his drink, the big burly fellow named Dobbs who'd been at the table the night before came in, looked surprised, and joined him. "I thought you got off. Is the bar open yet?" he asked.

"Yep. Barkeep is getting me a ham and cheese. What made you think I was getting off so soon, Dobbs?"

"I seen you," Dobbs said. "At least I thought I did. I was coming outta the crapper when we put in along about two last night. I thought I saw you leave your stateroom. But when I called howdy, you just waved and sort of run forward around the corner. Didn't you go ashore after all?"

Longarm thought that was a stupid question, considering they were both standing there. But he said, "You must have seen somebody else. I stayed in bed through that particular stop. Did you really see him go down the gangplank?"

Dobbs frowned. "No. That's a funny thing, now that I study on it. I did follow you, or whomsoever, up to the bows. I wasn't being nosy, I just aimed to say adios. But there was only crewmen up there, rolling barrels down the gangplank to some other gents on shore. I didn't *run* the length of the boat, so I figured I'd just missed you . . . I mean *him*."

Longarm nodded. It was easy enough to see how Canfield had slipped over the side and simply waded ashore in the shallows in the gloom.

After being sent to his own stateroom by the skipper-lady, he'd likely hidden in Sylvia's while the boat put in at Willow Bend. Later, afraid the local law might get around to searching there, the two of them had decided to lure a dupe into Sylvia's, drug him, and use a less suspicious empty stateroom for Canfield to lay low in until they got to where he could get off. Longarm knew they couldn't have known when or if he had to take a leak, so Sylvia had been prowling about looking for anything in pants. *She* might have had a chance to roll Donovan's body overboard yesterday. Of course, a gal would have attracted attention on the cargo deck, had anyone seen her. But if anyone had seen *anybody* moving about up forward, there wouldn't be any mystery, so what the hell.

Blue came back up with the sandwich and Longarm thanked and paid him. Two of the passengers who'd just boarded came in and leaned against the bar, farther down, so Blue went to serve them. Dobbs waited until Blue was out of earshot before he said quietly, "I noticed you called that nigger 'mister.' How come?"

"Ask Captain Grimes," Longarm told him. "She started it. Blue seems to think it's important, and it don't cost all that much to be polite."

"Oh, I thought you might be a nigger lover," Dobbs said.

Longarm picked up his vittles as he replied, "I ain't one for loving or hating anyone before they give me a reason. I don't like to jaw about whether Abe Lincoln was right or wrong so many years behind us all. I figure it was settled the hard way when Grant and Lee had that drink at Appomattox."

Dobbs shrugged and said, "That's as it may be. Personally, I rode for the South with Quantrill."

Longarm didn't answer as he chewed his sandwich. It wouldn't have been polite to point out to Dobbs that he had contradicted himself. Longarm had met many a man from the real Confederate Army who was still embarrassed about ragtag guerrillas who'd held up banks for Dixie. But Dobbs had started his brag and Longarm was hungry, so he just went on eating while Dobbs continued, "Yep, I was in the same troop as old Frank James. Knowed Cole Younger too. They was good old boys, no matter what you read in the papers these days. I mind one time when we was swapping shots with jayhawkers . . ."

The story went on, but Longarm was frowning about something else as he realized Donovan had called *him* a jayhawker *and* a Johnny Reb. That was another contradiction, now that he really studied on it. The pro-

Southern guerrillas in prewar "Bleeding Kansas" hadn't been the jayhawkers. John Brown and the antislavery terrorists had been the jayhawkers. And Donovan had hoorahed Longarm as an ex-enemy, claiming to be a Union man himself.

Of course Donovan had allowed he was from back East, and he might have just been mixed up about Kansas history, Topeka office or not. But Longarm resolved that he would definitely check the missing man out, as soon as he was in a position to send some coded wires.

To get Dobbs off the subject of how the South had really won the war, Longarm swallowed and said, "Last night, when they had that fight, I was seated directly across from Donovan and you were facing Canfield, right?"

Dobbs nodded. "I was, but what of it? It wasn't *me* as shot that gent under the table. You saw Canfield with the smoking gun in his fist. He admitted doing the deed!"

"Don't get your bowels in an uproar. Nobody's accusing you of anything," Longarm said, chuckling.

"Then what's your point, damn it?"

"My point is the angle of aim and view. From where I was sitting, I had to take it on faith that Donovan had been hulled at the waterline. You'd pushed your chair back, so you had a side view of him as he fell forward. Did you actually see him oozing some, or did you just buy his head on the table, like me?"

Dobbs frowned and said, "By Jesse Crawfish, I never *looked*, now that I study on it. But hold on. Them crewmen picked him up and carried him away. Wouldn't they have noticed if he'd been playing 'possum?"

"It would depend a lot on how good a 'possum he was. One had him by the boots and the other had him under the armpits, and they only carried him a few paces under the lamplight."

"I've had more than one deer get up and run off

78

long after I was sure I'd put it on the ground for keeps," Dobbs admitted. "But I still say your notion sounds a mite wild. Leaving aside the cold nerve it'd take to play dead in front of a whole roomful of folks, Canfield would have had to be *in* on it, wouldn't he? I mean, a man would know if he missed a man sitting almost in his lap."

Longarm said he reckoned so, and finished the rest of his sandwich. Dobbs was likely right. Sylvia had shown him the night before that she and Canfield planned ahead enough to have knockout drops on hand, and were flexible if things didn't go exactly right. Longarm suspected that he was trying to explain one thing that made no sense with other notions that, as Dobbs had said, led down even wilder trails.

So he put the mystery of the missing Donovan aside until he had a chance to ask some sensible questions.

It seemed to take a million years.

After the initial excitement, the trip up the Big Muddy settled down to a dull routine that helped explain why the old steamboat lines were losing passenger business to the railroads.

A steamboat was more comfortable to ride than a coach or train. You could walk about and pester or avoid folks, as the spirit moved you. The scenery would have been interesting, had not there been so damned much of it. Some days they'd pass high bluffs carved by the rains of eons into ogres' castles, Moorish cities, or the White Cliffs of Dover in that geography book. Along other stretches the river widened out into a big muddy lake with swampy edges. There were islands, forested or bare, and big rafts of floating timber that looked like islands until they moved. They met other boats coming down, and everybody tooted and waved. They put in at pretty little towns and ugly shantytowns. Both tended to get farther apart as they got farther upriver and the waterway started showing its bare bottom on more sandbars.

Longarm conversed most with those passengers who

seemed to be going the farthest. There was little sense in buying a beer for a gent who aimed to get off well before they reached the headwarters where the other boats had been hit.

After he'd heard Dobbs' version of the war a few times, Longarm took to avoiding him, even though he'd said he was going all the way upriver. The man just sounded too foolish to be up to anything slick, and whatever reason anyone had had for knocking off those other boats, they'd done it with considerable skill.

The Gilmore twins and old Lavinia Lee tended to sort of avoid Longarm. The older gal would nod her head to him as they passed on the deck, but the two young gals just prissed by like butter wouldn't melt in their mouths. They didn't exactly snub him; a gal has to notice a gent is *there,* to snub him. They were both pretty, and it was a shame a man would have had to climb up on a chair to kiss either one. How they navigated with their noses aimed at the ceiling was a pure mystery, but Longarm wouldn't have worried about it if the damned boat had been a mite bigger.

But as the suffering that Sylvia had put him through wore off, and Longarm found himself sleeping alone night after night, those gals he kept tripping over just got prettier and prettier . . . Come to think of it, Lavinia wasn't bad. Her few wrinkles were friendly in cruel sunlight and hardly worth mention under lantern light. Her dark brown hair was a mite frosted, but it made her look distinguished, once a man studied on it. He knew she owed some of that hourglass figure to whalebone and Charles Goodyear, but he'd undressed enough gals to know she'd unwrap nicely anyway, and he admired the way she walked. He figured she was on the near side of fifty, and if there was anything more exciting to take to bed than a willing virgin, it was an older, experienced gal who still had her shape. But it didn't look like there was any decent way a man was going to cut Lavinia out of that little herd she ran with, even if she did smile at him in passing. It was sort of funny. Lavinia was supposed to be chaperoning the two young gals up the river. But they were chaperoning *her,* too. He was pretty sure he'd have been able to get closer to her, had she been traveling alone. No sensible older gal was about to give two young snips a chance to gossip about her, though. So he decided he'd best hold himself pure for his true love, Miss Ellen Terry. He'd never met the English actress except in the pages of the *Police Gazette,* but she was one of the most beautiful women he'd even seen, if they hadn't done something to that photograph, and it was starting to look as though he had as good a chance with Ellen Terry as with any woman aboard this damned old steamboat.

He got to see more of Captain Grimes too, as they met at mealtimes, and Gloria Grimes kept getting better looking with each bend of the river, too. She wasn't around as often or as much. When she wasn't eating or sleeping, she was up in the wheelhouse. She was built more boyishly than Lavinia and the twins, and the river winds and bright sun had tanned her face more than current fashion decreed. Her nails were cut short and her hands were harder than most females liked their hands to be, but Longarm liked her eyes. They were clear, keen green, and he could see there was a brain inside her head, looking out through them. Longarm admired smart women, even if it did complicate romance a mite. By the time they were approaching Milk River, he'd about decided that if Ellen Terry never invited him to tea, Captain Grimes would do as well. He'd seldom had so many nice choices with so little action.

Chapter 5

Milk River, Montana Territory, was where the new Great Northern Railroad parted company with the upper Missouri after running side by side with it for a hundred and sixty-odd miles. Longarm had wondered at first why the *Minnitipi* hadn't met the mail train at Williston, North Dakota, when the river swung around the big north bend and locomotives started tooting at them from the high bank. But he'd learned to keep his mouth shut and his ears open even when he wasn't undercover, so he saved himself from getting hoorahed as a greenhorn by figuring it out himself.

The tracks didn't follow the river bend for bend; they cut across the rolling prairie. The smoke plumes of the trains they passed, going both ways, indicated that a speed of forty miles an hour was about average, with the Iron Horse getting up to sixty on long flat stretches. The poor little *Minnitipi* walked upstream doing less than ten as she threaded her way among the rafts and bars in the ever-increasing current. So even though the Post Office could have put the mail aboard sooner, they sent it on by rail as far as Milk River and saved a mess of days. It was good to see that Uncle Sam had somebody working in the post office who could read a map. Mail headed west the day the *Minnitipi* clawed her way past Bismarck could catch up with her at Milk River. Once it boarded the steamboat, it was anybody's guess when it would arrive at the head of navigation. Longarm admired Captain Gloria Grimes, but he could see there had to be a better way than this pufferbilly steamboat to get the mail through.

The mail car they were supposed to meet up with wouldn't arrive for a couple of hours yet, so Miss Gloria decreed a longer than usual layover and Longarm went ashore with the other passengers. The others likely wanted to stretch their legs. He did too, but he had more important business. As he strode along the landing he spied a couple of unshaved, ragged waterfront loafers seated on a pile of buffalo bones. He figured they were waiting for a flatboat to load. Bones gathered off the prairie came free for the labor, and even downstream at the bone-meal mills they weren't worth all that much, so Longarm reached in his pocket for a nickel as he stopped and asked the two shabby gents which way the Western Union office was. One just looked away. The other asked, "Who wants to know?"

Longarm frowned and said, "Never mind. I'll ask somebody more polite. I can see you're both busy as hell, and some kid could likely use the tip."

He walked on, not looking back. A familiar voice called out, "Behind you, Deputy!" As he turned, he saw the bone loaders coming at him, both carrying buffalo thighs like clubs. He didn't figure they aimed to load them on a flatboat.

Longarm stood his ground as he smiled warmly and let his frock coat fall open to expose the grips of his .44. They stopped a few paces off and stood there glaring at him. He saw that the man who'd shouted the warning was Blue, the barkeep from the *Minnitipi*. As the black man came along the path, one of the louts growled, "You got a big mouth, nigger."

Blue didn't swerve around them. He headed to join Longarm as he smiled and said, "You'd best stand aside, country boy. There's a steamboat man a-coming through."

They didn't like it much. Both braced themselves and raised the bone clubs as Blue placed a hand on his hip pocket. Longarm snapped, "That's just about enough, everybody," as he drew his revolver. "Why don't you boys just go sit on your bones or something? Mr. Blue can show me the way to the telegraph office, and you've proved how cross-grained you are."

One of them started edging away as his sidekick spat in the dust like a schoolyard bully and stayed put. But when Blue walked past, he didn't do anything.

As the barkeep fell in beside him and they walked away, Longarm holstered his gun and said, "Thanks. I never expected a shabby tramp to come up behind me. They must be drinking something mean as hell."

"Drunk or sober, they was flatboat trash," Blue said.

"Is that what the fuss was all about? I could see they were gleaning the few crumbs left on the Buffalo boom. You steamboaters must be in mighty fearsome competition with the old flatboaters, now that railroads are taking so much fast freight away from you both."

Blue nodded sadly. "That's true. Nobody's been able to work steady as a flatboater since old Nick Roosevelt took the first steamboat down the Ohio, long before the War. Kids and old boys nobody else would hire still run a cargo like firewood or bones down the river on a one-way craft. They bust the flatboats up for lumber to sell as well."

"How do they get back up?"

"Some of 'em don't. They's drifters who just work here and there as folks see fit to hire 'em. If they have a home port upstream, they buy passage on a steamboat or walk like anybody else. Sometimes a steam pilot will sign one on to work his passage. Captain Gloria don't. Her daddy, Big Bill, taught her long ago that most flatboat men are trash."

Longarm filed that away. He didn't know much about the economy of the Big Muddy, but he'd learned long ago not to dismiss a man as good or bad just by the work he did. He could see how the easy drifting life with the downstream current could attract a man who wasn't one for hard work. He could see how many a man who'd been turned down as a worthless bit of flotsam by a proud steamboater might hold a grudge too, and Blue had just said some of them made it back upstream, one way or another. A man had plenty of time to brood, trudging day after day along the bank as he watched the steamboats gaily passing by.

Blue pointed out a distant hanging sign as they came to the corner of the main drag. "I've time for a drink before I send my wires," Longarm said. "You've been serving me many a drink aboard the *Minnitipi*, Mr. Blue. It seems only fair for me to wet *your* whistle for a change."

But Blue shook his head emphatically. "I thanks you, but I'd best go on down to the part of town where they serves gentlemen of color without fluster."

Longarm didn't argue. They were about as far north as you could get without permission from the Northwest Mounties, but that was the way the world was, and Blue seemed philosophical about it, so they each went their own ways.

Longarm didn't stop as he passed the open swinging doors with the honkytonk piano tinkling inside. He'd only mentioned the drink to be polite, and no matter who was sitting atop the piano in tights, the boat was fixing to leave soon.

He went to the telegraph office and sent a long night letter to his "Uncle Billy" in Denver. The code was simple, but the clerk who would send it later, when the rates went down, would likely wonder why he'd been so long-winded, even in a night letter. He asked his office to inquire about the late John Bishop and double-check with Topeka about the hot-tempered Post Office dick, Donovan. He said to wire the answers to Fort Benton, up the river. Then, after he'd handed over the long message, he asked the man behind the counter if he had any messages for anyone called Lansford.

The clerk brightened and said he had. They'd been waiting for him for days. Longarm tipped him and strode out to find a place to read them. The saloon with the piano sounded like as good a place as any. So

Longarm went in, ordered a beer, and took it to a corner table. He'd been wrong about the lady in tights atop the piano. There wasn't one. A sad little man chewing on a matchstick was all alone at the piano, playing pretty damned cheerfully considering the place was nearly empty.

Longarm took out the wires and scanned them, balling each sheet up and tossing it in a nearby spittoon as he finished it. Even if anyone was interested enough to fish them out of tobacco spit and read them, they were all in code too.

They were answers to the inquiries he'd sent from K.C., of course, but they didn't tell him much, decoded or no. There really was an agent named Donovan working out of the Topeka office, and nobody anywhere had a line on the two young galoots who'd tried to hold up the train, so nobody knew the identity of any others they might have been riding with. But Billy Vail agreed they didn't sound like the James Boys or any other sensible gang.

He sipped his brew, and as he read the last check-off he saw that he'd wasted a couple of questions in his night letter. Old Billy Vail was a sharp lawman, too. He'd double-checked with his opposite number in the Post Office Department. Inspector Donovan was really a Post Office dick, but he hadn't been assigned to this particular case!

Vail's coded wire said Donovan had asked for a month's leave and gotten it. He also sent a complete description of the moody Donovan and it added up. So Donovan had been acting on his own, it seemed. But why? If he'd been an ambitious kind, he might have heard of a big case and decided to horn in. Nothing much was going on around Topeka right now, and Donovan had been a pushy sort of jasper.

Dumb too, if that had been his play. Other federal agents might or might not welcome another gent into their game, if he showed some common sense and manners. Donovan had been on the prod and acting like a loudmouthed pain in the ass to everyone he'd met. Billy Vail's wire said he was a senior agent with a good arrest record. He sure had acted like a total idiot, though. Longarm thought of some more questions to add to his night letter, but decided not to bother. Vail and Topeka had already described Donovan as close as you could get without a photograph. It was possible that some wise-ass, knowing the real Donovan was on leave, might have decided to take his place for some reason. But if it had been a sensible reason, they'd chosen a piss-poor ringer. It was one thing to announce to everyone you met that you were a federal lawman, but it was another thing entirely to pick on grown men until one of them just had to shoot you!

As Longarm got rid of the last wire and lit a smoke, a tall man came in off the street and strode up to the bar. He ordered a drink, then turned around to survey the interior of the establishment as his eyes grew accustomed to the dimness. His gaze lit on Longarm, then went on past. The man frowned, gave a little start, and his gray eyes returned to gaze fixedly at the lawman. His tanned features split in a wide grin. Longarm recognized him at the same moment, but not fast enough to stop the man from saying loudly, "Longarm! You old rascal, what are you doing up here in Montana?"

It was Matt Kincaid, an army officer he'd worked with in the past. Kincaid was in civvies this afternoon, and as he picked up his drink and strode briskly over to the table, Longarm whispered, "I'm undercover, Matt. I'm using the name Lansford, should anybody ask."

"Lansford it is. We rode together in Easy Company a couple of years ago, right?"

Longarm noticed that Matt hadn't asked him what sort of case he was on. That was one of the things he liked about the big Connecticut infantry lieutenant. Matt Kincaid had gone to college, but it hadn't rotted his brains.

"Well, Matt," Longarm said, "this is a pure surprise.

Have you taken up an honest line of work, or deserted, or are you just dressed like a human being for the day?"

"I'm afraid the army's still got my raggedy ass, for what it's worth," Kincaid replied. "And the Good Lord and the War Department haven't seen fit to promote me yet, either. No, I'm just up here comparing notes with the BIA, and you know how skittish Indian agents can act when they see army blue."

"Mr. Lo acting up again, Matt?" asked Longarm. He knew Kincaid often served as liaison between War and BIA, since he knew his Indians from a hole in the ground and could work with other services without bragging too much about his own outfit being the only thing standing between civilization and utter chaos.

Kincaid said, "As a matter of fact, Mr. Lo has been quieter than usual. I was just over at the Belknap Reservation and I heard good things about you from the Indian police. Just what was it you did over on the Blackfoot Reserve that pleased everybody so?"

"Ancient history. Crooked land agent was trying to grab some Blackfoot grazing rights and I made him stop. Right now I'm on a mail job, riding as a passenger on a riverboat."

"Kimaho & K.C. Line?"

"You *have* done your homework. Are you sure this is an accidental meeting, soldier blue?"

Kincaid laughed. "Officer and a gentleman's honor. I had no idea you were on the case. We've been working with postal inspectors on it."

"The army's breeding mailmen, Matt?"

"No. If you know anything about the attacks upstream, you know some say it could have been Indians. Nobody's *seen* any Indians shoot up a steamboat, and I'm sure we've a handle on every band in the area. But the senseless savagery of the attacks sounds sort of Sioux to people who don't know them as well as you and I."

Longarm nodded. "I'm supposed to cover that angle too. Indians don't have a monopoly on senseless savagery. I've caught many a white man pulling stunts an Apache would consider crazy." Then he took a sip of beer and added, "I'm glad I run into you, Matt. I know damn few Indians could pull the wool over your eyes, and if you say they're in the clear—"

"Back up," Kincaid cut in. "I said no such thing. I said neither War nor BIA has any line on who'd been shooting up the Kimaho & K.C. boats. I never said it wasn't possible. You know how young bucks are, about trying to build a rep. I'm sure none of the chiefs or older medicine men are in on it. Sitting Bull reads the *Washington Post* and the *Army Times*. So the elders know it's an election year and that it makes sense to sit tight and see if the next administration will increase their allotments. But you know how little control they have these days over their young men."

"Yeah, it's sort of hard to look dignified when you line up outside the agency for your flour and beans. But a warrior who'd knocked off two steamboats should have publicly counted coup on his victories by now."

Kincaid nodded and said, "That's one of the things I've been checking out with the BIA. In the Shining Times, they'd be gathering at the Medicine Places for the summer Sun Dances about now, and of course our friendlies would be picking up gossip. But as you know, the Sun Dance is forbidden now by federal law. There won't be any real gatherings until just before the fall hunting ceremonies."

"You reckon they'll *have* a hunt this fall, Matt? I just passed a pile of buffalo bones being shipped for fertilizer. Some of them looked like they'd been out in the sun and rain a spell."

Kincaid sighed deeply, and a bit angrily. "Yeah, the herds have really been shot to hell. There was enough beef on the hoof out here to feed the Indians *and* the rest of us, if they'd managed the herds. But that's ancient history too. To answer your question—yes, there will be a fall hunt. There aren't many buffalo left, but the BIA allows Mr. Lo to let off steam at the bird migration and so forth. We in the army sincerely wish him well. If you have to issue the Indians government ammunition, it's sort of comforting to see them blazing away at ducks."

Longarm consulted his watch and saw that he had time for another round. But Kincaid declined with a shake of his head. "I've got a train to catch in a few minutes. Speaking of trains, you might look into the Great Falls & Yellowstone, Longarm."

Longarm frowned as he studied his mental railroad map and said, "There ain't any such line, Matt."

Kincaid nodded and said, "I know. It makes one wonder. A syndicate from the East just outbid the Great Northern for the right-of-way on a spur line running up the headwarters of the Missouri and then following the Front Range cross-country, down to the new Yellowstone Park."

Longarm traced the imaginary route in his head before he observed, "That don't make much sense, Matt. I can see how someday when the country gets more settled, they'll have a line following the Missouri past the fall line and over the mountains past Butte. The Anaconda & Pacific joins up with the UP down there, so a northern way out would be profitable. But tearassing southeast from Great Falls to the headwarters of the Yellowstone don't add up. Hardly anybody lives in that foothill country. Who the hell and what the hell would a railroad carry?"

Kincaid nodded. "That's why the older lines didn't fight too hard for the route, Longarm. I was talking about it to a Great Northern man the other day. He says they were planning to run a spur the way you said, in a few years when it would pay. He said they felt sort of wistful about being outbid on parts of the upper Missouri, but that this new outfit was welcome to most of their projected route. He said if you come back a hundred years from now you won't find a railroad running through such rough and empty country."

Longarm chewed on his cheroot and said, "He'd

likely know how to make money running a railroad. Of course the steamboat still makes a modest profit on the mails up to the foothills."

"Modest is the key word, Longarm. A steamboat doesn't pay land taxes on its right-of-way. It has no tracks to maintain. If the Kimaho & K.C. was hauling enough mail and cargo to be interesting, there'd already be a rail line up to Great Falls and beyond."

Longarm started to ask the army man how he felt about railroad men trying to put the little pufferbilly *Minnitipi* out of business, but he didn't. The answer to that question was obvious. As Jesse James and lots of other folks kept complaining, the rich railroad moguls had enough congressmen on their payrolls to run the tracks just about anywhere they wanted to. No railroad line had to sink a steamboat to take its trade away. Once they had the Iron Horse running alongside, the race was to the swift. The Post Office would just naturally give the mail-hauling contract to those who could deliver the fastest, and a locomotive could leave the *Minnitipi* in its dust at its slowest uphill pace. It'd make more sense for a steamboat line to wreck a train. Folks like the Vanderbilts and Huntingtons didn't hire guns to put shoestring rivals out of business. They didn't have to.

He saw that Kincaid was watching the clock over the bar, so he said, "I've seen enough of Milk River too. But before we part company there's a favor I'd like to ask. I've been trying to figure out how to do it discreet, but an old army man could get into the records without attracting as much attention."

"Sure, Longarm. Who do you want me to check on?"

"That pilot of the second boat, Johnny Bishop."

Kincaid frowned and said, "He's dead, isn't he?"

"It could fall off the log either way." Longarm explained his suspicions about missing bodies and what Blue had told him about Miss Gloria's husband.

Kincaid looked interested. "I was at the Point with

a fellow who's a colonel in the Michigan State Militia now. They'd have the records of the old volunteer regiments. But it would help if we had more details than just a name."

Longarm nodded. "If Bishop was a licensed river pilot, he must have filled out a mess of forms. Ain't the Army Engineers in charge of navigation on interior waters?"

Kincaid nodded and said, "Good thinking. The states license pilots out of their home ports, but they send a copy to the Corps of Engineers. So the army has a record somewhere of Bishop's physical description, date of birth, and so forth. It'll help in matching him up with his claims about the War years. It's going to take me a few days, but if he marched with the old Michigan Volunteers, we'll soon know it. We'll know if he's on their list of deserters too."

"I doubt he'd boast of an outfit he deserted," Longarm pointed out. "Most deserters who jaw about the War at all say they served in some other outfit entire. Old Blue is a smart gent and Southron-raised. If he thought Bishop was a Southron he must have had a reason."

"Try it this way," Kincaid offered. "If Bishop was a 'galvanized Yankee,' they could both be right."

Longarm puffed pensively at his cheroot. "Are we talking about those Confederate PWs who signed up with the Union?"

Kincaid nodded. "Yes, when the Sioux rose under Little Crow and started killing settlers in Minnesota while the War was going on. The Union had all these Johnny Rebs at Sandusky, south of Detroit, with damned few Union troops to spare for Indian-fighting."

Longarm nodded and said, "I read about it. They stuck a mess of Confederates in blue uniforms and sent them by lake steamer to help fight the Sioux. But how would that put old Johnny Bishop, reb or no, in the Michigan Volunteers?"

"Easy. Nobody was about to arm and equip a whole

regiment of rebel PWs. The galvanized Yankees were parceled out among militia outfits. Two Union men to every reb, with Union officers and NCOs, of course. It'll be on record in Lansing, if that's the answer to a Yankee Wolverine who had a Southern accent."

"What happened to the galvanized Yankees, after they hung Little Crow?"

"Nothing much. It would have been sort of shitty to send a man back to a prison camp after he'd fought Indians for you. The Southerners were enlisted as Union volunteers with the understanding that they'd not be sent to fight their former comrades under Lee. In fairness, they chalked up a fine record against the Sioux, who must have been confused to hear the rebel yell in the Land of Sky Blue Waters. After Little Crow's bands were rounded up or driven farther west, the galvanized Yankees served as frontier troops in the Northwest until the war was over. Then most were mustered out with honorable Union discharges. Some put in for veterans' allotments and got them. A lot of them stayed in the North as homesteaders. You can see why, of course."

"Yeah. It would have been sort of hard to explain blue britches to the good old boys around the general store in Dixie, whether you'd fired on the Stars and Bars or not. If it turns out that Johnny Bishop was one of those galvanized Yankees, Blue and me will owe him some apologies for being so suspicious. But I'd still feel better about the gent if somebody could point out his grave to me."

Kincaid muttered something about his train and rose, saying, "I'll check it out for you. But you may be barking up the wrong tree. A lot of people have vanished forever in the Big Muddy, Longarm. The odds are ten to one against a body being recovered in any condition to be identified, if it ever comes up again at all."

They walked outside together and shook hands before each went his own way. Captain Grimes had said she aimed to leave in what was now less than an hour, so Longarm headed back. The buffalo bones were still there when he reached the landing. The two loafers who'd been looking for trouble weren't.

He went aboard the *Minnitipi* and climbed the steps to see if Blue had beat him back to the bar. The black man wasn't behind the bar; Gloria Grimes was. She'd poured herself a most unladylike double whiskey, and when Longarm asked if she was serving, she did so. But she slopped his suds as she slammed the schooner down in front of him, and when he tried to pay she snapped, "Don't be an ass. I own the boat."

He didn't answer as he picked up the wet schooner. Her expression softened just a bit. "I'm sorry. It ain't your fault and I had no call to flare at you like that."

"I can see somebody put a burr under your saddle, ma'am. Is there anything I can do to help?"

She shook her head grimly. "Not unless you run the post office. I told you all we were stopping here to meet the mail train, remember?"

"Yep. I noticed a mess of trains beat us this far west, too. No offense."

Gloria muttered something unladylike indeed under her breath and said, "I just came from the post office. They said the mail I'm to deliver hasn't arrived yet. The government promised me some federal agents too. They're with the mail sacks."

Longarm sipped his beer, then asked, "When is their train due in, ma'am?"

"Tomorrow morning, goddamnit to hell!" she snapped. Then she added, "Excuse my cussing, but I am purely fit to be tied."

"I can see you're as mad as a wet hen," he admitted, "but I don't reckon the other passengers will be all that sore. We've all been cooped up in a small space for days and they might welcome an overnight stop in an exotic port of call."

She shook her head. "The hell with the passengers. It's my poor little bottom I'm worried about."

Longarm had noticed that her bottom was right

handsome, but he suspected she wasn't talking about her own. His surmise was confirmed as she went on, "The river is dropping a good six inches a day, and from here on it's too shallow for comfort even at high water. On a good trip we can figure on grasshoppering her over some bars near the mountains, but if we don't get going soon, we'll never get her past Eagle Butte."

Longarm read his mental map before he asked, "That's about two days short of Kimaho, ain't it, ma'am?"

"Make it more like a week and change. The Big Muddy winds a mite from here on. We can count on three feet of water most places from here to Eagle Butte. We'll never make it around the Big Bend, upstream from there, if the river drops another foot before that infernal mail arrives."

"Has it ever happened before, Miss Gloria?"

"Yes. And it costs like hell to pack the mail and cargo the rest of the way by mule."

"I can see how it might. You can't hardly make a profit if you deliver steamboat mail by pack train, can you?"

"Why did you think I was drinking alone?" she asked. "We don't just lose money if we get stuck in the mud. We lose time and goodwill. It's no secret that the only thing keeping us in business is the mail contract, and the settlers up in the foothill country are already broody about waiting as long as they do for their letters."

He sipped his beer and asked, "What do you aim to do if the mail train don't beat low water, ma'am?"

"What *can* I do? I'm damned if I do and damned if I don't. If we push off now, we'll arrive empty-handed. If we get stuck in the mud above Eagle Butte, we won't arrive at all, or at least not by water or on time. I don't know which I hate worse, the mule ride or the same stale jokes as we drop off a mail sack at each country post office."

Longarm said, "This ain't my business, ma'am, but

ain't you doing things the hard way when the river fails you? If I was running this line and I found myself stuck on a bar short of my goal, I'd see if I could hire me some freighters to deliver further up. Then I'd turn around and head back down to make up for the loss on more civilized parts of the river."

She snorted derisively. "It's a good thing you're not running the Kimaho & K.C., then. You'd have no trouble at all getting sweet-talking mountain freight contractors to take your cargo off your hands."

"In that case, what's the problem?"

"Getting the business *back,* of course! Have you any notion how many mule and wagon freighters have been trying to take my mail franchise away from me? No, sir. Nobody is about to deliver my mail and cargo but my own self."

He smiled sheepishly and regarded the bottom of his beer schooner. "I can see I haven't been keeping up with the transportation business. I'd clean forgot there's more to this race than steamboats agin locomotives. Neither Butterfield nor Wells Fargo run their long stage routes anymore, and the Iron Horse just killed off wagon freight on the Santa Fe Trail. There must be a mess of muleskinners and wagonmasters looking for business these days."

She nodded. "Of course. They're fighting tooth and nail for the mails and freight where neither the rails nor a river runs, and the territory keeps shrinking. So you can see why, if I have to hire mules, I hire them in my own name."

"Have you had much competition up in the head-water country, from rival freighters who take the slower land routes?"

She said, "More than you can shake a stick at, damn it! Aside from mule packers and a wagon outfit, we've been running neck-and-neck with a shoestring stage line that keeps trying to steal our mail franchise between Fort Benton and Kimaho. Their Concords make about the same time, once the river braids out under us. When we really hit low water, they naturally beat us."

"What keeps you in good with the Post Office? Seniority?"

"Partly that. Mostly a matter of distance. As you see, we can pick up here, over a hundred and fifty miles further east than the stage line runs. We'd beat them to Fort Benton even if they had a line this far out on the High Plains. So we gain a few days on them, counting the whole run. They keep trying to buy in. They say it would make more sense if we ran the mail as far as Eagle Butte or Fort Benton and turned it over to them to go the rest of the way by stage. They say I'm just being a stubborn she-male. But I mean to stick it out anyway."

Longarm thought before he asked, "*Wouldn't* you both make out better that way, Miss Gloria? If you split the run, you'd have fewer low-water worries and they'd be saved maintaining way stations out on the prairie. It sounds practical for each outfit to run where it can run best. You on the water and them over the hills."

Gloria took a slug of her own drink before she said, "No. Two ways. I don't just deliver mail; I carry heavy freight to folks who need it at a price no stage or packer could match. The mail franchise is the icing on the cake that keeps us in the black, when the durned old river behaves! Since I have to get there anyway, I might as well have it all."

"That sounds reasonable. What's the second reason?"

"Call it woman's intuition. I just don't *like* the rascals who own that infernal stage line. My daddy, Big Bill, said he didn't trust either one of 'em far enough to spit, neither, and what my daddy said is good enough for me." Then she fixed Longarm's gaze with her own, and said, "You sure do ask a lot of questions, Mr. Lansford. You did say you were a cattleman looking for new rangeland, didn't you?"

Longarm just nodded and decided he'd asked enough

questions for now. They finished their drinks and Gloria Grimes said something about going off to bed. He didn't think he ought to ask any questions about that, either. She'd likely have told him if she meant to include him.

Chapter 6

Longarm found himself almost alone in the salon at suppertime. The prissy little gent who'd been at the table before the card game heated up was there with a little brown sparrow who'd turned out to be his wife, according to Blue. Lavinia Lee and the Gilmore twins were there too, at another table. Most of the other passengers had gone ashore, since they were male. A man never knew when he'd get a chance like Milk River again.

Anyplace where riverboats and trains met up near a cattle town had to be well furnished with improper entertainment. But Longarm had already seen the best saloon. It was sort of seedy, and his job called for him to keep an eye on the steamboat, even if it made him look like a sissy.

He knew Gloria Grimes was catching up on her sleep so as to be fit for the hard haul ahead, come morning. But most of the crew had taken shore leave. Blue was off wherever gentlemen of color got laid in a river town, and the bar was manned by a surly white boy who probably would have gotten in trouble if they'd let him ashore anyway.

Longarm finished eating and went out on the far side to watch the sun go down across the muddy water as he had himself a smoke. He couldn't tell whether the water level was dropping or not. The river rolled past like bean soup. When the breeze shifted, it smelled like rotten eggs. Every once in a while something floated by, outlined darkly by the setting sun. But there weren't as many logs and sawyers this far up. The river had narrowed some as they rode up it. They'd lost the waters of the Yellowstone more than a hundred miles downstream, and now they'd lost the inflow from the Milk River too. So the Big Muddy was still muddy, but it wasn't as big. Longarm knew they'd be passing the outlets of the Musselshell, the Judith, the Crow, and the Arrow by the time they reached Eagle Butte. So he could see how the Big Bend, around to the south, figured to run a lot lower and slower. The main stream was fed by snow melting off the Rockies, far to the west, and by this late in summer, most of the snow that was going to melt had done so. The glaciers on the high peaks didn't contribute much to the summer runoff.

Lavinia Lee and the twins walked past him. He straightened up and touched his hatbrim, and the older gal observed that it was a lovely evening as they passed. He didn't argue. They passed too fast.

As he admired the view from the rear until they'd rounded a corner, he saw a couple of deck chairs aft, not far from his stateroom door. They hadn't been there before, but it looked like a handy place to sit until he bored himself enough to turn in. He'd been sleeping more than usual of late, and it was still early, but there wasn't much else going on.

He lowered himself into one of the deck chairs and leaned back to smoke some more. The sun dropped behind the foothills to the west, painting the sky and muddy water red and gold while a horned lark sang sadly from the rail of the Texas deck above. Longarm always felt sort of wistful in the gloaming. It was a pretty time of day, but it could remind a man of other nights when he'd been alone. Somewhere on shore a piano was tinkling like a distant music box, and Longarm resisted the temptation. He knew the siren calls of a dusty little cow town all too well. The lights and music lost their magic when a man drifted in too close. The so-called fun of Saloon Row was like a shabby, painted whore; it lost its charms when you were close enough to kiss it.

The horned lark serenaded him again and Longarm growled, "Oh, shut up, I know I could have settled down a long time ago and had me a regular home to come home to in the evening. But *that*'s a siren song too. Right now, all over this land, there's many a drifting tumbleweed staring at the lights in the windows and wondering what he's missing, and there's ten times that many trudging home from factory, farm, or mine, and wondering why the hell he never ran off to be a cowboy when he grew up, like he'd planned. Go home and kiss your wife and kids, you fool bird. If it was all that great, you wouldn't be out here whistling so lonesome."

Lavinia Lee came around the deck again, alone. Longarm started to rise as he wondered idly where her charges were. It might make more sense to stay on his feet if the fool woman meant to pace the deck all night.

"Please don't rise on my account, sir," she said, and then she sat down beside him in the other chair. So he didn't.

He studied the smoke in his hand and she said, "Heavens, you really are a gentleman of the old school, aren't you? I wouldn't have joined you if cigar smoke offended me, Mr. Lansford."

He hadn't known she was joining him, but he put the cheroot back in his teeth and let her have the floor. She said the sunset was beautiful, which sounded pretty ordinary. Then she said, "I've been trying to have a word with you, sir. You see, I have a bit of a problem on my hands."

Longarm said, "My pleasure, ma'am. What's wrong? Has some gent been pestering you and the twins, or do you need me to fix something?"

She laughed. "As a matter of fact, I do have something you might be able to fix. But I hesitate to ask, since we hardly know each other."

He said, "Well, just call me Custis and ask away. I'm fairly handy with tools."

That seemed to strike her funny for some reason. She sort of choked as she said, "I thought you might be equipped with the tool we need." Then she looked about, as if to make sure they were alone and unobserved, before she added, "Dear me, it seemed so simple when I tipped the deckhand to place these chairs here. Now that we're face to face, I feel awkward."

Longarm blew a smoke ring over the rail at the river and kept quiet. He could think of a dozen reasons why a lady might admit to having trapped a man alone like this, now that she'd admitted as much. But none of them were very proper. He was in a position to make a total fool of himself if he was wrong, and if he was right, he knew a man could spook a skittish female by saying the wrong thing too soon.

She waited a long tense moment before she caid, "You may have noticed my two younger traveling companions."

"Yes, ma'am. A couple of handsome young ladies."

"I'm taking them to relations up the river. I'm, ah . . . responsible for them."

"I figured as much. But you said you had something for me to fix. I ain't much on chaperoning."

"To be frank, neither am I," she said. "I thought I could handle them. One of them is a dear little thing, but . . . . can I trust you not to repeat any of this?"

"Mum's the word, ma'am. Which one's giving you a hard time?"

She laughed again and said, "I'm not going to *tell* you. That's the point! It came to me a day or so ago that the fact you don't know one from the other offers a way out of my, ah, problem. You see, *one* of the twins is, uh . . . very naughty."

Longarm frowned into the sunset and said, "I can see why you don't aim to tell me whether it's Cindy Lou or Mary Jo. But I'm still puzzled about what you want me to do about it. Is it your plan to have a grown man take one young lady over his knee, incognito?"

Lavinia said, "You're getting warm. Obviously no man who didn't know for certain which twin he was, ah . . . *fixing* could repeat a tale that would ruin both of them."

He said, "I got that part figured out. What am I supposed to do to the wicked one, ma'am?"

"Well, I thought if it wouldn't be too much trouble, you might fuck her as a favor to her sister and me."

Longarm choked and nearly bit his cheroot in two. When he recovered he said, "Sorry ma'am. I must have wax in my ears. You'd best repeat that."

Lavinia said, "I know it sounds shocking. But I can see you're traveling alone, and *somebody* has to do it before she gets in a real mess."

"You sure chaperone funny, ma'am. I thought your job was to keep young gals from being trifled with like that."

"It is, damn it. The girl is simply sex-mad. Every time I turn my back on her she starts up with the nearest thing in pants. She's been with two men I know of since we came aboard at K.C. Fortunately they've both gotten off downriver, and of course neither can say now whether it was Cindy Lou or Mary Jo he had his wicked way with. God knows *who* she'll be after now, and some of the men left on board will be getting off with the three of us. You know what *that* could lead to in a small town."

"I reckon I do. I'd be a liar if I said I hadn't admired all three of you, and a sissy if I crossed my legs and blushed. But are you sure your notion is the sensible answer, ma'am? A gal that pretty is going to get in all the messes she wants to, no matter what you do, and playing God can backfire."

"I just want to deliver the two of them safe and sound," Lavinia insisted. "I'll be coming back down the river in a few days and they'll be on their own. I don't care what they do after that. But I mean to have no snickering whiskey drummer or crewmember bragging about his conquest as we disembark. So will you do it?"

Longarm took a long drag of smoke as he tried to figure out any way that this could be interfering with the U.S. Mail. His common sense told him to avoid crazy ladies, but he knew she'd be mad as well as crazy if he said no, after she'd put her cards on the table the way she had.

He sighed and said, "I ought to have my head examined. But like I said, a pretty gal is a pretty gal and my folks never raised me up to be rude to ladies in distress. What's the play? Do we all get together for a drink and let nature take its course?"

Lavinia said, "Heavens, no, that would hardly be discreet. Why don't you go in your stateroom and just wait. I'll send her in to you."

"She knows about your plan, ma'am?" Longarm asked incredulously.

"For Heaven's sake, call me Livvy. Of course she knows. Her innocent sister doesn't. So, at breakfast—"

"Say no more. Ships that pass in the night. I never knew what a bull at service felt like before. It's sort of interesting, now that I study on it."

Lavinia Lee stood up, so Longarm did too. He stepped over to his stateroom door, remarking as he did so, "This is pure insanity, but you can send her when you've a mind to."

She looked shocked. "Oh, I dasn't, until it's proper dark."

As he opened his door, he saw that she wasn't leaving. She looked both ways and then she shoved him inside, followed after him, and closed the door behind them.

There was little light coming through the jalousies, so he struck a match and lit the bed lamp. Lavinia Lee said matter-of-factly, "As long as we're waiting, I'd best examine you."

"Beg pardon, ma'am?"

"Take off your clothes, Custis. I'm a practical nurse."

"I can see you have practical views, uh, Livvy. But what do you aim to examine me for? I ain't sick."

"I'd better be the judge of that. I want you to service one of my charges. I don't want you to give her a dose of the clap."

"Aw, hell," he said, "I'm losing interest in this whole notion by the minute."

"What's the matter? Have you something to hide? Take off your clothes."

"Not hardly. Not by myself. It sounds indecent."

"Oh. Would it help if I took my clothes off as well, before I examined you?"

He laughed. "It would sure cure my shyness, but I ain't sure we'd get much examining done."

Lavinia Lee began to unbutton her bodice as she said, "Well, if it's the only way to put you at ease for a proper examination, I'll just have to accommodate you."

He stood there thunderstruck, until he saw she really meant to strip. "I'll blow out the light," he volunteered, but she said, "Leave it on. How am I going to see what I'm doing in the dark?"

By this time she'd shucked the dress and was in her chemise, drawers, and corset. She left her hair pinned up as she turned her back to him and asked, "Would you be good enough to unlace me?"

So he unfastened her corset, noticing how thick his fingers felt all of a sudden, and as she dropped the corset over the foot of the bunk, he got to work on his own duds.

She beat him. As he sat on the bunk to shuck his boots, she stood over him stark naked. A thin line of hair ran from her navel to the thick muff between her thighs. He'd been right. Her pubic hair was frosted with gray, like the pelt of a silver fox. He felt a mite better. She was a salty old gal who'd done this sort of thing before. He wondered if either of the twins had any idea where she was as she said, "There, lean back and let's have a look at you."

Then she dropped to her knees between his own and took him by surprise by grasping his shy, limp shaft firmly and rubbing it as she scrutinized it with a critical eye. Reliable as usual, it rose to the occasion and she said approvingly, "Good. I can see it's healthy, and it ought to be big enough for that saucy wench."

Then she let go, got to her feet, and picked up her chemise.

His eyes widened in disbelief. "What the hell are you getting dressed for?"

"I've finished the examination," she told him in a businesslike manner. "You have neither clap nor crabs, and I'm sure the child will enjoy you."

"What about you?"

She looked sincerely puzzled as she replied, "Me? Heavens, you don't think *I* would have an affair with a total stranger, do you?"

As she started to slip the chemise over her head, he rose and stepped over to her, saying, "Hell, I don't feel all that distant, Livvy."

Then he hauled the chemise off her and threw it aside as he pulled her close to him and kissed her, his erection trembling between her thighs. She kissed him back right nicely, stood on tiptoe, and moved her hips until their pubic bones made contact. He accommodated her by bending his knees on either side of her straight legs.

When they came up for air she said, "This is really quite improper. I didn't proposition you for myself! What about the poor child who needs your . . . My God, it's *grown* since we started this conversation, hasn't it?"

Silently he picked her up, carried her back to the bunk, and put her down. "Now really, this is not the way I'd planned this at all," she said, sounding somewhat flustered.

He didn't answer. The soft lamplight was kind to

her, and despite a few frayed edges, she was still pretty enough to be doing this in broad daylight. So he ignored her innocent protests as he wrestled her gently into position. "Oh, dear," she said, "I do think I'm being raped."

He knew they both knew better, but some gals liked to think like that. It excused them to their mothers and Queen Victoria, most likely. And despite her repeated protests that this whole deal was a medical examination gone awry, he noticed she came up to devour him with her hungry wet love, all the way to the roots, even before he'd settled his weight in the saddle.

Lavinia made love like a lunatic mountain lion who'd been saving it up for the right mate. Her seniority made her soft skin looser than that of the lean and muscular man who'd mounted her; he could grab a handful of it over each hipbone and pull her on and off like a glove. She suddenly went limp and gasped, "Enough. Save some for the children!"

He laughed as he came a second time, and then he asked, "*Children?* I thought you only had *one* other gal for me tonight, Livvy."

She said, "I was speaking metaphorically, you animal. Aren't you satisfied yet?"

"No, are you?" he asked innocently, and she laughed and told him he was awful and he said she wasn't bad, either. Then she got on top. She leaned way forward, tickling his nose with a nipple as she snuffed out the lamp. He asked her why, since he'd admired the view. She said, "It's embarrassing when I sit up in the light. Surely you noticed my stretch marks?"

He kissed her dangling breasts and she giggled and said his handlebar mustache tickled. But she let him have his fill and he sucked on both in turn to keep them from being jealous, as she bounced up and down on him until she suddenly collapsed with a contented sigh atop him. He wasn't there yet, so he held her tight and kept bucking until she said, "Stop it. I promised not to be selfish."

He was pretty sure he was onto her game now. Poor old Lavinia was a mite long in the tooth and he had noticed even in the soft light that a couple of kids had flown under the bridge. Her younger charges were just the bait she dangled to get a man's undivided attention and a little harmless fun. She'd been afraid he'd laugh at her if she'd propositioned him for herself. She and the gals would be getting off the boat soon and she must have been getting desperate. But she was a nice old gal and he meant to do right by her. It was sort of flattering to any man to have a grown woman display so much ingenuity.

He was about to roll her over and finish right when Lavinia suddenly popped off him in the dark and said, "Behave yourself. I've got to slip my clothes on and fetch your real patient."

He lay bemused and erect as she swiftly donned her outer garb and balled her unmentionables up to carry. As she kissed him fondly in farewell, he said, "Lord of mercy, I thought you were joshing me! Are you serious about tossing a young virgin to the lions, Livvy?"

She laughed, sort of dirty, and warned, "She's hardly the one I'd call the victim. Leave the door unlatched and don't light the lamp. She's sort of shy. About *talking* to men, I mean."

Lavinia slipped out, after making sure the coast was clear. As she opened the door, Longarm saw that it was pretty dark outside now. He lay on the bunk in bewildered anticipation. Then, as time and his erection passed, he began to have sane second thoughts. Livvy might have just wanted to slip back to the quarters she shared with the twins before they wondered where she was. Livvy might have set him up for something less friendly than a visit from a young nymphomaniac. He was stretched out naked and unarmed behind an un-latched door!

He swung his bare feet to the door and reached for the derringer he'd tucked between the mattress and the headboard, muttering to himself, "You're getting mighty suspicious in your dotage, old son."

But then he rose and dragged the bedside chair into a corner, out of the line of fire should anybody kick in the door and point a gun at his recently occupied pillow. He might be being overcautious, but he was still alive, and more than one apparently friendly gal had set him and other foolish gents up like that.

So he perched naked on the edge of the bentwood chair, the brass butt of the derringer cool and comforting in his overheated palm. He was starting to want to smoke. He decided to give it a few more minutes before he locked the door, and then the hell with it.

He'd just decided old Livvy wasn't going to send back either a lover or a killer when there was a kitten-like scratching on the door and without waiting for an answer, somebody came in. A soft female voice breathed, "Lie still, cowboy. Aunt Livvy told you what I came for." So he didn't answer as he sat there listening to the rustle of poplin and silk until she whispered, "There. Prepare to meet your maker, handsome!"

He rose, aiming the derringer politely at the ceiling as he stepped over to the bed. The girl had bent over and was groping around in confusion among the covers on the empty bunk, whispering, "Where are you, damn it?"

He cupped one of her hipbones in his free hand as he placed the gun on the bed table. "Oh, what a novel approach," she murmured, and got her knees on the edge of the mattress as he put himself in place and grabbed the other hipbone and thrust home.

It was a pleasant surprise for both of them. The experienced woman who'd just left had been what a man might call satisfactorily tight. The twin, whichever one she was, was almost too tiny for a grown man. Her hips were like a fourteen-year-old's and he'd have accused himself of child molesting had Livvy not told him how far he was from the first man she'd ever done this with. She proved her older mentor's tale when, after the first shock passed, she thrust her tailbone up and wiggled saucily, whispering, "Oh, yes, all of it, as deep as it will go!"

He reached forward to get a better grip and saw that she still had her corset on. He got a good grip on the whalebone-ribbed cinch and hauled her back hard. It made a right convenient handle. "Do you aim to leave that thing on, ma'am?" he asked.

She said, "Of course. It takes forever to lace me into it. Do you have to chatterbox while you work? I didn't come for conversation, cowboy!"

So he shut up and started pounding her, a mite pissed off. He knew she'd probably mean-mouthed him like that because she preferred brutal loving, and the odd combination was sort of interesting. He grinned down at her barely visible pale rump as his eyes grew more accustomed to the nearly total darkness. Someone had lighted a hurricane lamp on deck and the jalousied slits in the upper door panel gave him just enough to go by. Because of her youth and the tightly cinched corset, her waist was wasplike indeed. He could put his thumbs together on her spine and almost touch his fingertips together across her belly. He wondered if that was what made her feel so tight inside. Her innards had to be shoved *someplace*. "Oh, I'm almost there and I want to turn over and do it right," she said breathlessly. So he let her. She rolled on her back with a foot braced out to either side of his on the floor and her tailbone off the edge, as he lowered himself to enter her. The view from this side was even better. Her cameo face was sort of wilful and pouty as she stared up at him like the brazen young hussy she was. So he didn't bother to kiss her as he got back in the saddle, his own legs stiff and a bare foot braced wide against the floor for some no-nonsense screwing. The corset only came halfway up her ribcage, so her firm little cupcakes were bare. It was fun to watch them bounce like gelatin desserts as he started hammering her. Her eyes opened wide and she gasped, "Oh, God, that's

110

marvelous! I knew you'd be good the first time I saw you, but this is almost too much!"

"Am I hurting you?" he asked, moving more gently.

"Yes, but I *love* it! Don't hold back, damn it. The next man might be a sissy. I don't mind a few bruises."

That sounded more crazy than reasonable, but he did his best to please her. Despite his earlier tussle with Lavinia, he had no trouble staying interested. Normally, Longarm was a gentle lover. He genuinely liked women and he knew he was bigger and stronger than the average man. It felt wild to just screw the hell out of a sort of nasty little thing who looked like a snooty virgin but acted like a tough-deadline whore in bed. He had a good head start on her, so she naturally came first, bucking like a mule being whipped with a prickly pear. Then, as she throbbed contentedly around his shaft, she purred like a kitten and raised one leg at a time to hook her ankles around the nape of his neck. He hadn't noticed until then that she still had on her high-button shoes. It felt funny, but it sure placed her at a new and interesting angle. He was practically stubbing his toe on her hard little cervix on the bottom of each stroke when she suddenly clamped down so hard it almost hurt. She tried to straighten her legs as she came a second time, which would have pulled his head off by the roots if it had worked, and he fired hard inside of her in mingled discomfort and pleasure.

For some reason he felt a mite out of breath now, so he suggested they move into a more natural position and recover as they cuddled. But Mary Jo or Cindy Lou or whichever one she was said, "You rest up and get your second wind. I have to tinkle."

He rolled off and lay on his back near the bulkhead as he said, "There's a thunder mug under the bunk, honey."

She sat up, saying, "Don't be vulgar. The convenience is just around the corner."

"Yeah, but you'll have to get dressed, and what the hell, it ain't like we're strangers now."

111

She laughed. "I can peel as fast as I have to. But it's nice to see you're still anxious. I'll be right back, cowboy. If you can't wait, just start without me."

She'd been slipping her poplin duster on as she spoke, so she jumped up and dashed out like she really had to go pretty bad. He figured that tight corset might have something to do with it. He'd never figured out why women wore the damned things. He didn't know a man who'd throw a pretty gal out of bed for an extra couple of inches around the gut, and corsets made gals faint a lot, even when they weren't all that excited.

He wondered if he had time to grab a smoke. He decided to pass on the notion. If she got back before he'd recovered his wind, he was in trouble enough. He grinned like a coyote in the dark as he considered how Lady Luck treated a wandering man. Like that horned lark had been saying just before Lavinia sat down beside him, most sundowns sent a single man to bed wistful. But for some reason, when there was one gal available, there seemed to be more than you could shake a stick at. Life was like that. Unfair as hell.

The door opened again, breaking into his revery. Longarm said, "Howdy. Long time no see."

The girl slipped out of her duster with a warning whisper. "Quiet. Some people are walking the deck outside. I had to wait and wait until it was safe to sneak in here."

Then she was all over him, sobbing and panting as she kissed him hungrily. He enfolded her in his arms, and as he ran his hand down her spine he noticed she didn't have the corset on any more. He ran his fingers down past her tailbone as he said, "That's better. Where'd you leave the corset, honey?"

She answered, "Corset? Oh, I left it in my stateroom."

"You went back there? I know your Aunt Livvy knows, but what about your prissy sister?"

The girl in his arms huffed and said haughtily, "Let

112

her wear her own corset, darling. Don't worry about her. She's too dumb about these things to be believed."

Longarm didn't believe. They were playing a pretty slick little game, but he was a man whose job called for suspicion beyond the usual call of duty. He knew, even before he was in her, that this was the second twin.

They looked and even felt identical, so most men they pulled this on probably bought their tale. The three roving sex maniacs were playing a carnival shell game with one innocent virgin as the nonexistent pea. He had to admit it was practical as well as funny. Lavinia didn't care about her own reputation, since a sophisticated older gal could cope with gossip. By saying that one twin was wild and the other innocent, they assured that their victims would be cautious later, in public.

As he mounted her, the latest arrival hissed and cautioned him, "Ooh, not so hard. Let me get used to it."

So he went into her gently, and even though they were peas in a pod between the legs, it felt different. This Cindy Lou or Mary Jo seemed softer and more innocent. He knew she was no such thing, but she probably liked men and was more romantic than her sister. She was less acrobatic and more loving. She caressed his back and buttocks with her hands and kissed nicely. It took longer for him this time. In fact, if it hadn't been for the novelty he'd have been willing to pack it in for now. But though the other two had more than sated him, he liked this one the best. He had to hand it to old Lavinia for orchestrating it like this. Like the salty old girl had figured, any hard-up gent could get it up for a reasonably good-looking older gal and keep it up for a pretty young thing. This one was the extra-sweet dessert you had to taste even if you were stuffed. She didn't move her slim hips demandingly. She just sort of milked his shaft with what felt like sliced peaches preserved in sweet slippery syrup, and sobbed nice things as she came herself, repeatedly. He joined her on the third or fourth climax, and while it came as a surprise that he still could, it felt so good it hurt. They lay still, entwined in one another for a long sweet glide down from the stars. Then she said, "That was so lovely. Can we do it again?"

"I'd sure admire to, honey. I ain't sure I can."

She sighed and disengaged herself enough to fondle him with her soft hand as she said, "Oh, the poor little thing. Its wing must be broken."

That felt swell too. So he kissed her some more. She said, "Aunt Livvy swore she'd been good this time. Was my— I mean, was I rough on you before I went out for a moment?"

"I don't talk about other ladies, ma'am. Let's just float with the current and enjoy the here and now of it."

"Oh, you're so understanding," she said, then she started kissing her way down to her hand and its contents.

She even did *that* sort of sweetly and innocently, like a bride experimenting with the first one she'd ever seen. Longarm knew no shy virgin had ever shown such skill, of course, but as he ran his fingers through her unbound hair it was hard to keep from saying all sorts of dumb things and easy to pretend she was really that gal all men dreamed of meeting up with, the skilled and responsive virgin. He knew that sooner or later some poor fool was going to marry this one and think he'd struck gold. Longarm was already jealous of him. He knew there was no such critter, of course, but if he ever did settle down for keeps, it'd be with a good girl who made love like this bad girl.

She moved her lips skilfully until he was as good as new, and then she rolled atop him to settle down on him with a contented little sigh. "There, it's all better, dear. I 'spect you think what I just did was very wicked, don't you?" she asked with mock shyness.

114

"No. I'd call it pure considerate," he replied.

She laughed and started moving up and down with a sort of gyration while he relaxed and fondled her bobbing breasts. She said, "I guess I am a wicked girl, but you see . . ."

He put a finger to her rosebud lips and said, "Hush, honey. You're no more wicked than I am. It takes two to do it, and you don't hear *me* complaining! Someday folks may act more natural, but I understand your problem. You just go ahead and enjoy yourself and I won't say anything dumb at breakfast in the morning."

For some reason that seemed to drive her wilder and she said all sorts of dumb sweet things as she rode his broomstick over the moon.

It must have been ten or so when she suddenly pushed him away and said, "I have to go. It's getting late."

"What's the matter? Do you turn into a pumpkin at midnight?"

"No, but the others worry about me and I'd never be able to explain if another passenger saw me out so late."

He doubted that her wild twin and lively chaperone worried all that much, but he was feeling as wrung out as a dishrag by now, so he didn't argue as she sat up and started to get dressed. When she'd slipped the poplin duster over her naked body, she bent to kiss him good night. Naturally he ran his hands over her, and naturally her firm little curves felt different under the smooth cloth, so naturally he just had to run a hand up under her skirt. That felt different too.

She laughed and said, "You're just dreadful. Let me go." And then as he kissed and fingered her, she sighed, "Oh, all right, but I'm not sure it's proper."

Then, as he hitched her skirt up around her naked rump and mounted her again, she said, "Oh, it feels so naughty with your naked body against my bodice and all." So they said good night properly.

But after she'd left, Longarm locked the door. He wasn't sure the three of them were through with him for the night, and if Lavinia came back for seconds, it would kill him.

Chapter 7

Everyone was discreet as hell at breakfast, considering. Captain Gloria Grimes was up and having flapjacks at her table, which was the one nearest the door. She looked rested and chipper, and when she invited Longarm to join her, he did. Lavinia Lee and the Gilmore twins were at a table on the far side, gazing innocently down at their breakfast plates. He tried to pretend they weren't there, but it wasn't easy. He wondered which of the seemingly identical twins had been the salty one and which the sweet one. It wasn't likely that he'd ever know; the three of them were getting off at Eagle Butte. When he asked Gloria what time she meant to reach there, she said, "About now, had that fool mail been waiting here like it was supposed to. I'm going up to the depot in a spell to see what's holding things up."

"I'd be proud to escort you, ma'am," he told her. "I just had a look at the river. It looks about the same as it did last night when I turned in."

"Did you sound the depth with a lead, Mr. Lansford?"

"No, I just went by guess and by golly."

"You don't follow the channel by guess and by golly, sir. You have to go where there's at least mark twain."

She hadn't invited him to come with her to the railroad tracks, but he noticed that she dawdled over her coffee as he ate his flapjacks. So he gulped his own coffee fast and said he was ready.

She didn't say she wanted him to come along, but she

117

didn't say he couldn't, so he did. He noticed that a couple of crewmen and the mate—a young, quiet gent called Jim Truman—were tagging along in their wake as they left the *Minnitipi* and walked up from the landing.

As they passed the Western Union office, Longarm was sorry he hadn't known they'd be stuck there overnight. Any answers to the questions he'd sent the day before would be waiting for him upriver and around the Big Bend, and from the way Captain Grimes and Jim Truman were talking, it wasn't a sure bet they'd ever get there. Gloria did all the fussing, but her mate kept nodding, so he must have agreed with her. Jim Truman was a licensed river pilot too. By the time they reached the depot, Longarm was as anxious as they were to see the train that was due any minute from the east.

He and the other men stood on the sun-bleached wooden platform while Gloria talked to the stationmaster. Longarm knew the crewmen had come along to handle the mail sacks and any baggage that might be arriving with possible passengers. He tried drawing Truman into a conversation, but it was like talking to a telegraph pole that grunted once in a while.

After a while they saw a smoke plume beyond the first rise out of town, and Gloria rejoined them as the train pulled into the station. She stared at the red cowcatcher on the Baldwin diamond-stacker and muttered, "Durned old railroads. They think they own the whole blamed country."

Longarm didn't argue. She was not only a lady; she was right. As a lawman, he knew that technically some other folks controlled a good share of these United States, but the railroad barons and their kin didn't seem to notice. He'd met folks who said they were Vanderbilts or Huntingtons as theough they expected a mere federal deputy to drop to one knee.

The train rolled in and hissed to a halt in a cloud of steam. They'd been standing where the mail car stopped, so nobody had to move much as the mail car door slid open and a clerk called down, "Howdy, Captain Grimes. I hope you brung a cart. You got a mess of mail to deliver this time."

As he and his helpers started tossing down gray canvas sacks, Gloria told her crewmen to fetch a hand-cart from the stationmaster. Then she called up, "Where are the postal inspectors they were sending out with the mail? Back in the Pullmans?"

The mail clerk replied, "No, ain't you heard? Frank and Jesse James are at it again, further east. They helt up the Glendale train again and the whole world is hunting for 'em!"

Longarm called out, "Hold on, this ain't the Missouri Pacific."

The clerk nodded. "I noticed. All trains was halted whilst the law wired back and forth to get a line on which way they was riding. That's why we're so late. Posse lost 'em near St. Joe, and as they seem to have gone to earth, things are getting back to normal."

"What happened to my infernal mail guards, then?" Gloria complained.

"They're with the others, searching high and low for the James Boys, I reckon. I understand your problem, ma'am. I mentioned the Kimaho mail as they was parting company with us. They said Uncle Sam was sending somebody from the Justice Department to give you a hand. I reckon they thought the James Boys in the hand was worth a maybe in the bush."

The crewmen came back with the handcart and started loading it while Gloria stamped her foot and swore, "Damn it, we had us a federal man on board, but he got hisself shot and throwed overboard. How am I to deliver so much of this stuff unguarded, and how come there's so much this trip?"

"Can't answer either way, ma'am," the mail clerk replied. "I told you the Post Office dicks rode off after Jesse James, and it's agin the law to open the mail. Somebody must be advertising something. There's a sizable packet to every crossroads post office you service up the river."

Gloria stared morosely at the growing pile of mail sacks on the borrowed cart. Jim Truman shuffled his feet, looked off into the distance, and said shyly, "We could leave it in the post office here, Miss Gloria. Our contract don't call for us getting kilt, and they promised us an armed guard."

Gloria shook her head bitterly. "The mail can't wait and neither can we, for the river's dropping whilst we jaw about it. We'll just break out the Winchesters from the arms locker and issue one to every man on board."

She turned to Longarm and asked, "Are you any good with a rifle, mister?"

"I shoot tolerable," he said.

"I figured as much, from the hang of your sidearm. If the rascals hit us again, I mean to give them a dusting they'll remember."

Longarm nodded in agreement as some folks who'd gotten down from the train came toward them. There were five of them—two women and three men. The more noteworthy gal of the two was a Junoesque, brassy blonde wearing a big hat made of ostrich plumes dyed pink. Her travel duster was dusky rose, and she packed a furled parasol that matched her hat.

The other gal was small and dressed sensibly in a dark poplin duster and a veiled straw boater. It was hard to judge any woman's shape under the baggy dusters they wore when traveling cross-country, but Longarm could see that neither of them were deformed and the little one was sort of pretty, as far as he could tell behind that dusty lace. The big blonde wasn't as beautiful as she seemed to think she was. Nobody could have been. But she'd have been all right, had she scrubbed off some of the travel soot and heavy makeup.

Two of the men were nonedescript gents in the store-bought suits that traveling salesmen wore. The third was the human male's challenge to the peacocks. He had on a checked suit and a gold-brocaded red vest

120

that could blind you in the sunlight. He had gold chains draped across his barrel chest and diamond rings on both pink, pudgy hands to match the locomotive head-lamp he used for a tie pin. He wore his expensive, dove-gray derby at a jaunty angle and when he smiled, the sunlight glittered on a big gold tooth with a dia-mond set in it. He smiled a lot, like a snake-oil drum-mer. But when Longarm ran the rest of the florid face through his memory files, he drew a blank. The man was all flash. His chubby face looked like a fresh-cured ham with a gilded smile.

The flashy dude spotted the pilot's cap on Gloria and asked her if she had any connection with the Kimaho & K.C. Line. When she nodded, he introduced himself as T. J. Porter of the GF&YSRR.

Longarm knew that was the unborn railroad that Matt Kincaid had told him about. He didn't say any-thing. He wasn't supposed to be interested in anything but rangelands up the river.

The mail cart was nearly loaded, so Gloria said she'd take them all to the *Minnitipi* if they'd just follow her. The big blonde complained, "Do you expect us to *walk?* There ought to be a station wagon!"

Gloria smiled sweetly and replied, "I know, but there ain't. My hands will see to your luggage, if that's what they're unloading down the platform. The boat landing is downhill, but if you want, I 'spect I can carry you piggyback."

The blonde drew herself up and said, "Nobody talks to me that way, my girl."

"I just did," Gloria said. "And I ain't your girl, I'm the skipper of the *Minnitipi,* and we're pulling out as soon as we load up. You can just do as you've a mind to."

Then Gloria turned and headed for the river, not looking back. The flashy man smiled at the blonde and said, "I told you that folks were a bit boorish out this way, my dear." Then he turned to Longarm and

121

said, "Be good enough to fetch us a hansom cab, will you, my good fellow?"

Longarm smiled benignly. "I reckon you're a good fellow too, but there ain't any cabs for hire hereabouts."

"Are you being impertinent too?"

"Nope. Just being my ownself. Before you really say something silly, I'd best tell you I ain't a deckhand. I'm a passenger, first class. That's the only class there is aboard the *Minnitipi*. So I'd simmer down polite if I was you."

T. J. Porter stared hard, and for a moment Longarm saw something he hadn't expected in the pudgy man's oyster-gray eyes. Porter looked like a puffed-up, harmless dude. But Longarm had met killers before, so he recognized the flicker of movement deep inside Porter's eyes, like the shadowy turn of a shark in deep water.

Porter must have been a good judge of other men too. He took Longarm's comment with good grace. "Right. I fear we're all a bit on edge from the long trip." Then he offered an elbow to the blonde. "Come, my dear, we don't have far to walk. I can see the steamboat's funnel from here." She unfurled her parasol and allowed him to help her down from the platform as the others started to follow. Longarm saw that the less flamboyant gal had no escort, so he stepped down first and turned to offer her a helping hand. She took it with a demure murmur of thanks, but she ignored his proffered elbow as they walked after the others down the slope. Longarm introduced himself, using his assumed name, and she said she was Miss Sue Ellen Brooks. He asked her if she knew the big blonde ahead of them, and she made a slight face as she replied, "We exchanged a few words on the train. Her name is Daisy Melrose, if you're interested. I see most men are."

Longarm was pretty sure he knew what kind of words they'd had. He watched the big blonde swivel her shapely caboose under the loose duster as he said, "I can't speak for other gents, but she ain't my type. I've always been more partial to little quiet gals."

Sue Ellen smiled and said, "Down, boy. I'm spoken for in Kimaho, and he's almost as big as you are."

He glanced sidewise at her pert profile, and chuckled. "We'll get you there, and I'll be proud to shake his hand. I admire a gal who puts her cards on the table before the stakes get foolish."

She slipped her hand into the crook of his elbow. "I thought you might. I can see you're a ladies' man, but you look intelligent enough to understand an honest answer. Life would be so much simpler if everyone could speak frankly, don't you think?"

He nodded, although he wasn't sure he agreed completely. He was glad this one had told him right off that he'd be wasting his time, but he wasn't sure he'd like it as a steady diet. The nice thing about having to guess was that everybody got to daydream some. He knew a mess of gals he had to leave alone because they were tied up with a friend or worked too close to his home office. It'd be awful if he knew for sure that none of them liked him at all!

They arrived at the landing, and as he helped Sue Ellen aboard, he spied one of the Gilmore twins staring down at them from the passenger deck. Naturally he couldn't tell whether she was the sweet one or the mean one. She didn't look too pleased right now, whichever one she might be.

Everybody went upstairs, and Gloria's purser took Sue Ellen away from Longarm to show her to her stateroom. Gloria herself had climbed up to the Texas and was making ready to cast off as soon as the mail and luggage were aboard, so Longarm went into the salon.

He found Blue behind the bar, so he nodded and ordered a beer. No woman ever bellied up to a bar, even in Dodge. But one of the Gilmore twins came over to him anyway and murmured, "You rat."

Blue stared at the ceiling like there was something interesting crawling across it. Longarm took his beer and Cindy Lou or Mary Jo over to a nearby table and plunked her down, saying, "You can't stand at a bar, damn it."

She said, "We won't be getting off for hours, and already you've started trifling with another girl!"

He saw that old Lavinia had partly told the truth. The twins were smart enough to play their game with cool heads. As Lavinia had said, *one* of them was wild as hell! "Simmer down," he told the girl. "In the first place, that lady I helped aboard is engaged to a man who'll be meeting us up the river. So 'trifle' is too strong a word for helping her up the gangplank. In the second place, fair is fair. I disremember exchanging eternal vows with the three of you last night. Where in the U.S. Constitution does it say you get to screw your way across the country, but that nobody else can play?"

She said, "All right, I'm jealous. I thought what we had was better than usual, and I wish we weren't getting off at Eagle Butte. So there."

He patted her hand and said, "That's a warm and friendly thing to say, honey. But you do have to get off and I have to stay aboard."

"Custis, I think I'm falling for you."

"That's downright flattering. I'm going to miss you too. But that's the bitter that goes with the sweet when you play the game of love-'em-and-leave-'em. But look at it this way. If it never hurt to drop out of the game, the game wouldn't be worth playing."

"I know," she sighed. "Aunt Lavinia said I was acting foolish. What time are we supposed to arrive at Eagle Butte?"

He looked out the window at the sun. "Not as late as we ought to, if your mind is as dirty as mine. It'll be after sundown, but nobody will be turning in as we approach a main stop."

"I'll come to your stateroom as soon as it gets dark."

"I'd like that, but you ain't listening, honey. A mess of folks are getting off with you all at Eagle Butte.

124

They'll be pacing the decks like caged-in tigers, and you'll be spotted for sure as you slip out. Captain Grimes ain't sure what kind of a run we'll have today, either. So the exact time of arrival is up for grabs and she'll have linemen up in the bows, facing aft as they yell up at her. You're going to have to learn to quit while you're ahead."

She made a beestung pout and said, "I don't care if I get caught. I want some more. I liked it when you did it to me while I had my clothes on. It's given me all sorts of saucy notions I've never tried yet."

Longarm was a mite surprised. He'd thought he was talking to the bold one. This development made it even harder to say no. But he tried. "Listen," he said, "you're getting off at a little river town, with other passengers who'll be your new neighbors. I'd love to hear some more about your saucy notions, but somebody has to be the grownup, so I reckon it'll have to be me. It's over, honey. It hurts me to say that too, but facts is facts."

She said, "I'll come to your stateroom during dinnertime. Nobody will see me. They'll all be in here stuffing their faces."

"Hell, that's high noon!" he protested. But she insisted urgently, "All the more reason we can get away with it. Nobody expects people to do this sort of thing in the middle of the day. It'll be easy. We'll sate ourselves all afternoon and I can slip out just at sunset, when the light gets tricky. Should anybody see me slip out and around the stern, they won't be able to say for sure it was me." Then she giggled and added, "Even if they see me up close, they won't be sure whether it's me or my twin. I'll come to you when they ring the dinner bell. Be sure you're waiting for me there."

Then she got up and slipped out just as T. J. Porter and the brassy blonde came in, so Longarm couldn't follow. He nodded to the other passengers as they passed. He didn't think it was the blonde who was giving him a hard-on, so he realized with a sigh that he'd probably be waiting in his cabin when the time came to take his beating like a man.

The *Minnitipi* made good time out of Milk River, considering all the fuss about low water that he'd heard. Still, it seemed to take an unusually long time for the sun to reach high noon, for some reason. Longarm paced the deck, smoking furiously and telling himself he was being foolish as he watched the rolling, tawny rises pass astern. They put in near the Musselshell, just long enough to throw a mail sack and a barrel of nails ashore and load some fuel. Longarm noticed they were loading coal instead of cordwood this time. When he asked a deckhand about it, he was told they didn't dig it there. There were coal seams at the water's edge, upstream, and local settlers rafted it down to the prairie ports. Most of the crackwillow and cottonwood had been cut around the settled landings by now, and neither kind of wood burned long or hot enough when the Wolf Wind blew down from the north.

The dinner bell rang as they steamed out into mid-channel again. Longarm did some mental arithmetic and calculated that they were making almost fifteen miles an hour, since it had been well after sunrise when they left Milk River. Allowing for bends, they'd be in Eagle Butte just about sundown, give or take a spell either way. He didn't see the twin on deck, and he knew it would attract even more attention if *he* went to *her* door.

He moseyed to his own door and stopped with a thoughtful frown. Longarm had a habit he didn't advertise about doors he locked behind him. He liked to stick a sliver of matchstick in the jamb near the top hinge, when he locked up.

So he knew right off that somebody was in his stateroom when he spied the empty space where the sliver had been lodged. There was nobody on the port deck; they'd all gone in to dinner. At least, almost all of them had. He drew his Colt and tried the knob. It was un-locked. He moved in fast and slid his back along the wall to avoid outlining himself in the doorway as he covered the interior. The naked lady in his bunk said, "Oh, you startled me, dear."

He holstered the gun and shut the door and locked it behind him. "That makes two of us. How the hell did you get in here?"

She said, "I tried my key, and guess what? It worked. What are you waiting for? Take off your clothes. I want you so bad I can taste it."

He thought about the lock as he took off his gun rig and started shucking the rest. A lot of hotels were like that too. They bought three or four kinds of cheap locks and trusted that as long as they didn't install two identical ones side by side, nobody would notice. It was sobering to know he'd been feeling safer than he should have, but now that he knew his lock couldn't be trusted, he could figure out a dozen ways to live with that.

He climbed in and took her tenderly in his arms, remembering that she was the one who liked it that way. He kissed her and said, "Well, as long as you're here . . ." But she turned her head away and grabbing him between the legs, said, "For God's sake, are we going to have a conversation or are we going to fuck?"

He blinked in surprise as she rolled him on his back and mounted him before he was fully aroused. She grinned down devilishly and growled, "Oh, that's bet-ter. I'll teach you to look at other women, cowboy!"

She did, too. She was pretty in the daylight, and a man could forgive mean talk when a spicy wench who looked like an innocent young virgin started riding him like he was a brass pole on a merry-go-round and she was a painted pony. But this sure was confusing. He was sure it had been the *nice* one who'd liked it with her duds on, just as he was sure *this* had to be the hard-boiled twin. What she wanted felt great, but she was using him and abusing him as if he was the cow-

127

town whore and she was a young and randy trail herder who hadn't had it for a month. The softness of her thighs and the way her little titties bobbed as she damn near raped him kept him from feeling too womanish, though. She suddenly stiffened with a silent scream of pleasure, digging her nails into his chest and sobbing, "Harder, you son of a bitch. I'll kill you if you ever stop!"

That was just bragging, of course. Eventually they took a breather and she cuddled against him while he had a smoke and fretted about the arrival time up the river. She started to cry unexpectedly, and as he comforted her she fondled him and went all kitten-soft in his arms. As she started to lick his chest like it was a bowl of milk, he said, "Let me finish this cheroot. You were wearing your corset the first time last night, weren't you?"

She purred, "Yes. I was in too great a hurry at first. But you were right, dear. It was nicer with it off. Your body feels so nice against my bare tummy. Why did you take me again after I'd started to dress? I liked it, but it felt awfully strange."

He watched a smoke ring drift lazily toward the ceiling as he considered that he might not be as smart as he'd figured, after all. He'd been sure they'd switched on him when she or her sister had ducked out for a moment. But she didn't just have an identical twin, she had two completely different personalities. Old Lavinia, for God's sake, had been telling him the truth! It was a most unusual experience, all things considered. He snuffed out the smoke and asked, "Are you Cindy Lou or Mary Jo, in case I want to write?"

She giggled and said, "You'll have to guess. I promised Aunt Livvy I'd never tell. Do you know what I want to do now? I want to put on my shoes and stockings. Then I want you to lace me into my corset, tight, and do it to me standing up."

That sounded fair, so they tried it. They wound up

with her lying on her back and him skinning his knees on the floorboards, and she said she really liked the way they thudded on the downstrokes. He was afraid somebody would hear them, but she said they'd likely think it was the engine.

After they'd finished that way, she let him put her back on the bunk and undress her properly while she cooed at him. When he was ready for more, she'd gone all soft and sweet again. It was a hell of a nice way to finish off, but finish they had to, and even she was getting nervous now, as folks walked by the door.

So as Longarm recovered, she suddenly sat up and started dressing. He said, "It's early yet."

She turned and looked at him fondly. "Thank you. You've been very sweet. Will you do me one more favor?"

"Sure, if I'm able," he said. "I've about run out of ideas, though."

She said, "I don't want you to say anything or even look at us when the three of us get off this evening. Don't say anything now. Just lie there and let me walk out of your life, as though we never happened."

She'd said not to speak, so he didn't. He knew what she meant. He reached across to his shirt and fished out another smoke as she finished dressing. As he lit up, she rose and stepped over to the door without looking back. She cracked it open, peeked out, and then suddenly she was gone. Forever, it would seem.

Longarm told the rising smoke, "That sure was a nice dream, crazy as it might have been."

Then he finished his cheroot, washed and dressed, and stepped out into the afternoon sun. The *Minnitipi* was passing the same tawny rises it had been passing all day, and the river just rolled under them, quiet and full of silt. He walked forward and leaned against the rail to watch upriver. A while later, when Lavinia Lee and the Gilmore twins passed him on their before-supper stroll around the deck, he touched his hatbrim and the three of them just smiled shyly and kept going. As he watched them from behind, he had no idea which twin was the good girl and which was the bad girl.

Maybe it was better that way.

Chapter 8

The Big Muddy made a wide turn near Eagle Butte because a range of hills tried to drive it up to Canada along that stretch. Time and the patient waters of a million spring thaws had won out, but the channel narrowed between steep banks as the *Minnitipi* neared Eagle Butte. The river ran shallower here too. They'd lost the waters of the Arrow an hour or so downstream, so as the *Minnitipi* put in at Eagle Butte just after sundown, the paddlewheel was churning up as much mud as water.

Longarm didn't watch the twins disembark. He bellied up to the bar and asked Blue if it was open. The black man said it was and poured him a beer. As Longarm paid, Blue looked uneasy and told him, "Captain Gloria knows."

Longarm sighed and swore softly under his breath. He'd told Cindy Lou or Mary Jo, or whoever, that they were making too much noise. He asked the barkeep, "Is she, uh, really sore about it?"

Blue considered before he replied, "She didn't *sound* angry. Mayhaps puzzled would be more like it. She said she was a mite surprised that you was that kind of rascal."

"Took it like a good sport, huh?"

"Yessuh. Captain Gloria has a tolerable sense of humor. She just laughed and said it only goes to show that you can't tell a book by its cover."

"She laughed, huh? Well, I can see how lots of folks might find my foolish ways amusing. I'd disremembered

131

she used to be married up, and lots of funny things must happen aboard a steamboat, now that I study on it."

The flashy gal and the man called Porter came in. The barkeep and Longarm were alone in the salon while everyone who could be spared smashed baggage and shifted cargo, so Blue went to serve them. The quiet little spoken-for gal, Sue Ellen, came in alone, looking undecided as to where to sit. Longarm went over to Sue Ellen and said, "There's a table here by the windows, ma'am. You just tell me what you want and I'll have Blue get it for you."

She took the seat he'd indicated, but dimpled as she asked, "Heavens, are you a waiter too?"

They both knew she was just funning. She said she'd like some sarsaparilla if they had it, and Longarm went back to the bar.

Blue came back, frowning and muttering under his breath, so Longarm knew they hadn't called him mister. As he slammed their orders on a tin tray, Longarm told him the other gal wanted root beer and that it would be on him. Blue nodded and took the other drinks he'd built over to the brassy blonde and her flashy companion.

Captain Grimes came in just then, and he thought she was going to have a drink too, but she walked right up to him and said, "There you are. You'd better come with me, Mr. Lansford. I may have need of your peculiar talents after all, this night."

Longarm shot Blue a quizzical look, but the barkeep had his back turned to them. So Longarm followed the tomboy captain outside. "Let's go to my cabin," she said as she indicated the steps up to forbidden territory. He let her go first and followed, admiring the view as he climbed behind her. The gal he'd had that afternoon had been petite and small across the beam. Captain Grimes was taller but even slimmer. He wondered what her long legs looked like. He wondered if he was still man enough to do a lady right if she offered to show him.

They got to the flat Texas deck and she led him to a little cabin between the wheelhouse and the smoke funnel. It was dark inside, but she struck a match and lit a hurricane lamp on the wall above her bunk. It had a feather mattress and was covered with a quilted spread. She pointed at it with her chin and said, "Set yourself down and make yourself to home while I slip into something more comfortable. There's a bottle on the bedstand, if that's your pleasure. But go easy on it. We may face a long hard night."

Longarm sat down, but ignored the bottle she'd pointed out. He already regretted the beer he'd just had. Gloria stepped into another space with a curtain over the doorway, and he heard the rustle of clothes coming off and rolled his eyes heavenward as he thought, *Lord, you really have a peculiar sense of humor. It ain't that I ain't grateful for such pleasures as we seem about to receive, but no joshing, Lord, couldn't you sort of spread things out a mite?*

As she did whatever she was doing in there, Gloria called out, "I wish you'd told me right off what sort of man you were. It sure could have saved us a heap of shilly-shalling."

He said, "Well, I don't like to brag on my private life, ma'am, and some folks act sort of shocked when they find out I ain't as dumb and innocent as they might like me to be."

"I can see how that might happen," she said, laughing. "I think, since we'll be a mite closer from here on, that we'd best call one another by our Christian names, Custis."

He said, "That's fine with me, Gloria. Who, uh, told you about my wicked past, if you don't mind my asking?"

She called back, "Oh, some of the crew were already suspicious. But I wasn't sure until I forced it out of Blue. Mr. Blue doesn't miss much."

"I know. I thought he was a friend of mine too."

"Don't be cross with him," she said. "I told you I forced him to tell me. He was quite upset about it. But after all, his first loyalty is to me and mine, and anyway, had he kept your secret, I wouldn't have been able to use you tonight, and I *need* a man right now."

Longarm scratched his head vigorously. That damned Victoria Woodhull must have started something with her scandalous books. "Well," he said, "I can't say I'm not flattered, Gloria, but I am a mite surprised. I'd have thought that if you were that hard up for a man, you'd have worked something out with old Jim Truman by now. He's right next door in the wheelhouse, ain't he?"

He heard her snapping something open or shut as she laughed and said, "I was considering Jim. But he's sort of young and callow. Jim's a good river pilot, but you're more the sort I really need."

"Well, I do my best," he told her as he started to unfasten his gunbelt.

At that moment Gloria parted the curtains and came out wearing a whipcord riding habit and boots, and carrying a braided leather crop.

He stared up at her dumbstruck. Finally he said, "I'll go along with the unusual, but I don't reckon I'll go along with whips, if it's all the same with you!"

She frowned and asked, "What are you talking about?" as she turned to open a cupboard across from where he sat on the bunk. He had no idea what else she needed. He stood up and stepped over to her. He was about to take her in his arms from behind, with a hand cupping each tomboy breast, when she turned around holding a Winchester and handed it to him, saying, "Here, it's loaded, but the safety's on."

He took the weapon, but asked, "What in thunder do we need guns for? I ain't *that* hard to convince."

"Stop funning about," she said as she took another rifle from the rack for herself and added, "Let's go."

"Go where?"

"Up the bank, of course. I don't see how we're ever going to make it around the next bend. So I have to hire mules, like I told you. Goldfarb, the man I usually rely on, died this spring, and his son is being stubborn as hell. I have to get the mail up the river one damned way or another. I'm hoping that when he sees me with a federal agent backing my play, he'll be more willing to hire me his mules."

Longarm laughed a bit wildly, and she frowned up at him and asked, "What's so infernally funny? I *need* that mail contract, damn it!"

This made him laugh even more. Finally he quieted down enough to say, "I know. Is that what Blue just told you, that I was a federal man?"

"Of course. That's what you are, aren't you? Blue said he'd seen your badge. I know you've been acting awfully sneaky for some fool reason, but it's time to stop this pussyfooting about and deputize me some mules!"

He said, "While we're going I'll explain why we ought to do it less openly." Then he started to giggle like a kid again. She asked why and he answered, "Never mind. I might have made a hell of a mistake, but I didn't, praise the Lord. Let's go see about some *real* jackasses."

Longarm could see why Gloria had felt the need of a male escort as they strode along the waterfront of the little river port. Eagle Butte was a cow town soaking its feet in the river, and it was Saturday night, but nobody trifled with them. Even a drunken buffalo skinner knew better than to trifle with two folks packing rifles.

As they headed for the outskirts of town, which seemed to be only spitting distance from the center of this teeming metropolis, Gloria simmered down about her notion to have the law on Goldfarb, Inc. after he'd explained that first of all it wasn't a federal crime to refuse a lady the hire of a mule, and second, it made sense to hold your cards close to the vest until you knew who else was playing.

He asked her what made her feel the need of manpower to back her play, since her late father had dealt with the packmule outfit in the past. She said, "Young Mose is mean. My daddy told me wrong about *his* skulking cap."

Blinking in puzzlement, Longarm said, "His *what*?"

"You know. Them skulking caps that gentlemen of the Hebrew persuasion wear. My daddy said old Mose Goldfarb was an orthy-something-or-other, and that he'd never been cheated by a Hebrew who wore a skulking cap and kept to the Old Country ways. He said it wasn't true that they sacrificed rabbits and kidnapped Christian gals. He said he'd dealt with lots of old-fashioned gents like Uncle Mose and that he'd never met up with a mean one. What do *you* think, Longarm?"

"Careful what you call me in public; I'm still undercover, you know. I know what your dad was talking about. The only really mean Hebrew I ever met had shaved off his beard and changed his name from Rhinegold to Ringo. I bought these pants off an orthodox gent in Denver, and the seams ain't ripped yet. What happened to old Mose?"

"He was killed in a hunting accident this spring. His son, young Mose, runs the business now, and like I said, he's mean."

They passed a sign that read: *Ticket Office, Amalgamated Stage Lines*. She pointed up at it and said, "They're mean too. Come out here a few years ago with a busted-down old Concord and eat up all the smaller lines until they just about control land travel in these parts."

Longarm didn't answer. The stage line's rough-and-ready business methods had been in the papers that Billy Vail had given him. The laid-off Wells Fargo men who'd started the line had a reputation for hard-driving business methods, but they'd never killed anybody except a few road agents who'd tried to hold them up. Billy had said they struck him as the sort who'd run you out of town in a daylight face-off. He'd followed their paper trail all the way back to the time they'd worked for Wells Fargo, and they'd never been caught doing anything sneaky. They were just plain ornery.

They came to a frame house tacked to the wall of a big barn surrounded by corrals, and even though it was getting pretty dark by now, he could see that the corrals were empty. There was a porch light over the doorway of the house, so he could see the gent sitting on the porch in a rocking chair fairly well. As they approached, Gloria said, "That's him. Young Mose."

The man rose as they came to the steps and Gloria introduced them, leaving out the fact that Longarm was a federal lawman. Young Mose Goldfarb didn't look all that mean or all that young. He was a heavyset man on the sad side of forty, with a luxurious black beard and bushy hair that framed the skullcap Gloria had mentioned.

He smiled sort of pleasantly, considering, and said, "Listen, Miss Gloria, what can I tell you? I'd have saved the mules for you if I'd known you were coming, but do I have a crystal ball?"

"What happened to your mules, Mr. Goldfarb?" Longarm asked.

"Nothing. They're packing lumber up the valley for another customer. You people just missed getting them. I hired them out this afternoon."

Gloria stamped her foot and said, "You knew the water level was going down and that I'd be coming up, young Mose!"

He shrugged and replied, "Do I look like a river-boater? Who else looks at the river? Business is business, Miss Gloria. The building contractor who hired my animals didn't haggle over the price, and it's not often I get the chance to hire out every beast at once. Can't you get pack animals from the livery down the road?"

"You know durned well the livery only hires horses out local," Gloria snapped. "I've tried afore to get them to let me take critters up the river, and they've always said no. Twenty miles outside the township line is their limit. Besides, horses don't pack as good as mules in rough country."

"So listen, why don't you make a deal with the stage line? I'm sure they'd carry the mail up to Kimaho for you, Miss Gloria."

"Oh, *sure* they would! They'd be proud to get the mail franchise away from me too. I only carry the mail because I average speedier delivery, young Mose. The Post Office knows that come hell or low water, I've always got the mail up the river one durned way or another. If I start using the coach service, somebody in the Post Office is bound to wonder why they can't deal direct with Amalgamated and cut out the middle woman."

Goldfarb looked at Longarm. "She makes sense," he sighed, "but what can I do?"

Longarm asked, "Would I be far wrong in suspicioning that the gents who hired your mules this afternoon might have acted out of malice aforethought? You'd know if they were working for the stage line, wouldn't you?"

Goldfarb frowned and replied, "As a matter of fact, the builder who hired all my mules to haul lumber has put up some bridges and way stations for the stage line in the past. But what makes you think he cornered all the pack brutes in town to hurt Miss Gloria here?"

"You don't haul lumber from the prairie to the mountains," Longarm said. "You cut and mill the logs in high country and carry them *down* the valley."

Goldfarb struck his forehead with a palm and said, "Oy! That's right! But listen, who asks such questions when a man comes to you with a good business proposition?" He turned to Gloria and added, "Look, give me a day or so and I'll see if I can line up some other animals, all right?"

She said, "I don't have a day or so. We're just going to have to go up the durned old river the hard way before it shallows even worse. Come on, Custis. I mean to show you some shoal piloting you'll want to write home about!"

As they left, she was still cussing young Mose Goldfarb. Longarm said, "You may be being hard on him, Gloria. What makes you suspicion him of hiring out his mules to hurt you? He's in the business of hiring out mules, and it's first come, first served, ain't it?"

"His daddy, old Mose, would have known the *Minnitipi* was due in with the mail and the river dropping. He knew Amalgamated was out to do us wrong, too. There's something mean and sneaky about young Mose. Call it a woman's intuition if you like, but I always feel like he's undressing me with his eyes."

"Well, a pretty gal has to live with that, Gloria. Don't take this wrong, but most of us gents stare a mite harder than we likely should."

"Oh, young Mose ain't interested in my body. I always get the feeling he's wondering if I'm wearing a money belt under my skirts. His old dad was a fair-dealing man. The first thing young Mose did after he took over was to raise all the freight rates and stop giving credit."

"He talks friendly."

"Talk is cheap. Wait till you sign a contract with young Mose! Folks sure do miss his daddy around here, now that he's gone."

"Well, don't forget that prices are rising everywhere, now that the pinch of the seventies seems to be over," he reminded her. Then he chewed absently on the edge of his mustache as he mulled over a thought that had just occurred to him. Finally he said, "You say old Mose was killed in a hunting accident, Gloria?"

"That's what they tell me. Seems that old Mose and young Mose were out on the prairie on horseback, when the old man was shot for an elk, accidental."

Longarm's eyebrows rose. "An elk, on the open prairie?"

She nodded. "Ain't it peculiar? There was some ugly talk about it at the time, but the coroner was finally convinced it was an accident. Young Mose witnessed for the one who did it."

Longarm looked hard at Gloria. "This gets stranger and stranger. Young Mose witnessed *for* the jasper who shot his old man?"

"Not all that strange, considering," she said. "It was the town halfwit, the Peterson kid. What seems to've happened is that young Peterson came over a rise with his rifle and let fly before he'd studied on what he was shooting at. The coroner's jury acquitted him, but the kid ain't allowed to hunt no more."

Longarm ran the tale through his head again. He was paid to be suspicious. Then he shrugged and said, "Well, if the dead man's son and the local coroner were satisfied, it must have been just one of those dumb things that happen when you let a halfwit loose with a gun. Young Mose sounds like a good sport, considering. I'd have likely gunned the Peterson kid, idiot or no, had I just seen him kill my father."

She said, "Oh, young Mose gave him a good licking and dragged him in to Eagle Butte by the scruff of his neck, packing old Mose across his own horse. The Peterson kid was bawling and carrying on awful, according to them who saw it. Young Mose had busted his nose and gave him a black eye. But he said he'd quit when it came to him that he was beating up a halfwit."

"You mean young Mose didn't know the Peterson kid?"

"I reckon not. Young Mose had gone back East to learn bookkeeping, so he was away when the Peterson kid started shaving and hunting rabbits. He said when it first happened he thought they were getting bush-whacked by some kind of ants."

"Anti-Semites?"

"Yeah, that's what he called 'em. He said when he was in the army, them ants hoorahed him awful for being of the Hebrew persuasion."

Longarm nodded as they saw the steamboat landing ahead. He remembered the one Jewish kid in his old outfit during the War, and how some of the old boys had acted sort of dumb. Longarm had never had any trouble with old Iz. He'd been a fair soldier, and they might have gotten friendlier in time, had it not been for that enemy sniper at Shiloh. Some of the old boys who'd teased old Iz had later said they were sorry when they saw how bravely he died with that minnie ball in him just above the belt plate.

They got to the steamboat and Longarm asked how soon they'd be shoving off. Gloria sighed and said, "Sunrise. No pilot born of mortal flesh could take a sternwheeler around the big bend in the dark."

So he saw her to the Texas steps and told her he'd mosey back to town and ask some questions along the main drag.

He didn't know it was a mistake, if it was one. Later he'd realize it would have happened on the boat anyway. But he swore softly under his breath and tried to crawfish backwards out the swinging doors when he stepped into a saloon and spotted the gambling man, Canfield, at the street end of the bar. Canfield saw him at the same time and spoke out sharp and loud enough to make the men around him freeze as he said, "I've been looking for you, Lansford!"

Longarm moved sideways away from the doorway as he smiled and said, "Howdy. I see you made good time up the river."

Canfield stepped away from the bar to face Longarm, and as his lavender-gray frock coat fell open, Longarm saw that *he* was wearing a cross-draw rig now, too.

Longarm kept his voice light as he said, "I see you're loaded for bear."

Canfield replied, "Not a bear. A wolverine who's been pissing in my bed."

The other men in the bar started edging away, and the barkeep sighed and started to take down the mirror hanging behind the bar as Longarm said, "That could get a gent riled up. Is it anyone I know?"

"You shave in a mirror, don't you? We're wasting time, you bastard. Sylvia told me what you done to her."

"You ain't thinking, old son," Longarm said levelly. "I'll tell you man to man that I have never trifled with another man's woman without an invite. As to what old Sylvia might have said I did or didn't do, we both know that gals don't talk personal to a man unless they want to see him get his fool self killed."

Canfield smiled crookedly. "We'll see who gets killed, you slippery bastard. You'll not talk your way out of this one. So fill your fist whenever you've a mind to."

Longarm shook his head. "I can't hardly do that, old son. This ain't Dodge in the seventies, and even if it was, I'd be a fool to give you a self-defense if you won."

"You yellow-bellied bastard! You *owe* me a fight, goddamn your eyes!"

"Nobody here owes anybody a fight. You've never done anything to me, Canfield. As to what you may think I've done to you, you ain't got as much call to revenge as you might think. I don't talk about a lady in public, but take it from a man who means you no harm, nothing happened down the river that hasn't likely happened many a time before."

Longarm had meant that neighborly, but he saw there was no reasoning with a Samson who'd been hoodwinked by a Delilah. Canfield went for his gun.

Longarm didn't consider himself a killer. He'd never gotten any pleasure out of gunning a man. That was what made him so dangerous. Canfield, on the other hand, was worked up and too anxious. So his hand whipped across his belly in a blur and gripped his gun butt with an audible slap, driving the weapon deeper into leather for the fraction of a second it took him to reverse direction.

Longarm drew like the professional he was. His first shot filled the room with smoke and echoes just as Canfield's gun cleared its holster. Longarm fired twice more, dancing the gambling man down the bar like a ballerina spinning on her toes until he faced the other way, fell forward like a tree going down, and died with his face in a cuspidor near the brass rail.

"I sure am sorry about that, Canfield," Longarm said as he thumbed the spent rounds out of his cylinder and reloaded, leaning against the bar. The barkeep came up to him warily and said, "You're going to have to talk to the law about what you just done, stranger."

Longarm said, "I know. That's why I ain't running out the door. You'd better fix me a boilermaker with Maryland rye whilst we're waiting. If the gent on the floor owes you anything, I'll pay his tab. We used to be friends."

When the town law arrived, Longarm said he wanted to make a private statement. So they went to the back room and told the gents who'd been playing cards through it all that the game was over. As soon as they were alone at the table, Longarm took out his wallet and said, "My office gave me a rundown on all the lawmen I might meet going up the river, so I know you, and now you'd better know me." As the town law studied his badge and credentials, Longarm added, "I'd take it neighborly if we could settle this without telling the whole world I'm a federal agent."

The Eagle Butte lawman handed him his wallet back and said, "I'll fix it with the coroner. From what the gents from the saloon told me when they came to fetch me, I reckon it could be put down as suicide, once you study on it. Did that gambling man know you were a U.S. deputy?"

"Yes. He must have. He went through my possibles

aboard the *Minnitipi* the other night, and he gunned another federal employee down the river before that. He made *that* look like a fair fight too."

"Well, I'll send some wires and see if he was really a gambling man or something more serious. Who was the gal you two had words over just before he committed suicide, Marshal Long?"

"I ain't sure. You see, he really was a damned good card mechanic and she was traveling with him sort of sneaky. I don't know if she knew how often he killed folks. I found her sort of a friendly gal. She did try to put me to sleep with drugged brandy, but we sort of kissed and made up. I suspicion she was just his shill and play-pretty."

The town law frowned and said, "I ain't one for butting in on another man's case, Long. But it reads two ways to me. Canfield could have meant to gun two federal lawmen. On the other hand he could have just been sort of moody. If you trifled with his woman, he might have had it in for you, badge or no. How do you reckon he found out about you and the gal?"

Longarm shrugged. "She might have talked in her sleep. He might have just made that up as an excuse to pick a fight. How in thunder can anyone say what a man who wears a purple suit might do?"

"Well, he sure has stopped, whatever it was. Do you reckon his saucy traveling companion is anyplace hereabouts?"

"I misdoubt it. To meet us this far up the river, Canfield must have been riding lickety-split. I'll write you down a description before I go, but I suspicion neither of us will ever see old Sylvia again."

The town law said something about having to tell the local coroner the truth, but that he could vouch for the coroner as a discreet cuss.

Longarm said, "Billy Vail told me you were a good old boy. It wouldn't be fair to leave you here empty-handed in an election year. Let's talk about somebody you *might* be able to arrest."

He saw that he had the other lawman's undivided attention, so he said, "If I were you, I'd look deeper into the accidental death of Moses Goldfarb. Before I ran into Canfield just now, I'd jawed some with folks who live around here. They told me young Mose left Eagle Butte years ago to go to college in the East."

The town law looked at him blankly. "Sure, so what?"

Longarm said, "College courses only last four years. Mose has been gone since before the War."

"Hell, that ain't no mystery, Marshal Long. I know for a fact that young Mose got drafted into the Union infantry and fought at Cold Harbor."

"The War's been over for fifteen years. Folks say old Mose had given his son up a long time ago as killed in the War. This gent everybody *calls* young Mose just got here about a week before the old man was killed in that funny hunting accident. Billy Vail tells me you're a Methodist, so I'd better tell you something. Orthodox Jews don't hold with hunting. It's against their religion. They can't eat a critter that wasn't killed proper by a rabbi."

"Do tell? How come old Mose and young Mose was out hunting that morning, then?"

"I don't think they were. I think the man we know as young Mose got the old man to just go riding out across the prairie for some other reason. He might have been planning the deed. He might have just got lucky. When the halfwit Peterson boy took a wild shot at them and then ran off scared, I think young Mose shot old Mose, then chased the village idiot down and whipped him silly until the Peterson kid couldn't rightly say what had really happened. If you'll think back, young Peterson said more than once that he hadn't really aimed his gun at anybody. But who listens to the village idiot, right?"

The town law frowned and said, "Hold on, now. Are you accusing young Mose of gunning his own father and framing the kid?"

Longarm shook his head. "He didn't gun his father. He wasn't the old man's son. I figure the *real* young Mose died in the War, like his father thought. The man running the business right now must have known him in the army, and when he found himself out in these parts he looked the old man up."

"Now hold on, damn it. The Peterson kid is the village idiot. Old Mose was a smart old cuss. Even after twenty years or more, a father would know his own son."

Longarm nodded and replied, "Sure. You're forgetting that the old man died just a few days after the man who calls himself young Mose got here. Old Mose never introduced him to anyone in town as his son. I checked on that. Old Mose was sort of an outsider in a Methodist town. He lived on the outskirts too. This old army pal of his son looked him up, likely saying he was Jewish too, and the old man hired him or just took him in for a spell. Couple of days later the old man was dead. So the ringer took over the whole kit and caboodle, claiming to be somebody he wasn't. If you go back over your homework, you'll find that the first time he *said* he was young Mose was when he brought the body and the halfwit in. Before that, nobody in town remembers jawing all that much with him. They remember seeing him around the old man's spread. They remember him sitting on the porch with the old man. But that's all! Nobody had any dealings with young Mose until he took the business over uncontested."

The Eagle Butte lawman was paid to be suspicious too, so he studied some before he shook his head and said, "It's thin air, Long. I can see how the gears fit together, but I can't see how how to make it tick loud enough for a grand jury to consider. You have to admit there's not a shred of solid evidence that young Mose ain't who he says he is."

Longarm said, "There must be some other followers

146

of the Herew faith within a day's ride. I'd start by calling them as friends of the court. Then, of course, I'd check with the War Department to see if Graves Registry has a record of where they buried the real Moses Goldfarb. He'd have been home a long time ago if he wasn't buried some damn place."

"I like the army notion. Try me on calling in Jewish witnesses again."

"The man calling himself young Mose ain't Jewish. Not a practicing Jew, at any rate. He wears a beard and a skullcap, but he just told Captain Grimes and me that he hired out all his mules this afternoon.

"So what? That ain't against the law."

"It is to an orthodox Jew. This is Saturday. The Hebrew Sabbath runs from sundown Friday to Saturday night. No Jew who followed the ways of his faith would touch money on the Sabbath. They ain't even allowed to cook a meal or ride a horse. By Friday evening they're supposed to have all their chores done so they can spend the Sabbath in rest and prayer, like their Good Book says. Doing business on a Saturday afternoon would rank with eating pig's knuckles and fornicating with their sisters to serious Hebrew gents."

The town marshal slapped the tabletop and grinned broadly. "Hot damn! I just remembered, now that you mention it!" Old Mose Goldfarb did shut down on Saturdays! It riled enough folks in town for them to remember it, too! I'd better go arrest the son of a bitch."

"I'd build me a better case first, if I were you," Longarm cautioned him. "He ain't going anywhere to-night. The army records office will be closed tomorrow. I'd wait until I had an address for the real Mose Junior's body before I made my move. That murderer imitating him don't know he's under suspicion, but he'd only need a day's lead and a shave to make arresting him complicated as all hell."

The town law agreed. So they shook hands as they

wished each other good hunting, and Longarm ducked out the back way to head back to the steamboat.

A light was burning in Gloria's window, but it was late and he knew better than to go up to the Texas uninvited. He went to his own stateroom instead. As he strode the deck he didn't see any other passengers about, but the vessel bubbled and squeaked as they kept the fire going under her boilers, and down below he heard men shifting cargo. They seemed to be moving stuff forward, which would trim the bow lower than the stern and slow the *Minnitipi* down some. It seemed crazy until he considered the advantages of running on a sandbar with the bow low and the rest of the hull and paddlewheels a few inches higher in the water when you wanted to back off.

He fished out his key and glanced automatically at the match sliver he'd wedged in the jamb. Then he froze in place. Because it wasn't there.

"Aw, shit, not again," he breathed as he drew his .44 and quietly tried the knob. The door was locked. He swore, put the key in, and twisted it as quietly as he could, standing to one side. Nothing happened when he shoved the door open and slid inside fast, dropping to one knee in a dark corner. He said, "I can see you. And this is getting mighty tedious."

Nobody answered. As his eyes adjusted to the light from the open doorway, he saw that nobody else was in the room. Slowly he got to his feet. He closed the door before he struck a match to light the lamp. There was a faint, funny buzzing. Most folks might have taken it for some shipboard sound.

Longarm wasn't most folks. He backed away as far as he was able and held the match high as he heard it again. It was under the bed, and it was a big one, from the sound of its rattles.

The match burned out in his fingers, so he lit another as he hunkered down at a safe distance and peered under the bunk. Two mean little eyes peered back at him, glittering in the light as the diamondback that was coiled under the bunk stuck its tongue out at him and buzzed again.

"Howdy, snake," he said. "We have us a problem here, don't we? I can't fire into the decking. There's folks on the far side. Let's study on this. I can see you're more scared than I am. But then, nobody carried me on board in a sack and throwed me into a dark room. I sure wish snakes could talk."

The critter just watched his match flame, coiled and ready. Longarm went outside again and took a red fire bucket filled with sand from its rack on deck. Then he stole a hurricane lamp too. He went back inside, and after making sure the rattler was still under the bunk, he placed the hurricane lamp on the floor in a corner. Then he took a running leap and landed atop the bunk as the snake under it buzzed hysterically.

He bounced up and down, creaking the springs as he watched over the side. He felt it strike at the springs a few times, which must have smarted. Then the big diamondback slithered out from under the bunk and he yelled, "Freeze, you son of a bitch!"

Snakes were deaf, he knew, but as it picked up the vibrations of his voice and sensed him above it, the diamondback recoiled into a neat ball of wary, hissing hate. Longarm dropped the bucket over it, open end down, and all but the whirring tail was trapped inside. The snake made a dull clunking noise as it banged its fang-filled head against the metal of the bucket.

"I know just how you feel, old son," Longarm said as he held the bucket's rim against the flooring and slid it across the room and out the door. There was still nobody out on deck. Longarm slid the bucket to the edge, and while the bucket wouldn't fit under the turned balusters of the railing, he could safely lift the rim on the far side until the snake got the idea and slithered out to drop with a faint splash in the water below. As the current carried it downstream he knew it wouldn't make it ashore until it was too far off to

149

pester anyone but prairie dogs again. He put the bucket and lamp back where he'd found them and locked himself in for the night. He knew it was a waste of time to question innocent parties. Anyone on his side who'd known there was a diamondback in his room would have said so. It'd be interesting to see who would be most surprised when he turned up at breakfast.

Chapter 9

Longarm woke at first light to the churning of paddles, and knew they were under way well before breakfast time. He washed up, shaved, and dressed. As he stepped out into the cold gray dawn he saw he'd beaten the sunrise. The sky was rosy pearl to the east and the river ran like old pewter that needed polishing. When he found himself alone in the empty salon, he went back outside. A deckhand who must have been looking for him said, "Captain's compliments, sir. Miss Gloria wants you to join her topside in the wheelhouse."

Longarm nodded his thanks and went up. He found Gloria alone at the big wooden wheel. She said, "I wanted to talk to you some more last night. How come you didn't say good night?"

He said, "It was late. I can see you turned in early, if you ever sleep."

"I'm used to piloting with sand in my eyes. What's this I hear about you having a gunfight ashore?"

"I ran into Canfield again. Guess who won."

"I know who won, damn it. What on earth were you fighting about?"

"I ain't sure. He wasn't in a talking mood. How does the river look to you this morning, Gloria?"

"Low. You see that silver streak in the water over yonder?"

"Yeah, it's sort of pretty in the half-light. Like somebody rubbed a streak of polish over duller metal."

She said, "It's a snag. Mean old waterlogged tree

151

just waiting to spear some steamboat's poor hull. See that fresh dirt caved out of the bank on the starboard? There used to be a landmark tree over there. Big dead cottonwood that glowed sort of silvery itself, in the twilight. I have to remember it's gone now, when I make this run again."

He moved closer and stared over her shoulder as they steamed up the river. She was slim-shouldered, as well as far shorter than he was. The big wheel seemed to be giving her a hard time. He asked her if he could help, and she told him, "Touch my spokes and I'll flay you alive! I don't mind strong current where the river narrows like this. It's the wide, lazy flats that kill most steamboats."

They were rounding a bend and he asked her if that was the big one she'd been talking about. Gloria laughed. "Heck, no. The Big Bend is a mess of *little* bends, twisting around them hills to our port side. We'll be swinging the other way in a minute, if we're lucky."

As new water came in view, Longarm could see that the river widened some here, and Gloria pointed dead ahead and said, "See that tumble-boil up yonder? That's where the water's running over a ledge of solid shale. There's usually a mark and a half of water over her, but like I said, the durned old river's dropping fast."

He stared at the line of bubbling water ahead and said, "I know this ain't my business, Gloria. But you seem to be headed for that underwater ledge at full steam ahead."

"Don't try to teach your granny to suck eggs," she said. "The ledge ain't straight across the channel, and the nice thing about a tumble-boil is that the water's always deeper just downstream. Now hush, I've got me some piloting to do!"

The *Minnitipi* moved ever closer to the tumble-boil, and Longarm started looking for something to grab hold of when they hit. Then, as the blunt bow almost kissed the downstream bubbles, Gloria spun the wheel hard over and they sort of skidded broadside and seemed to be headed for another crash into the far bank. Something solid thudded against the bottom of the hull. "Rock," she said laconically, as she swung the wheel the other way.

The *Minnitipi* seemed to pause for breath as she hung in a slick, smooth stretch of water moving faster than the rest. Then they were moving up the river again and she said, "There's only one gap in that infernal tumble-boil. My daddy taught me long ago how to pass there when the water level's low."

"There ain't any straight way through, huh?"

"Not that anyone's ever found, and a mess of boats have gotten banged up looking for her."

They started moving faster, and when Longarm commented on it, she explained, "We're in a stretch where the bottom's deeper between shoals. The trick now is to build up speed before the next bottom-banger."

He noticed she was swinging around what seemed a perfectly innocent stretch of smooth, deep water, but he didn't say anything. He was glad he hadn't when she said, "New sandbar building up there. Most fools can see the riffles when a snag or bar is fixing to surface, but it slicks like that when the obstruction's just at steamboat-killing depth."

They made another bend, and again the river widened beyond what looked like the ripples of a breeze on a quiet millpond. Longarm could see that the wind wasn't blowing against the current, though, so he wasn't surprised when Gloria said, "Hang on. We're going to feel a bump."

He reached just over his head to grab a rafter as the *Minnitipi* lurched under him like a buckboard hitting a pothole. She laughed and said, "That ledge is always covered with sand." Then she reached for the brass engine telegraph beside her wheel and moved the lever to half speed. She tooted her whistle, and when a crewman ran out on the bow and looked up at her, she

153

slid the glass open and called down, "See if you can find me a channel, Tom."

The crewman unwound a weighted line from around his waist, swung the lead, and cast it ahead of the bow. As the boat glided past the line he called up, "Mark twain and a quarter."

Gloria swore under her breath and signaled Dead Slow. Then she said, "You may as well have breakfast, Longarm. We're not going anyplace fast or interesting for a spell."

"I don't understand. I make that over six feet of water, and we only draw three, right?"

"It's a good thing you ain't piloting this steamboat," she said. "A mark is three feet on the lower river. Up here it's two. So we're clearing the bottom by fifteen inches, and that's in the infernal *channel*."

"Now you've really got me mixed up. I always thought a mark was half a fathom, no matter where."

"Hell, if Tom had his line marked in feet or fathoms, he'd call out feet or fathoms. The lead line's knotted and each knot is a mark, naturally. As you go upriver the marks get closer spaced. Below St. Louis the main channel runs nine feet deep. Up here the best we can hope for is five. It saves counting to mark the line accordingly."

The lineman called, "Mark twain and shoaling."

Gloria grabbed the engine telegraph and said, "Damn. We'd best tread water and study this. I've seldom seen it so shallow in this stretch."

She swung the wheel, and as the bow seemed to drift to starboard she called down, "Sound that slack just this side of that boil, Tom!"

The lineman did, and called up, "Mark twain and a half, Captain."

She grinned and said, "There you go. There's a big rock up a ways that scours the bottom to her downstream lee. Now if only I can sneak up the scour without hitting the infernal rock . . ."

Longarm could see she was right; it would take some

time to round this particular bend. "How long do you figure it will be before we reach Fort Benton?" he asked, and she said, "All day, if we're lucky."

"Gloria, Fort Benton ain't more than twenty miles from here as the crow flies."

"I know. The *Minnitipi* ain't a crow. Neither is the river. The Big Muddy hairpins north over twenty miles and then winds like hell a good thirty or more to the south. You think we're going slow now? Wait till we make the Big Bend."

"Hmm, are you putting in anywhere soon?"

"If I don't run aground first. There's a post office at a settlement just up a couple of bends. Why?"

"I'm sort of anxious about some telegrams I sent. They'll have sent my answers to Fort Benton. I thought I might hire a mount and cut across."

"It's rough country," she said.

He gazed to the west out the side window and said, "It just looks like rolling prairie to me. I've been through the canyonlands on a mule."

"I ain't talking about your falling off a bluff. It's the folks and critters that are rough. I hear tell there's a herd of unshot buffalo still roaming the deep draws inside the Big Bend. They say there's unreconstructed Injuns hunting them too."

"I was told the BIA and the army know where all the bands are this summer," he said.

She snorted. "Yeah. They told Custer to expect maybe thirty or forty lodges on the Little Bighorn too. You'll likely save some time by riding across the short way, if you don't get scalped. But I'd study on it before I left the river if I was you."

Gloria wasn't him, but Longarm said he'd think about it anyway. Then he excused himself and went down to see if there was anything left to eat. There was. He had ham and eggs while the lineman outside kept calling out "mark twain" until it sounded like he was advertising old Sam Clemens' books.

Most of the others had already eaten. T. J. Porter

155

and the fancy gal in the ostrich hat were drinking at the same table as though they'd never left it since he'd last seen them. But of course he knew that neither one had been in the salon when somebody shoved that snake in his stateroom.

When he'd finished breakfast, T. J. invited him to join them, so he did. The big buxom blonde was still named Daisy Melrose, which sounded made up as well as silly. When Longarm said he was aiming to get off at the next landing and take a shortcut over to Fort Benton, the railroad man said, "I've got a telegraph message I'd be obliged if you'd send for me. One of the crew just told us there was no telling when we'd make the next real town. I'd be happy to make it worth your while, of course."

Longarm told the man he'd do it, but that he wasn't a paid messenger. He said he'd take money to pay Western Union, but that was all.

T. J. smiled and said, "Oh, it won't cost nothing at this end. I'll write it down and you can send it to my Chicago firm, collect."

Longarm agreed and T. J. took out a paper pad and a lead pencil. As he wrote his telegram, Longarm felt somebody rubbing knees with him under the table. He didn't think it was the railroad man. He looked thoughtfully at Daisy Melrose and she just smiled innocently and said, "You'll meet us all again at that other port, won't you, sir?"

He said, "Yep. Captain Grimes says they'll tie up for the night at Fort Benton. After that it's just a two days' run to Kimaho."

She sort of sucked his kneecap with the crook of her soft leg as she said, "I'll be so relieved to get off this tub. I'm looking forward to seeing the Great Falls of the Missouri, if I can find someone to escort me there."

"Kimaho ain't too close to the Great Falls, ma'am," Longarm told her. "We leave the main channel just below the township of Great Falls and cut up Kimaho Creek to the settlement named the same. The waterfall

156

is in a canyon nobody lives in. It's a couple of hours' ride from any town worth mention."

"Really? Maybe I'll pack a picnic lunch."

Longarm wondered how all this was going down with T. J. Porter. The railroad man wasn't deaf and he'd been buying a lot of booze for the gal. But T. J. just went on writing until he got done, and when he folded the message and handed it to Longarm he was smiling. So Longarm smiled back and put it in his inside coat pocket.

The gal left one knee over Longarm's, but stopped rubbing as T. J. ordered another round and began to brag about all the wonders and cucumbers the GF&YSRR was going to bring to Montana Territory. Longarm asked him if he was a surveyor and T. J. said, "Lord, no, I'm an executive. This is a closing trip I'm on. We have to line up our right-of-way. So I've been sent to spread good cheer and option money among the settlers."

"You're carrying hard currency in these parts without a bodyguard?"

"Of course not. We pay by check. Most of the land we need is public domain, of course, and Montana Territory is only too anxious to see us lay our tracks. The tricky part is that folks who settle new country tend to choose carefully. It seems somebody owns every pass and ford our engineers have picked out for us. So we have to buy off a lot of clods."

Longarm nodded and said, "I can see how a man holding a bottleneck could hold up a railroad almost as good as Jesse with a gun." But T. J. laughed and said, "Fortunately our plans are flexible. There's always more than one way to skin a cat or route a rail line. It's a matter of simple economics."

Daisy caressed Longarm's knee with her leg as she said dryly, Mr. Porter knows a lot about economics. He's explaining it to me. A lot."

T. J. didn't get her drift. He said, "It costs money to go around a ranch or settlement. It costs money to buy

157

a right-of-way through. So the set price is sort of automatic. We're willing to make a deal for a convenient route. But if they ante the stakes too high, we can always build around them. We've had to point that out to a few folks, but most of them can count."

Longarm nodded and said, "I'd say most small towns would *want* a railroad station."

"Exactly," T. J. replied. "Everybody knows a settlement can't send much to market if it's tucked off in the back of the beyond. We don't have much trouble convincing the merchants and bankers in the towns. It's the ranchers who can be muleheaded. They say our whistles spook their stock, and that they can always drive their own critters to market when the time comes. But this trip I'm authorized to settle it with fair-sized checks. So, come this time next year, you'll see the Iron Horse this far west."

"How do you figure it'll get here? On a steamboat?" Longarm asked.

"Of course. The rails will have to be shipped up the river too. We've already contracted with a local lumber outfit to furnish the ties. We're still dickering about the coal. There's a lot of coal in those hills up the river. But you Westerners are used to mining for gold and silver. No offense. It's hard to convince some folks that coal is a cheap bulk product. So far all the bids we've gotten have been way out of line. But I'm sure one outfit or another will see the light. If push comes to shove, we can always dig our own infernal coal. Our surveyors found a couple of seams on land we already have lined up."

The big blonde yawned and said, "I think I'll lie down for a spell. I can't fathom what's suddenly made me so sleepy."

She didn't ask if Longarm wanted to join her, but the way she hauled her leg off his was as good as an engraved invitation. Both men rose as she left the table, and as she sashayed out, T. J. sighed and said, "Nice, huh?"

"You saw her first," Longarm said.

The railroad man laughed and replied, "Don't hold back on my account. I'm a happily married man, and I've got a bad back too. Let's have another drink."

Longarm said he'd be proud to pay for this round. But just then a crewman came in and told him, "Captain's compliments, sir. We're putting in just long enough to toss a mail sack ashore. So she says if you aim to disembark, you'd best get a move on."

Longarm nodded thanks and told T. J., "I'll buy you that drink in Fort Benton, if either of us makes it."

Longarm spied no buffalo as he rode across the whipped-up sea of grass on the calico gelding he'd hired at the landing. The livery had thrown in a stock saddle with a busted tree and told him he could leave the whole kit at another livery owned by the same folks in Fort Benton. The Winchester lying across his knees he'd borrowed from Gloria.

The country was more rolling than it looked from the river, but not really busted up too badly to beeline. So he did, walking the gelding up the steep slopes and letting him trot down. It was the trotting that made the broken saddle tree something to cuss over. The split wood under the leather hadn't been noticeable when they'd put it aboard the calico for him. He couldn't feel it give at a walk. But he'd known the first time he trotted that the forks had parted company, likely from somebody trying to rope a locomotive or something, tie-down-style. The saddle would get him there, but it wasn't meant for serious riding. Every time he stood in the stirrups to ease his balls, he heard it crack some more. If it every really gave, he'd be sitting there like a big-ass bird with a slack cinch and the longest stirrup leathers in the world. But what the hell, the sun told him he was still moving a lot faster than the steamboat, and going in a straight line.

He hadn't thought to bring along any other reading material to pass the time as he rode over a lot of nothing much, so he took out Porter's message. It wasn't sealed, and of course the railroad man expected him to read it when he sent it, anyway.

The night letter was addressed to the railroad's office on State Street in Chicago, and read:

WILL MAKE FINAL OFFER TO TOWN COUNCIL HIGHWOOD WELLS STOP SUGGEST WE LAY TRACKS THROUGH WALTHAM IF THEY WONT LISTEN TO REASON STOP COAL OFFER BY EDWARDS AND SONS GOOD BUT COAL INFERIOR STOP CAN I MAKE BETTER OFFER OTHER MINE QUESTION MARK T J

Longarm shrugged and put it away. The blonde had had a point, it seemed. He squinted as he found the two towns drawn on his memorized map. They lay fairly close together to the south of the Missouri and on the way to the headwaters of the Yellowstone. T. J. was right. It didn't matter much, to the railroad, which way they went. He knew T. J. was right about Western coal outfits too. He'd almost gotten himself killed getting between mine owners and strikers, down the Front Range near Pueblo that time. Folks who'd come west yelling, "Pike's Peak or Bust!" didn't see fit to dig anything out of the ground for the same wages as they'd been paid back in Penn State or West-by-God-Virginia. But that was T. J.'s problem, not Longarm's. He'd have never built such a fool railroad anyway.

Longarm frowned and reconsidered that angle as he walked the calico up a rise. He knew that more than half the profit in Western railroad building lay in the land they wrangled over for their right-of-way. The federal and local governments fell over one another granting land to railroad builders to pay them for their Christian charity in bringing Civilization and such to the benighted frontier. The railroad barons owned mines, timber, town sites, water, and grazing rights too rich to put a sensible price on, even after they'd sold off blocks of land to furnish customers for their rail traffic. Any idiot could die rich, once he had that first rail franchise.

He knew the GF&YSRR wasn't on the Big Board with railroads like the UP, the B&O, or the SP, and despite his bragging, T. J. seemed to be on a tight budget. So how could a small railroad playing for big stakes profit by putting Gloria's steamboat line out of business?

"They can't," he told himself. "The lonesome route they say they mean to follow don't compete with river traffic. T. J. had said they'd need the riverboats to haul equipment up the valley. T. J. could be fibbing about some things, but rails and locomotives sure have to get up to the headwaters *some* damned way."

He figured that as long as he was suspecting Porter, he'd roll him over a few times and look at him from all angles. So he tried to figure out how the planned railroad could profit by interfering with the U.S. Mail. They weren't asking for the river mail. Since the tracks would cross the river like the top of a big T, the GF&YSRR would get mail from the post offices near the river to deliver farther along the Front Range. That took him back to the stage line, which was in more direct competition with the steamboats. But he didn't like them much as suspects. Any shoestring stage outfit that could afford a private army wouldn't *be* a shoestring stage line. Like Gloria, they were barely staying in business, and both would benefit by the coming of the railroad. Everybody in the territory would. All forms of transportation tended to make folks richer if they'd gotten in on the ground floor in virgin territory. He couldn't see how any settler, miner, rancher, or whatsoever could object to the railroad, the stage line, *or* the river traffic.

He was still pondering this as he topped the rise. Then his eyes widened as he muttered, "Oh, shit!" and reined in.

The tipi ring in the draw below consisted of two dozen lodges. They were decorated with green paint, which meant they were Arapaho, and Indians of all ages and sexes were spilling out of them, meaning they'd spotted him.

Longarm considered his options. They were all disgusting. If he turned tail and made a run for it, the Arapaho might chase him and they might not. If they chased him, they'd catch him as soon as his saddle fell apart. If they didn't chase him, it meant they were friendlies and that he'd be late getting to Fort Benton while they had a good laugh on him. So he sat his mount on the skyline and stared down thoughtfully at the Indians, who were just as thoughtfully staring back up at him.

None of the braves were running for the ponies tethered near the downwind side of camp. He didn't see green stripes on the ponies, either. It was hard to tell from up here whether the braves were wearing paint or not. They were probably making up their minds on that point.

He shrugged and heeled his mount down the slope to them, riding in as though he'd expected to see them there. As he reined in again politely, a pistol-shot's distance from the nearest lodge, a delegation of older men walked out across the summer-killed grass to meet him. An old gent wrapped in a red and green tartan blanket wailed out, "Hear me! The guns you gave us don't shoot straight. Half our matches don't light. There is sand in the sugar from the trading post. We are very cross."

Longarm was glad these folks, or at least their chiefs, could and would speak English. He knew they liked the sound of formal speech, so he fancied up his grammar to oblige them as he began: "The Great White Father has heard that his red children have been saying this. Tell me what the traders have done wrong and I will put your words down on paper and send it to my chief."

He wasn't supposed to be posing as a BIA man, but he could see that these rascals were off the reservation and hadn't seen fit to inform their agent. He knew that most Indians would rather use a BIA man as a Santa Claus than scalp him. That was why the BIA was always telling the army that gents like Red Cloud only wanted peace. A piece of this and a piece of that. A man they took for BIA was seldom molested. Other strange whites, alone, with horse and guns, tended to get lost on the prairie a mite.

The tribal elders talked it over in their singsong dialect, and then the one in the Scotchman's blanket said, "I am Raven Laughing. I am not an evil person. Come. We shall smoke together while I tell you all the bad things other Americans have done to us."

Longarm dismounted, and a young buck came over to take the reins. The Arapaho was missing an eye, and the saber scar had left his mouth twisted in an eternal mirthless grin. He said, "I like this horse. Maybe I will own this horse someday."

One of the older men spoke sharply to him in Algonquin, and the scar-faced buck shrugged and led Longarm's mount away, still grinning despite the naked hate in his one good eye.

Raven Laughing led Longarm to a four-point Hudson's Bay blanket spread on the grass near his lodge. They sat on it together as the others hunkered down around them. A squaw brought a lit pipe from the chief's lodge and he puffed it hard before handing it to Longarm. The tall deputy ignored the bitter kinnikinnick they'd adulterated the more expensive tobacco with. It made the cornsilk he'd smoked as a boy seem downright luxurious, but a guest in an Indian camp had to allow for the tastes of folks who put flour in their coffee and black powder in trade liquor. Raven Laughing watched approvingly as Longarm said, "My brother's smoke is good," and handed the pipe on to the next victim.

"We can prepare a tipi and a woman for you, if you have ridden far," Raven Laughing offered.

"My heart smiles to see I am among such good people," Longarm replied, "but I can't stay long among my brothers. I have to go to Fort Benton, where the Singing Wire can carry their complaints to the Great White Father."

That seemed to strike them fair enough. So as Longarm took out T. J. Porter's message and wrote on the back with a pencil stub, they took turns accusing the BIA of everything but the common cold. Most of it was just the usual carping of a once-proud people forced to live as wards of the state. He skipped some of their complaints and noted a couple of real irregularities. He genuinely felt that some Indians had gotten the short end of the stick and the law was the law, no matter who bent it out of shape to make a dollar. So, while he was a fake Indian agent, Longarm meant to put their more sensible gripes on the wire. It never hurt Interior to know that Justice was reading over its shoulder from time to time.

The scar-faced buck came over and squatted across from Longarm, staring hard and thoughtfully with his one good eye as the lawman joshed with the older men. Longarm knew he spoke good English, and the saber cut indicated a more than passing acquaintance with the U.S. Army. Longarm nodded at him and asked his name. The Arapaho said, "I used to be Dancing Fox. Now I am Iron Head. I count coup on the American who broke his long knife on my skull. He died screaming like a squaw. I was bleeding. My eye hung down my cheek on its stalk. I killed him anyway. I killed him slowly. I like to hear my enemies cry."

Longarm shrugged. "Well, some men collect stamps. Everyone to his own fancy, I always say."

Iron Head said, "Hear me. I do not think you are from the Indian agency. If you are from the Indian agency, prove it to me and my brothers."

Raven Laughing scowled and said something to the

younger man in his own lingo. Longarm laughed easily and told them, "That's all right. I wouldn't want you boys to think I was a British spy. I'll just let Iron Head read my ID. You can read, can't you, Iron Head?"

Iron Head didn't answer, so Longarm knew he was home safe. Modesty was not considered a virtue among Plains Indians. Iron Head would have bragged some if he'd been able to read.

Longarm took the federal ID card out of his wallet and threw in a couple of business cards to pass around. The Indians examined them gravely and passed them back. Longarm put them away and said, "I have to ride on now. I will tell the Great White Father everything you have told me."

Iron Head didn't offer to fetch his horse, but another young gent did. So Longarm waved to everybody and rode out the far side of the camp feeling sort of smug. He didn't look back. It was considered impolite. So he was well on his way when he finally did rein in on a rise and spotted someone trailing him.

It was one Indian on a black pony. He dropped down in a draw when he saw Longarm stop ahead, but Longarm had seen enough of him to know it was Iron Head. Some men just never learned, it would seem.

Longarm rode on as if he hadn't noticed. An hour later he spotted the Arapaho again, ghosting him to his left, a dark blur against the skyline glare to the south. He knew that by now the Indian had seen that he was beelining west-southwest for Fort Benton. And sure enough, the next time Iron Head came up for a peek, he was just as obviously trying to head Longarm off.

Longarm rode on, studying the matter. He could avoid the fool Arapaho easily enough by dog-legging around him, but playing tag was only fun for kids. He had a steamboat to catch.

He tried to put his brain in the other man's skull, as thick as it was. He knew it would be an even fight if they met on open ground and the Indian knew he was

165

packing a Winchester. The ambush would be at the first brushy creek he came to next. More than one prairie stream ran off the high ground of the Big Bend to join the Big Muddy. He topped a rise and paused thoughtfully. The draw beyond held no water in its palm. There was a mess of tumbleweed windrowed along the bottom, but it wasn't thick enough to hide a man, let alone his mount. The tumbleweed balls formed flattened spheres of dried twigs, about two feet in diameter. They were piled high enough in places to make Longarm thoughtful as he investigated. But Iron Head wasn't in that draw.

That settled it. Longarm knew he would be in the next one. Leaving his own mount down the slope, he crawled up through the grass and had a look over the rise. There was a double hedgerow of cottonwood, crackwillow, and underbrush winding along the bottom of the draw to the west. Naturally, Longarm couldn't see hide nor hair of the Indian or his mount. But if Iron Head wasn't laying for him down there, he wasn't really serious.

Longarm slid back down to his horse and said, "Well, the sun says we can't hang around here much longer, Calico. So here's what we're going to do."

A few minutes later, down in the crackwillows, the man called Iron Head grinned crookedly in anticipation as he saw Longarm stop his mount on the rise above, a little to the south of where Iron Head had been expecting him, but not too far to cut off without breaking cover. The white man always stopped to look around like that. But this time he seemed to be taking his time. Had he seen something? Iron Head knew he was a very good skulker. The hated white man couldn't have seen *him*.

Leaving his black pony tethered safely to a willow, Iron Head started moving south along the line of brush, intently watching the figure on the rise up there. What was he doing? Why didn't he move? He'd said he was in a hurry. Was he going to just sit up there all day?

The Indian slipped into a new vantage point and rose gingerly behind a bush, his own rifle at port arms across his naked chest. The dark, still rider hadn't moved yet. He was probably worried about the brush down here. Iron Head waited. He knew that sooner or later the white man would either ride back the other way or come on down. If he rode the other way, Iron Head would follow. If he rode into the ambush, he would die sooner. The day was young and this was a good hunt.

A voice behind the waiting Indian said, "Howdy."

As the Arapaho started like a deer and whirled around, Longarm fired from the hip and kept doing so until he had the Indian on the ground, with the rifle he'd been packing lying too far off to worry about. Then Longarm lowered the hot muzzle of his smoking Winchester and strolled over hatless and coatless, as Iron Head tried to raise his head, failed, and gasped, "How did you *do* that?"

Longarm stopped a few paces off and told him, "Oh, I stuffed my frock coat with tumbleweeds and perched my hat on top, like when you make a scarecrow. What you were scouting up yonder is still there. I led the calico up, crawling on my belly, and left the whole shebang there for you to study while I run down a ways and circled in behind you. You're hit pretty bad, old son. I just don't know what I'm to do with you now."

Iron Head coughed weakly and said, "I'm not afraid to die. I knew someday one of your kind would kill me."

"Fair is fair, Iron Head. When a man is right, he's right. You might have made it if you'd had sense enough to quit while you were ahead. But it's a mite late now, so we'll say no more about it."

"Are you going to finish me off, or are you going to just stand there and watch me die, you big coyote?"

"Can't say," Longarm answered. "I don't like to shoot a man when he's down. But I sure don't want your kinfolks after me for what just happened. I reckon I'll leave the dying up to you whilst I have a smoke. I'd offer you one, but I can see I hulled a lung."

"Hear me, I want to die. I want to die now. I have great pain."

"Don't worry, you'll get there in about an hour at the rate you're bleeding. I'd like to help you out, but it was your idea to start this slow-death bullshit."

Chapter 10

Fort Benton was either a cow town or a military reservation, depending on which end of the main street you were on. Longarm didn't want to talk to the army about killing Indians, and he already knew they weren't keeping very good track of the live ones. So he rode the hired calico to the livery and got rid of it before he went to the Western Union office.

Despite the fooling about with Arapaho, he'd beaten both the sunset and the *Minnitipi* by a good three or four hours. He picked up the wires they were holding for him at the telegraph office and sent Billy Vail a progress report, which didn't take many words. Then he sent T. J. Porter's wire for him and, while he was about it, turned the paper over and got off a stinging night letter, collect, to a gent he knew in the Indian Bureau. All but one of the Arapaho he'd met up with had treated him right, so it was only fair.

The post office was still open, so Longarm went there next. He didn't want to identify himself to the postmaster, but he had to. They'd never have answered his questions, otherwise.

The postmaster was an owl-eyed little cuss who'd not met many government men from other parts. So he acted flattered and invited Longarm into his private office. He poured the lawman a drink, and Longarm gave him a cheroot. As soon as they were settled comfortably, the tall deputy brought the older man up to date on his recent adventures. Patting the sheaf of telegraphs in his side pocket, he added, "You'll be glad to know that Inspector Donovan ain't dead. He's been located at his home in New York State, where he *said* he was going on his vacation."

The owlish postmaster blinked and asked, "Then who in hell was the jasper the gambling man gunned aboard the *Minnitipi*?"

"Don't know," Longarm said. "Nobody's found the body yet. But I'm pretty sure somebody hired him to take the real Donovan's place, knowing he wouldn't be in Topeka to answer any inquiring wires. My office sent more on the late gambler, Canfield, too. He'd been drove off the big steamboats on the lower river for having a mean disposition. The gent calling himself Donovan wasn't the first man Canfield gunned in a game of cards. He came after me for a piss-poor reason too."

"You mean he wasn't in on anything with the fake Donovan?"

"Nope. Like I said, Canfield was just mean and I was just lucky. The way I put her together, the man pretending to be Donovan was a hired gunslick, sent to stop me. He knew who I was. He knew I had a rep for fighting back if somebody really pushed me. So he started pushing. I was sort of confused about another lawman acting like a cow-town bully. So I likely confused him some by taking his guff."

"How come he got into it with Canfield if he was after you?"

"He didn't mean to. He was on the prod and expecting me to explode in his face any minute so's he could gun me legal. He was tossing off one insult after the other, and I reckon he never expected a man in a purple suit to get so excited when he let some of his bile spill over on the other gents in the game. When Canfield called him, he just swatted at him as an unimportant fly. Only the fly turned out to be a hornet, and that was that. He probably died surprised as hell."

"How do you reckon his body wound up amongst the missing, Longarm?"

"Canfield rolled him over into the water on his way to my empty stateroom, I reckon. It was taking a dumb chance. Gloria Grimes might have spotted him, had she been looking down instead of up the river. But we know Canfield took dumb chances, so what the hell. Let's get to more important matters, like the shot-up steamboats and mail floating down the river. I was hoping you could tell me something about that mail."

"I'd be proud to, Longarm. But there ain't much I can tell you. You already know what they done. They tore open the mail sacks, ripped most of the letters in two, and scattered 'em to the four winds. Twice."

"Was the mail coming up the river or going down?"

"Coming up, now that I study on it. Why?"

"Why, indeed? I just lost another thread I'd been spinning. The railroad outfit has been paying folks up the river for options, services, and such. I thought maybe somebody wanted to rifle the letters with checks in 'em. Anybody who'd lost money in the mail would have said so by now, right?"

The postmaster nodded. "I follow your drift, but you're right about it not going anywhere. As a matter of fact, I'm sort of proud of the U.S. Post Office, considering. We recovered more than half of the letters from the water, torn up and soggy as they might have been."

"Hmm, does that mean they were delivered?"

"Well, some envelopes were missing contents and some letters were torn in two and, hell, they was all messed up. We sent back as many bits and pieces as we could find a return address for. A lot was never claimed."

The postmaster reached into a desk drawer and took out a cardboard box. He placed it on the desk between them, and Longarm saw that it was filled with bits of paper with postmarks on some, but not enough in the way of an address, either way, to consider delivering anywhere.

The postmaster said, "We're keeping these in case

anybody comes forward. There's a little writing in some of the torn letters inside. Folks who were expecting a letter from the East are welcome to fish around until they find a hometown postmark."

Longarm nodded and asked, "Do you keep a record of those who find anything?"

Looking self-satisfied, the older man replied, "Better than that. I keep a record of everyone who's asked. Folks down the river are still finding soggy envelopes in the shallows or on a fishhook."

He reached in another drawer as he said, "Everything is up to date here in Fort Benton. We got us a typewriter and carbonized paper. So you can keep these."

Handing Longarm two sheets of onionskin paper with barely readable lists of typed-up names and addresses, he said, "There might have been some folks who didn't know they were due to get a letter. But everyone who says he was expecting mail is on one list or t'other. The first list is claims for letters aboard the boat Big Bill was piloting. The other's missing mail from Johnny Bishop's boat."

Longarm scanned the thin crumpled papers, folded them with a nod of thanks, and put them away in his side pocket. The postmaster asked if there was anything else he could do for him, and Longarm said he couldn't think of anything. So the older man said he wanted to go home for supper.

They walked out front together and split up. The sunset was as red as clotted blood as Longarm walked down to the boat landing, watching his own long purple shadow preceding him. When he reached the river, the *Minnitipi* was nowhere in sight. He found a nail keg near the water's edge and sat down to have a smoke and read the wires he'd collected. He was pleased to see that Matt Kincaid had responded quickly to his request.

Another long shadow joined his, and when Longarm looked up, a man dressed like an undertaker said, "I

172

understand you were a passenger aboard the steamboat *Minnitipi.*"

Longarm nodded up at him and explained how he'd ridden across the Big Bend. The man handed him a business card, saying he was the Kimaho Coal & Lumber Company and that his name was Gower Powers. He took it back after Longarm read it, and said, "My betrothed, Miss Sue Ellen Brooks, is supposed to be coming up the river aboard the *Minnitipi,* and I wondered if you could confirm it for me."

Longarm nodded again. "Yep. I can say for a fact that your gal is likely to get here any minute. I congratulate you, too. She's a nice young gal."

Powers didn't smile or frown. He didn't look warm-blooded enough to do either. Sue Ellen had said she was spoken for, but this was ridiculous. Even in the warm light of sunset the man looked like he'd died and been embalmed at least a week ago. Longarm hoped for her sake that the gent she'd come all this way to marry up with was rich. There had to be some reason for a decent-looking gal to look at him.

But Longarm considered himself a polite cuss, and it wasn't a federal crime for a homely man to wed a pretty gal. So he said, "There's a railroad gent named Porter aboard the steamboat too. T. J. Porter of the GF&YSRR. You ever hear of him?"

Powers grimaced, which made him look even spookier, and said, "I know his outfit. They've offered me a coal contract. The same old song and dance about not wanting to pay top dollar, but willing to keep me busy."

"I worked for a boss like that once. What are you getting for your coal these days, if you don't mind my asking?"

Powers shrugged wearily and said, "It's no secret. I'm digging my seam at fifty cents a ton, FOB the shaft. Are you in the market for some coal, Mr. Long?"

"Not hardly," Longarm told him with a chuckle.

"My landlady in Denver gets her coal for two bits a ton, last time I asked."

Powers shrugged again. "She's lucky. The railroad quoted me some such price. They don't understand my problem. With the cattle business starting to boom, a man can make a dollar a day just sitting on a horse. To get him to load coal costs more. Those railroaders will find that out, once they get down to building on the ground instead of in the air."

Longarm said, "Old T. J. told me his survey teams have found coal outcrops on the right-of-way they aim to follow."

The cadaverous Powers shook his head and said, "They told me that too. I said they were welcome to dig their own coal. It's a matter of simple arithmetic. I have a going business with a developed strike. I know what it costs to dig the stuff out of the ground. Nobody in these parts can do it cheaper."

"Are there other coal mines close enough to matter?"

"Of course. They all charge the same, and my coal's a higher grade than some I could mention. I can see you're making the same mistake the railroad men have been laboring under. Finding coal in the Front Range is no big deal. The cost is in the digging it out."

Stepping closer to the water's edge, he stared down the river as he muttered, "Damn, where's that pokey steamboat?"

"Miss Gloria said she aimed to make it here to Fort Benton this evening, and the sun's still above the horizon line. I can understand your anxiety, though, meaning no disrespect to Miss Sue Ellen. She's anxious too. She told us on board that you'd be waiting for her. But while I'm asking questions, she said she was on her way to Kimaho, and your card says that's where you hail from too."

Powers turned his back on the river and said, "That's no mystery. Look at the infernal river. I knew the *Minnitipi* would never make it all the way up this time, so I came down here. That's my buckboard, yonder by that shed. I doubt Gloria Grimes will make it past the next bend upstream."

Longarm glanced over at the boiling red sunset as he opined, "I'd say it was raining over the mountains to the west, wouldn't you?"

Powers glanced westward and said, "All right, make it two, or even three bends, if you're a betting man. It didn't look like rain when I left Kimaho. If those thunderheads over to the west mean more than another couple of inches in the river by morning, I'll be surprised as hell. But that's not my worry. My buckboard rolls just as well wet or dry."

Longarm stared at the parked buckboard as he chewed his cheroot. Then he said, "Getting stuck here could be a problem for Miss Gloria Grimes, though. I don't reckon you freight any coal this far down the valley by wagon, huh?"

Powers smiled smugly as he replied, "On the contrary, I deliver coal all over these parts. As a matter of fact, that tipple you can just see, over there near that church steeple, belongs to me. You can't read the sign because the sun's aimed the wrong way."

Longarm chuckled and said, "I read the sign before, as I was walking to the post office from Western Union. The point I'm leading up to so polite is that you have freight wagons, and Miss Gloria has mail and freight to deliver. She might offer you a deal when they get here."

"Not a chance," Powers gritted, glowering. "Her late father and I settled that a long time ago. My wagons don't haul for the Kimaho & K.C. Line. *They* haul for *me!*"

"Do tell? They run back up the valley empty after they haul coal down here, don't they?"

"They do. I aim to keep things that way."

Longarm frowned thoughtfully up at the dark scarecrow figure. After a moment he said, "Well, I can see how you might not want to cross the rascals who've been raiding the U.S. Mail."

Powers laughed as harshly as a crow. "I've got a better reason than that. Aside from my coal and lumbering, I own shares in the stage line."

"I see. Business is business, eh?"

"Exactly."

Longarm was still trying to think of something nasty to say when there came a toot from downriver and the *Minnitipi* came around the bend, her smoke pink against the purple northeastern sky. Other townies were coming down to the landing now. Longarm decided to ignore the tight-fisted coal-and-lumber merchant. Powers didn't have his name on either list of folks who were missing letters. He and Sue Ellen must have settled on their wedding plans before the last two mail shipments. Or maybe they'd used the Western Union, although Powers looked too tight to send many wires.

Longarm rose with a thoughtful frown as he traced a mental line of telegraph poles down the river. Western Union wasn't having trouble getting messages east or west. There was an office in Kimaho too. The more a man considered, the less sense the whole thing made.

The *Minnitipi* shoved her blunt bows up on the mud slick and dropped the gangplank. Gower Powers went up it first as Longarm followed, still mulling over the trouble folks were going to to stop the mail when anyone could send an important message by wire.

He saw the spooky Powers on the steps, hugging Sue Ellen. And the pretty little thing was hugging him back.

It made Longarm feel plumb disgusted. Gower Powers looked as if a warm meal and a good lay would kill him, but that was the way life dealt the cards sometimes. At least she was getting a *rich* son of a bitch; he'd seen many a nice-looking woman throw herself away on a plain old son of a bitch. Women were funny that way.

Longarm found Blue almost alone in the main salon. Daisy Melrose was sitting at a corner table, nursing a drink and smiling at him every time he glanced her

176

way. Longarm bellied up to the bar and told Blue he'd admire a boilermaker, so Blue made him one.

The barkeep said, "Miss Gloria says she spotted rain clouds from the wheelhouse as the sun was setting. We ought to have six or eight inches more water in the river, come morning."

"I noticed. But we'll stay tied up here at Fort Benton for the night, right?"

The black man nodded and said, "Natcherly. The river's impossible by broad daylight, this far up. Did you get the wires and such you rode ahead to pick up, Mr. Lansford?"

"Yeah. You can call me Longarm now, though. It's tedious to use a made-up name when everybody knows who you are anyway. The army found out who Jim Bishop used to be too. You were right about him being a Southron. He was captured by the Union in Penn State. He started out the War with the Army of Virginia. Ended it like he said, fighting Sioux in the Michigan Volunteers. He was mustered out in the North and likely felt funny about going home to a burned-out plantation in blue britches. Lots of old boys just headed west when the mess was over."

Blue shrugged and said, "Well, if he's dead, I'm sorry I mean-mouthed him. If he ain't, I ain't."

Longarm didn't answer. He figured the odds were ten to one that Gloria's husband was on the bottom, somewhere down the river. It made no sense any other way.

T. J. Porter came in and joined them at the bar. He asked Longarm about the night letter, and Longarm said he'd sent it. T. J. looked relieved as he said, "I just bought a ticket on the stagecoach. They told me on shore that this boat don't figure to make the next landing, and what the hell, it's going to tie up here all night anyway. I can be almost to Kimaho by the time you folks cast off here. There's still time, if you'd like to keep me company, pard."

Longarm shook his head and said, "Thanks, but I'll

177

pass. Rain over in the foothills could make the difference in the main channel, and I'm in no hurry."

T. J. ordered a round of drinks for everybody anyway, and stepped over to Daisy's table to ask her if she wanted to keep him company aboard the stage. The big brassy blonde stared through him at Longarm as she replied, "I rode a stagecoach once. My back still hurts. I thank you, T. J., but I have a mess of luggage, and like the man says, there's no big hurry."

The railroad man looked at his watch, paid for the drinks, and finished his own. Then he said he hoped to meet up with them all again in Kimaho, and left. Longarm knew Daisy was expecting him to join her, since even a bold gal couldn't belly up to a bar. He was about to do so when Captain Gloria came in, looking bushed. Her pilot's hat was thrown back on her head and one auburn curl had come unpinned down over her ear. She still looked more ladylike than Daisy, but she came over to the bar anyway. There wasn't any way to stop her; it was her bar.

She smiled wanly at Longarm and told him, "I'm glad you made it. One of the boys on the shore just said a couple of hunters had seen Indian sign off to the east."

"Arapaho," Longarm confirmed. "Friendlies, mostly. I had a smoke with them this afternoon."

Gloria sighed and muttered morosely, "That's too bad. I was hoping they'd jump the stage. I 'spect you know the rats are deserting my hull before it's sunk. Just saw four passengers off. They had the nerve to ask for part of their passage money back, too."

"Did you give it to 'em?"

"Hell, no, would you have?"

"Nope," Longarm laughed. "Not if my boat was still afloat and able to keep going. They'll have a wet, uncomfortable ride. I figure it'll start raining down here too, in a little while."

Gloria brightened and said, "I know. I hope the stage trace washes out."

Daisy Melrose got up and approached the bar, saying, "I'll be blamed if I'll sit all alone. I hear there's a place in New York City where they have stools at the bar for customers to sit on. Have you ever thought about that, Captain Gloria?"

Gloria looked horrified and Longarm explained, "That wouldn't be right, Miss Daisy. Think how unsteady folks could get if they took to drinking while sitting down."

"Ladies are served sitting down, aren't they?"

"Well, sure they are. But folks served at tables can't drink two-fisted like you can over a bar. They do all sorts of wild, improper things in New York City, but you'll never see bar stools in more civilized places."

Daisy told Blue she wanted a standing-up drink, so Longarm glanced at his change on the bar and said it was on him. Gloria frowned and said all the drinks were on her, since it was her boat. She sounded sort of fretful, and Longarm wondered why. He'd competed with other *men* as to who was buying for a brassy-looking gal, but he couldn't fathom why Gloria wanted to pay for Daisy to get smashed.

The blonde raised her glass and said to Gloria, "Here's mud in your eye, honey." Then she asked how many stops and how soon they'd get to Kimaho. Gloria shrugged and said how soon was up for grabs, but that she figured on eight stops. If the water level was reasonable and the channel wasn't braided.

Daisy looked like she already regretted having passed up the chance to take the stage. Longarm said, "I talked to folks in the town some, while I waited here for you, Miss Gloria. There was anxious words about a place called Duckweed Flats. I can't seem to locate any such landing, though."

Gloria laughed loudly. "Duckweed Flats ain't a town, it's a stretch of the river. There's this bend where the banks widen out and the channel runs wide and shallow. You've seen the South Platte, north of Denver?"

"Yep. Rode across it many a time without getting wet. It's a mile wide and an inch deep, like they say."

"That's what it's like on the Duckweed Flats. It's really not that shallow, if you know your way across in a steamboat. My poor daddy showed me how years ago. The channel ain't in the same place from one summer to the next, but that's what makes piloting so interesting on the upper river."

"You sound optimistic, considering," Longarm said.

"Oh, Duckweed Flats is a bother, but there's nothing along that stretch as can kill a steamboat. It's all sand, with plenty of willow along the banks. We'll likely get stuck there, but you'll see it's no real barrier to a real pilot. Braided sandbars can't stop the *Minnitipi*. She sledges good."

Longarm exchanged glances with Daisy. He saw that she expected him to know what Gloria was talking about. He didn't, so he asked.

Gloria looked surprised that everyone didn't know how you ran a steamboat over dry ground. She said, "I told you there was willows along the bank up yonder. If push comes to shove and the main channel's just too shallow, I send some of the boys wading ahead with a few hundred feet of line. They tie up to a stout tree, I feed steam to the main windlass, and we just haul ourselves along the rope as the flat hull slides over the bars. It's a bother and it's slow, but like I said, no danger. It's the snags and rocks in deep water that worry a pilot."

Longarm asked her if she could show him these Duckweed Flats on her chart, and she said she could. Daisy looked sort of hurt when she wasn't invited to tag along to the Texas deck.

Longarm had thought it was just an oversight. But when Gloria took him up to her quarters and sat him down, she said, "I 'spect Miss Melrose is all right, if a man likes his women cheap and flashy."

He figured it would be more tactful of him not to reply to this. "You were fixing to show me your charts, Gloria," he said.

"They're in the wheelhouse. You just set and make yourself to home."

He did no such thing. As she left to duck next door, Longarm followed her. "The light's not very good in here," she said as she took a numbered roll from its pigeonhole over the chart table near the wheel. Longarm took it from her and unrolled it on the table. Then he struck a sulfur match on the table's edge and lit the oil lamp hanging above the table. She asked, "Wouldn't you have been more comfortable studying it in my quarters?" and he replied, "I didn't want to risk tearing anything, Gloria."

He stared down at the large-scale chart and made Gloria point out the stretch of river they were talking about. He saw that Duckweed Flats was between settled stretches of the valley. It was above the places where the shot-up and burned-out steamboats had been found. He didn't want to remind the girl about her dead father and possibly dead husband, so he didn't comment on what a natural place it was for an ambush.

Everyone had been assuming the boats had been hit as they put in to shore someplace. The pilots who'd known they had to slow down along the Duckweed Flats hadn't been consulted, since dead men tell no tales. He saw the way the banks were screened by natural cover, and how the marshy ground all around kept the local ranchers and hunters wide of the river as they rode up and down the valley. He didn't see, just yet, what he meant to do about his hunch.

Gloria pointed to the landing downstream from Duckweed Flats and said, "There's a place I suspicion. The man who keeps the crossroads store and post office there is a Mormon."

Longarm nodded. "So I hear tell. Both the postal inspectors and the Justice Department have looked into his background pretty good, though. He's sort of old, and if he's taken to robbing folks, it's a new notion.

He never did it before, and he's postmastered in a lot of places."

She said, "Just the same, I'm going to issue guns to my crew in the morning. You've still got that Winchester I loaned you, haven't you?"

"Yep. Locked it in my stateroom."

"Maybe you'd better bring it up here," she suggested.

Longarm glanced at her in the lamplight. The invitation in her moist eyes was easier to read than lots of smoke signals he'd spied on a distant rise. She was breathing kind of funny too.

Longarm said, "Well, it's your rifle, if you want to take it back and lock it up. But I'd be able to get at it a heap sooner if it was by my bed when I rolled out."

She didn't answer. She couldn't answer. She'd invited as much as a lady was allowed to, and the next move was up to Longarm. He knew that she knew that he knew and so forth. Life could get mean when a man used his brains instead of his glands to think with.

Something plopped against the wheelhouse window and he saw a raindrop running down the glass outside, like a tear. He said, "You were right about the rain." Then he rolled up the chart and put it away as he reached up to trim the lamp, saying, "I'd best get below before it really starts to come down."

Gloria stood between him and the door. The darkness seemed to make her bolder, for she flared, "I can see you want to be alone with that big cheap blonde."

"A man can't always be with who he wants to be with, Gloria," Longarm said. "I don't know if old Daisy is cheap or expensive. It was your notion to bring her up. I hadn't been thinking much about her, one way or the other."

Gloria's voice was bitter as she replied, "I'll bet. What's the matter with me, Custis? I know I'm sort of a tomboy and maybe I don't tart myself up in fancy perfume and paint, but—"

"Hold it," he said, placing a gentle hand on each of

her trembling shoulders as he added, "If it's any comfort, Gloria, I don't need perfume and paint to show me the way to the Promised Land. You know you're a nice-looking gal, and if I told you some of the things I've thought of while walking behind you, you'd likely slap me silly."

She swayed closer, or tried to. But Longarm held her, planted at a brotherly distance, and continued, "It won't work, Gloria. I know a widow gal can only mourn so long. I've comforted a widow or two in the past, so I know what *I'm* missing too. I'm going to hate myself for treating you like this, but—"

"How do you *want* to treat me?" she cut in.

"How I *want* to and how I *aim* to are two different things entire. I'll not deny that I'd love to haul you into bed and drown myself in you. But, having said that, I'll just go on down the stairs and we'll both behave ourselves."

"I don't understand," she pleaded, trying to move closer.

"I know you don't," he said. "That's why one of us has to act grown up. I ain't the sort of man you're looking for, Gloria."

"Don't you think I'd be the best judge of that, Custis?"

"Nope. You're packing too many stars in your eyes, honey. I like you, Gloria Grimes. You got grit and brains, and life's already stomped your pretty toes enough. Like I said, I'll surely hate myself when this is over, but you need a man that's permanent. I could promise you the moon, but permanent is one thing I don't carry in my possibles."

He thought he had it settled, so he let go of her shoulders. But she wrapped her arms around his neck and kissed him full on the mouth. Since he was a human being, he kissed her back.

When they came up for air, she said, "You can have me on any terms you want, darling!"

He shook his head again and said, "That ain't true,

even if you're too mixed up to see it. This has gone from adult conversation to needless cruelty, Gloria. We'd best part friends and say no more about it."

She didn't try to kiss him again, but her small breasts teased his chest cruelly as she pouted, "I'll bet you mean to have your way with that big blonde. The boys told me about you and those other gals."

He started to protest, then he saw that sometimes cruelty could be kinder, in the end. *Reason* sure wasn't working for him worth a damn! So he said casually, "I might try old Daisy on for size. No doubt she has her own needs too."

"You . . . bastard! What can she do that I can't, damn it? You know I'm no virgin. I mind I can do anything that tarted-up blonde can, and do it *better* too!"

Longarm didn't doubt that she was right, but he didn't say it. Gloria was a simple little gal who thought the physical part was all that mattered to a man. That was why she needed a simple man. Any other kind would hurt the hell out of her.

He kissed her gently on the forehead and said, "Let me go, gal. I was just funning about Daisy."

"I'll bet," she said, but she relaxed enough for him to gently unwind from her. He saw that it was raining harder, so he said something about not wanting to get wet and ducked outside before she could get set for another argument about his leaving.

It only took him a few seconds to make the shelter of the lower deck. Daisy was still in the salon, and drinking seriously. The blonde said, "Well, I didn't expect to see *you* again, so soon."

Longarm smiled down the front of her low-cut dress. "You noticed, huh?"

"Hell, cowboy, she was so hot for you that her skirts were smoking. What's the matter? Don't you like girls?"

"Let's find someplace where we can lie down and talk about it."

184

"Just like that? I'm beginning to get the picture. She threw you out for moving in too fast, huh?"

"You picture it any way you want to, Daisy. I can see this just ain't my night."

He took his beer to a table near the door and sat down to study the rain outside. It only took a few minutes for Daisy to join him. She sat down and said, "You shouldn't have spoken to me like that in front of the barkeep. I may not be as shy as that mousy gal who steers this tub. But I've got feelings too. How would it look if that colored man were to spread rumors about the two of us being more than just friends?"

Longarm laughed and said, "Hell, there's no such thing as a discreet romance aboard a steamboat. I've tried that, and it don't work worth a damn."

Daisy laughed too. "I know. That farmer's wife told me about you before she got off to take the stage. Why do you think I've been playing up to you? You look look like a real stud, and I just ran off from a husband who didn't have what it takes."

"Do tell? That's another apology I owe you, Daisy. I took you for, well, a business gal."

She laughed and said, "I've been that too, but I *like* it too much to make money at it! Are we going to sit here getting drunk while we tell each other the sad tales of our lives, or do you still want to lay down while we get to know one another?"

"Now you're talking. But it's only fair to warn you that I'm not in the habit of paying."

"Now you're *really* talking dirty," she said. "Do you want to make it your stateroom or mine?"

"Everybody knows how to unlock the door of mine. Let's see if we have better luck in yours," he proposed.

So she nodded and got up. As Longarm rose and followed her, he spied little Gloria farther along the deck, talking to one of her hands. She saw them too, and looked mad as hell when they ducked into Daisy's stateroom.

Daisy lighted the lamp, then trimmed it low as she

said, "Make yourself comfortable, cowboy. I'll fix us something to drink while you shuck those damp duds."

Longarm liked a gal who knew her own mind. He peeled off his coat and gun rig and draped them over the back of a chair. Daisy had her back to him as he palmed the derringer from his vest pocket before he took it off. He left his shirt and pants on, waiting politely for her to at least take off her big feathered hat. She handed him both glasses and reached up to unpin it. As her heroic bosom followed her elbows upward in the confined space, the effect was sort of startling.

He had ulterior motives in starting up with Daisy. But now that he studied on it, she wasn't hard to take. She wasn't nearly as pretty as little Gloria, but she was pretty enough, and looked as if she had a roguish sense of humor.

He'd learned the hard way about playing cards with strangers, or trusting a gal just because she invited you to come in and warm yourself. So he figured he'd better test her a mite before he leveled with her.

He put the glasses down and then fumbled them around as he took off his shirt before tasting one. Daisy never batted an eye as she started unbuttoning, so he knew she hadn't tried to spike his drink; she was willing to drink from either glass. She sat beside him in her unmentionables and started to roll down her stockings.

He let her see the derringer when he tucked it between the mattress and the headboard. She asked why, but didn't seem surprised when he said he didn't like surprises in his sleep. He didn't mention that he'd removed the cartridges, of course. So if she wasn't as friendly as she seemed, offering her such a good chance to get the drop on him would likely bring out any mean streak before morning.

She asked him to help her shed the corset. As he unlaced her, he mentioned casually that the reason he was so comforted by a handy gun was that he was really a lawman in disguise. He had his fingers against her spine when he said it.

"I might have known," Daisy laughed, but she didn't tense up. He unlaced her and she stood up again to let everything fall in a heap around her bare feet. Then she turned to face him, hands on hips, as she asked, "Well, are you going to make love in your damned socks?"

He told her she had a lovely body as he started shucking himself. She said he wasn't bad, either, as she stood there staring down at his tanned muscles in the soft light. He noticed she was really blonde, all over, He asked if she wanted the lamp out and she smiled wickedly. "No, I like to watch. What's the matter? Have you got something to show me that a man should be ashamed of?"

He did feel sort of silly as he peeled his balbriggans off and tossed them on the pile. Daisy licked her lips and said, "Oh, yes indeed."

So they both went crazy for a while.

Longarm was pleasantly surprised, considering that he'd seduced her—if you wanted to call it that—with ulterior motives. It really had hurt to turn Gloria down and there was no way, pounding the big blonde dog-style with the light on, to pretend she was a slim young tomboy. But Daisy had a lot to offer in her own right. She didn't say anything but "more" or "faster" for about an hour.

But finally even she had to rest, and as she snuggled against him, damp and jaded, with her sweat-limp hair across his chest, Daisy purred, "Oh, Christ, I can't begin to thank you, dear. I've been playing with myself since I married that awful little druggist, and the only man I've had since I left him didn't rise to my expectations. You have no idea how much I needed that."

Longarm patted her plump, soft shoulder and said, "I noticed you were sort of eager to make friends. You're a good old gal, Daisy. I like you and I just might take a chance on trusting you."

"Trust me?" she frowned, fondling him with her free hand as she asked, "What's left for us to trust? You know I don't bite. And you were nice about that position I found discomforting."

"It's early yet," he said, "so we'll have plenty of time for that sort of friendship, as soon as I get my breath back. But whilst we wait nature out, let's study on the future some."

She said, "Whoa, cowboy or whatever, I may have said some loving words in the heat of the evening's entertainment, but don't get the idea that this is more than just the here and now."

She played with his shaft some more as she added, "Well, mayhaps a weekend romance. But don't try to hold this kitten too tight. She just got out of the cage, and she's got some running wild to do before she settles down again."

He said, relieved, "Your words cheer me more than you can know, Daisy. You're a woman after my own heart, and that's the point I'm trying to make. I had no idea you were so wild and woolly. But now that I can see you are, it's given me some very sneaky notions."

She relaxed and said brightly, "Oh, you mean you want to try some different naughty stuff? Well, I'm willing to do anything that don't hurt. That damned little druggist I just wasted three years on went to bed in a nightshirt and said tongue-kissing was disgusting enough to get a person locked up."

"You told me he was odd," Longarm said. "By now, some of the others know I'm in here with you, Daisy. It's not too late. If I was to leave soon for my own bunk, they could say no more than that you was a mite improper."

"Hell, I don't care. I like to be improper!"

Suiting actions to her words, Daisy started kissing her way down his belly. Her long hair tickled as it trailed across his flesh behind her questing head. "Hold on now," he chuckled. "The point I'm making is that if

I'm still here come sunrise, there just won't be any graceful way for me to vacate these premises, Daisy."

She said, "I know. Who cares? I aim to screw you skinny, all the way to the end of the line!"

"Well, it's your reputation," he told her, and then neither of them could speak for a while, since they both had their mouths full.

Finally she collapsed atop him, moaning about how good it was to meet a man with imagination and understanding. Longarm kneaded her ample buttocks with his hands as she lay against him, and when he had his breath again he said, "Jesus, you're a killer. But you've got to admit we've gotten past pleasure and into showing off."

"I know," she agreed. "But it's sure been fun. Do you want to sleep now, darling?"

He said, "Like to. Can't. I got one last favor to ask before I let you sleep. I hope you're as sporting as you say."

"My God, do you mean there's something we haven't tried? Tell me what it is!"

So he did. And Daisy laughed like hell and said she'd do it.

Chapter 11

The *Minnitipi* left Fort Benton as soon as the rolling river water was distinguishable in the predawn sky glow. The young woman at the wheel was hurt, embarrassed, and mad as hell when they started out. By nine or so she was mostly just disgusted. It was a miserable morning. Veils of summer rain closed and parted over the channel ahead, and made for tricky piloting as well as a better crack at reaching the end of the line on a rising water level.

Her mate, Jim Truman, came up to relieve her as the *Minnitipi* reached the deep, straight slough above Moose Crossing. As he took the wheel and told her Blue was waiting breakfast on her, Gloria asked, in a desperately casual voice, "Are they still carrying on in that hussy's stateroom?"

Truman shrugged and replied, "Can't say, Captain. I don't listen at keyholes much."

Gloria started to stamp her foot, then thought better of it and stepped out of the wheelhouse. She knew she was acting mule-headed, but she walked aft in the drizzle along the Texas and went down the steps nearest the paddlewheel. As she moved forward, passing Daisy Melrose's door, she heard a soft, bleary voice singing:

"You naughty girl, her mother said,
   You've gone and lost your maidenhead,
      There's only one thing left to do,
         You'll have to sell your ring-dang-do."

Gloria grimaced and walked on, muttering darkly about the weakness of men in general and Longarm in particular. She walked into the salon and Blue brought a tray to her table. But Gloria said, "I reckon I'll just carry this up to the wheelhouse and eat it there, Mr. Blue."

"Mr. Truman can hold the channel long enough for you to eat right, Miss Gloria," Blue said.

She smiled wanly, got to her feet, and picked up the tray as she told him, "I know Jim's a good pilot. I just feel better watching the river."

She carried her tray outside. She knew she was being foolish to move aft with it, but she did. As she passed Daisy's door again, she heard:

> "They came by one and they came by two,
>> They came to laugh and they came to screw,
>> She caught the clap and the blue balls too,
>> And that was the end of the ring-dang-do!"

Gloria blushed beet-red and hurried on. She spilled her coffee going up the aft ladder, and the drizzle had chilled her ham and eggs by the time she reached the wheelhouse. She put the tray on the chart table and said, "I'd best take the wheel, Jim. We'll be coming to Duckweed Flats soon."

Truman said, "I'm in the channel. You ought to eat your vittles, Captain."

"I ain't hungry," she said sourly. "My belly has a big hard knot in it this morning, for some reason."

Jim Truman growled low in his throat and then said angrily, "It's your boat, so I'll not say how you should run it. But if I was the skipper, there'd be less singing and . . . whatever."

Gloria sighed. "It ain't for us to say what goes on in a private stateroom, Jim. You've issued the rifles like I told you to?"

Truman nodded. "Yes, ma'am. Every crewman has

191

a Winchester handy, where he can get at it sudden if the need arises."

He stepped politely aside as she took the spokes of the wheel from him and swung it experimentally. She said, "Good six inches under the hull on this bend. She'll bottom some, crossing Duckweed Flats, though."

"You want me to put the leadsman in the bows, ma'am?"

"No, Jim. I'll know when we ground. We'll come to a stop. There's only one oxbow to follow through the Duckweed. I can tell you now that we'll have to sledge around the main bend where the sand always settles."

She shot him a sidelong glance, hesitated, and added, "You can call me Gloria, if you've a mind to."

Jim Truman's expression didn't change. That was one of the nice things about Jim Truman, when a woman studied on it. Jim was a quiet, steady man who offered few surprises to a woman, either way. He was a good pilot, and sort of nice looking, and it might be time to let him have a mite more leeway in the running of things. "I reckon I'll eat after all. You can handle the wheel for now, Jim," she told him.

He just nodded as he relieved her. He suspected he knew better than she did why she was acting so friendly of a sudden. Jim Truman was a cautious pilot, so he figured he'd hold back on calling her Gloria until he sounded the channel ahead a mite.

Gloria ate half her breakfast and took the tray down to Blue. She felt sort of proud that she hadn't gone out of her way to pass Daisy's door this time. But she couldn't help asking Blue if he knew where Longarm had the Winchester she'd loaned him. After all, it was her infernal gun.

Blue put the tray on the dumbwaiter behind the bar and said, "That lawman ain't in his rightful stateroom, Miss Gloria. His bunk's made up and neither your gun nor his luggage seems to be in sight."

"My God, you mean he's *moved in* with that blonde hussy?"

Blue glanced away as he murmured, "Somebody has, Captain. She keeps sending out for drinks, two at a time."

Gloria shrugged gallantly. "Well, as long as they pay for them, it ain't for us to say how much a body drinks, or with whom."

But when she went out again, she couldn't resist moving aft along the passenger deck. She stopped by Daisy's door, lifted her little fist as if to knock, and then dropped it to her side with a defeated sigh. As she turned away, she caught the scent of those cheroots the tall deputy smoked, and as she left she heard a stifled giggle. Had they seen her shadow through the jalousies? It was enough to make a proper gal *die!* But they couldn't have known who she was. They might have taken her for some other snoop, she hoped.

Gloria mounted to the wheelhouse and stood at Jim Truman's side for a time, not saying anything. Jim just watched the channel. That was another nice thing about old Jim, when you studied on it. She spied a silvery slick in the channel ahead. Jim Truman swung the wheel and steered clear of the hidden snag without bragging that he'd seen it.

"I'm going to let you take her through Duckweed Flats, Jim," she told him.

He nodded, but said, "I'll never make the main bend."

She smiled, a trifle grimly. "I know. My daddy never made it when the water was this low. I'm going to oversee the bow crew and man the steam windlass. Take Duckweed at half speed, and when we hang up I'll send the boys across the shallows with the hawser to that big wolf willow we generally use."

Jim Truman nodded quietly, and for another space in time they just stood there. She was glad he didn't smoke on the bridge, either.

The *Minnitipi* swung around a willow-covered island and Truman gazed upstream at broader braided waters. Gloria was expecting him to say they were coming to

193

Duckweed Flats, but he didn't. He knew she knew where they were, and Jim Truman wasn't a man for wasting words.

"I'd best get down below," she said, and Jim moved the engine telegraph to half speed.

When he found himself alone in the wheelhouse, Truman let himself curse softly under his breath. His hands felt suddenly clammy on the wooden spokes. He knew he had to do this right, and the infernal river was spread out all to hell ahead. He knew the deeper water was always to the outside of the bends, but that was where waterlogged snags wound up too. He was glad Gloria wasn't there when he signaled dead slow. Some said he was a slow and pokey pilot, but he meant to get them there, and he was all too aware that they were above the bars where those other boats had been found, burned out and run aground.

A pilot was supposed to watch the channel, but Jim Truman found his eyes wandering to the willows along the shore. The riverbanks were far back and flat along this stretch. You couldn't rightly call the banks real banks; the water just silvered out among the willow roots. He knew he'd never hang a boat up in a willow tree, but he could see how those willows could hide most anything. If it was at all possible, he aimed to keep the steamboat at least a pistol-shot clear of any damned cover beside the water.

It wasn't possible. Jim felt the grit of sand against the starboard bow and swung off, crabbing aport and closer to the treeline as he followed the main channel. He got them another quarter-mile up the river and then, as the channel widened ever more and started to bend, the *Minnitipi* dug her blunt nose in and shuddered to a halt, her paddlewheel churning muddy foam in a gesture of futility.

Jim Truman swore and increased the speed. Not to move the steamboat; that was impossible. But every little bit helped. He saw four deckhands below hauling a thick manila line forward. One waved to him as they jumped overboard into the waist-deep water and started to struggle upstream with the hawser. As they waded, Jim saw that in some places the water was almost to their chests and in others it was only thigh-deep. The sand lay corrugated in riffles across the channel, but it wasn't bad. Once they had the line secured a thousand feet upstream, the windlass and paddles could horse them around in no more than three hauls.

Jim tooted the whistle for attention, and when a deckhand stuck his head in, Jim told the hand, "I want some men up here on the Texas, with rifles."

The other man nodded, then asked, "Have you spotted anything ashore, Mr. Truman?"

The pilot said, "No. When you spot things, it can be too late."

So the man went to get the riflemen, and by the time they were posted atop the *Minnitipi,* the wading hawser party had secured the line to the distant wolf willow and were standing clear on a bar. Jim Truman tooted a signal and the long slack line began to tighten up as, down below, Gloria fed steam to its windlass. The *Minnitipi* creaked and groaned as her protesting hull began to slither forward over the soft, sandy bottom.

They were two-thirds of the way, and Jim Truman had picked out another hitch farther around the bend, when all hell broke loose.

Truman telegraphed for reversed engine even as he realized sickly that he had no control of that. The paddlewheel could do as it pleased. The taught hawser was still hauling them bodily toward the treeline at an angle, and the treeline was exploding Indians like popcorn!

The line crew, way out in front, took off across the shallows, splashing, floundering, and swimming in some places. The Indians seemed to ignore them as they fanned out on the shallows and bars, yelling and shaking their guns like sticks. Jim Truman saw that he wasn't doing a thing to help at the wheel, so he let go the spokes and scooped up a rifle as he ran out the side door and knelt on the flat Texas, aiming up the fool hawser as it kept sliding the *Minnitipi* ever closer to the war party.

But then he heard the far-off, tinny sound of an army bugle blowing the advance, and he noticed for the first time that the Indians hadn't broken cover early and waded out across the flats to get at the steamboat. They were trying to get *away* from something!

Truman yelled out, "Hold your fire, boys!" as a ragged line of blue-clad, mounted troopers came out of the trees to splash at full gallop into the Indians! Truman spotted a tall, familiar figure dressed in tobacco brown aboard a borrowed army bay, and as Longarm fired one-handed with his Winchester to lay an Indian low, Truman said flatly, "That just ain't so! Everybody knows you're down in Miss Daisy's stateroom, singing about the ring-dang-do!"

But of course Jim Truman was wrong. The ambushers were more than a mite confused about it too, for as long as most of them lived. The bad thing about getting shot by a soldier in two or three feet of running water was that you tended to drown when you went down, no matter where you got hit, and the hardbitten troopers from Fort Benton shot pretty good.

As Longarm rode his mount along the shallow side of the channel toward the *Minnitipi,* the troopers were finishing off the few Indians who were dumb enough to be holding anything but their hands high.

Jim Truman saw Gloria Grimes running out of the bow. Of course the windlass had stopped, and they weren't going anywhere, so Jim went over to the ladder and went down to join them.

Longarm reined in, his boot heels just clearing the rolling brown water, and said, "Howdy. Anybody hurt aboard, Miss Gloria?"

The pilot shook her auburn curls and said, "No, praise the Lord and the U.S. Army as well as your ownself! But what on earth just happened?"

"Same thing that happened to your daddy and your

man, Miss Gloria," Longarm said. "I figured there was only one place away from any settlement that you could ambush a moving steamboat. I was sort of puzzled about Arapaho this far north, hunting buffalo where I saw no buffalo sign. So last night I snuck off with my suspicions to these army gents at the fort, and you can see how things turned out."

"You slickered us all!" Gloria laughed. "You had everyone aboard thinking mean things about poor Miss Daisy Melrose!"

Longarm glanced up to see Daisy grinning down at them from the passenger deck in her kimono. He nodded thankfully to Daisy and told Gloria, "I'm sorry if I caused undue alarm. The reason me and Daisy done it was simple. I knew the white boss of them Arapaho rascals had somebody keeping an eye on me. I knew that if I just slipped off the boat within a day's ride of any army post, they'd suspicion I'd put two and two together. So I asked Miss Daisy, as a public-spirited citizen of these United States, to create a military diversion. As you can see, it worked."

He turned in his saddle to stare upstream at the little knot of cowed Indians that the troopers were herding ashore. He said, "I sure wish old Raven Laughing hadn't insisted on going down with a gun in his hands. I'd have liked a few words with the rascal. None of those young bucks will be able to tell us much."

Jim Truman said, "I'm confused to see any Indians at all. Everybody kept telling us the Indians hereabouts were present and accounted for on the local reservations!"

Longarm nodded and said, "They were. Neither the Sioux, the Crow, the North Cheyenne, nor the Montana Blackfoot had anything to do with these attacks. The reason the BIA and the army didn't know about these Arapaho is that they belong way south, below the Yellowstone. They've been skulking well away from other Indians as well as whites. When I run into them the other day, they tried to slicker me. They sang the

197

old song of 'Lo, the poor Indian,' until they made certain I wasn't scouting for an army column. After I'd ridden on, they sent a warrior after me to kill me at a discreet distance from their camp. I went to considerable trouble to see that nobody would find his body soon, so they must have figured he got me and then lit out for their home reservation to establish an alibi. I was afraid they'd connect that passing stranger with the federal agent they knew was aboard the steamboat. But as you see, they didn't. I forgot to brag, back in town, about killing me an Indian."

Gloria shuddered as a soggy Arapaho floated by, facedown, and then she said, "I see it all now. Johnny and my poor old dad were massacred by Injuns. That accounts for them tearing up all that mail and scattering it on the waters. Everybody knows the rascals can't read or write."

Longarm said, "I've known more than one Indian who'd give the lie to that notion, Miss Gloria. But whether Raven Laughing could read or not is beside the point. They didn't interfere with the U.S. Mail just to be uncouth. They've been getting paid! Paid good, for Indians. I noticed some nice ponies with spanking-new silver-mounted bridles in their camp. Noticed they all had new blankets and such too."

Jim Truman gasped and asked, "You mean a white renegade has been behind all this, Longarm?"

Longarm said, "Well, Arapaho can be ornery, and the Lord knows they don't feel they owe the U.S. Post Office much, but yeah, I'd say some white man made it worth their while to come so far just to tear up letters."

"What you're saying, then, is that the man who hired these Indians had some good reason for interfering with the mails?"

"That's sort of obvious, ain't it? I'd like to borrow this rifle some more, Miss Gloria. I'll give it back to you at Kimaho."

Gloria said, "You're welcome to keep it forever. But

ain't you fixing to come aboard, Longarm? One of them soldiers can lead the horse back to the fort, can't he?"

"Ain't going back to Fort Benton, ma'am," Longarm informed her. "Going up the river alone, whilst they dispose of those left-over Arapaho. They said I could keep the horse too."

Gloria and Jim Truman exchanged glances. Then Gloria said, "We'll beat you up there, once we're past this shallow stretch."

Longarm nodded. "I know. I ain't in a hurry. I aim to stop along the way and jaw with folks."

"Do you figure the man behind all these attacks lives somewhere between here and the end of the line, Longarm?" Truman asked.

"Ain't sure. I have a list of folks who never got important letters they were expecting. Some names appear on both lists, which is sort of interesting, when you study the odds."

"You mean, if more than half the letters were recovered each time, and somebody's mail got stopped twice . . . ?"

"Yeah. It'd mean somebody had gone to a lot of trouble to keep a man from reading his mail. So I don't have to stop everywhere. Just at the interesting addresses."

Chapter 12

The *Minnitipi* ran out of river nearly five miles short of Kimaho, but that was close enough for folks to hire buckboards and such. The freight and mail were unloaded and packed into town too. The stagecoach had beat the steamboat by half a day this time, and they'd all beat Longarm up the river. He didn't show up for another thirty-six hours. The little steamboat had been horsed around in the shoaled-out river, and was on her way back down the Big Muddy by the time the tall deputy rode in on a jaded mount, looking trail-dusty and sort of pleased with himself.

The town of Kimaho was small, even by frontier standards. The most imposing edifice was a combined general store and post office. The retired Texas Ranger who owned and ran the store was also the local postmaster in consideration of past services, and because somebody had to be it.

Longarm left the borrowed army bay at the livery with instructions to rub it down good and water it gently. Then he cradled the Winchester in the crook of his left elbow and worked the kinks out of his legs by walking up the slope to the general store *cum* post office. As he passed the town hall, he spotted a notice announcing a meeting of the Kimaho Chamber of Commerce for later that evening. He grinned wolfishly as he clumped up the steps of the store and went inside. He waited politely until the old Ranger finished selling a bolt of calico to a nice-looking but obviously married gal. Then he told the postmaster who he was, and the old man led him back to an office in the rear.

Longarm sat on a barrel with the rifle resting across his knees, and waited for the older man to settle himself by a rolltop desk. Then he said, "First the good news. Some of your postal inspectors are on their way up the river after chasing a false lead about the James Boys."

The postmaster looked blank, so Longarm elaborated, "Some rascal sent a wire saying Frank and Jesse had robbed the Glendale train again. They hadn't. But it sure made your boys miss a lot of connections. I just checked in by wire, down the river a ways, and like I said, they're on their way."

The postmaster said, "I wish *we* had us a telegraph office here. Western Union says it don't pay to string wires this fur into the nowheres much."

"I know," Longarm agreed. "Now the bad news. There's no way in hell that any other federal men can get here in less than two days. Billy Vail says you were a tolerable Ranger in your day. I'm going to have to call on you and any other local men you can count on in what could turn out to be a noisy arrest."

The old man's face lit up and he seemed to drop two decades from his age. "Hot damn! A man sure gets tired of measuring calico and weighing groceries. You can count me in, and I know a couple of other old rascals who'd be proud to back your play. But just what sort of a play will we be backing, in case anyone asks?"

Longarm took out two smokes, handed a cheroot to the postmaster, and struck a light as he said, "I'd best start at the beginning. It gets tedious being told you're full of shit. Folks don't like the idea of arresting the Sugar Plum Fairy."

He lit the old man's smoke, then lit his own and leaned back to inhale some smoke before he said, "You just said the important part. There's no telegraph line this side of Duckweed Flats. I had to backtrack down the river to send my last wires, when they told me that

201

at a mine I visited. You see, I've been jawing with folks who put in claims for missing letters from the East."

"I've got the same lists here somewheres. Are you saying you recovered the missing letters, son?"

"Not hardly. They were never tossed in the river with the unimportant stuff. The gents who went to all that trouble to interfere with the U.S. Mail made a mistake they overlooked. The law of averages shouldn't have put the same addresses on the lists from two separate so-called Indian mischiefs. I started checking as soon as I noticed how the same folks kept missing their mail. It didn't take much longer to notice they all had other things in common. They were all property owners or local businessmen. A mess of them belong to your chamber of commerce that's meeting down the way this evening."

The postmaster's eyes narrowed as he replied, "I used to be a lawman. I see the pattern. But I'll be damned if I can see who's profiting by keeping local businessmen from getting letters from home."

Longarm shook his head and said, "Not letters from home, if you mean from relations back East. Like I said, I've been talking to some of them. They'd all sent letters of inquiry one place or another. Some of them sent serious letters. Most just asked business associates they knew in the East, sort of casually, what they knew about the GF&YSRR. Like me, they sort of wondered why a railroad company, even a new one, wasn't listed on the big boards of the Chicago or New York stock exchanges."

The postmaster's jaw dropped and Longarm knew he was in for a heated defense. Nobody likes to hear that there's no Santa Claus.

The old man held up a weathered hand. "Now just hold on a minute, son. I happen to be a shareholder in the Great Falls and Yellowstone!"

Longarm nodded and said, "I figured you'd be. Railroads usually hand out free shares to politicos, and the local postmaster's generally the party leader in town.

But what the hell, they didn't ask you to *pay* for your shares, did they?"

"All right, we both know how politics works. But you're still barking up the wrong tree. I know for a fact that the GF&YSRR ain't *sold* a single share of railroad stock to anyone in these parts!"

"I know," Longarm said. "I checked that out right off, as soon as I started to suspicion them. I knew they were up to no good when that T. J. Porter jasper went out of his way to let a federal agent read a telegram designed to make it look like they were fixing to start building. But, like you, my first notion was a stock swindle. I was thrown off for a spell when I couldn't find anybody they'd sold watered stock to."

"Back up," the postmaster said. "You're going too fast for me. What do you mean about them tricking you with a telegraph, son?"

"Oh, I was cutting across open country from Eagle Butte to Fort Benton. Old T. J. must have thought I was mighty stupid. He asked me to send a wire for him in Fort Benton. He didn't know I'd stumble over his hired Arapaho, and so of course he figured I'd read his message, as I did. It was just a brag about the doing of wonders and the eating of cucumbers, so I sent it for him."

The postmaster started to ask a question. Then he brightened and said, "Hell's bells, of course! He could have sent his wire from Eagle Butte! The wire follows the river, right?"

"Sure it does. Who the hell would Western Union service out in the middle of nowhere? The only reason anyone could possibly have for sending a wire from farther west and a day's ride later would be the one he had. He aimed to mix me up even more by feeding me false information. I'm almost sure he or his sidekicks sent that fake wire about a railroad holdup too."

The old retired lawman looked like he was about to ask another question. But he was starting to think like a Ranger again, and Billy Vail had said that in his day he'd been good. He reached in a desk drawer and took out a couple of stock certificates. As he handed them to Longarm he said, "You'll want these as evidence. Ain't they pretty? You must think I'm a foolish old fart."

Longarm shook his head. "No I don't. You and your friends up here never would have been dumb enough to *buy* shares in a railroad that only existed in a con man's head. As it was, enough of you wrote about it to friends and business associates back East to make the swindlers want to stop the mails from going through. Of course, nobody worked as hard at checking as they might have, had the scheme been a simple stock swindle. Most, like you, got your shares free. So, while it might occur to you to ask a few questions, it wasn't worth a ride down to the telegraph line, was it?"

"I see why they interfered with the mails," the postmaster observed. "You've convinced me the railroad is pie in the sky. Get to the good part. How in hell can a con man make money on a phony railroad unless he *sells* it to somebody?"

Longarm blew a smoke ring thoughtfully and said, "That's why I've called on you for help. It's going to be sort of embarrassing to a lot of folks as it is, and I'll need some confessions. So it's important as hell that we take at least T. J. Porter alive. He'll be at that meeting tonight. He's getting set to fold his tent like that A-rab and silently steal away with a carpetbag full of money. Western Union tells me he's already wired several thousand dollars east to his confederates in Chicago. But that's all right. The Chicago police department is fixing to arrest them when they try to cash the wires. *I* sent some wires too."

The postmaster shook his head in exasperation. "Damn it, you ain't listening to me, son! I know for a fact that the railroad hasn't even offered to sell no fake stocks or bonds. As a matter of fact, they've been laying out option money and signing contracts to buy coal, lumber, ties, and such! The meeting tonight is to decide on the location of the Kimaho rail depot. There's not an acre of ground inside the township limits that they won't have to pay hard cash for!"

"Not hard cash," Longarm said. "Post-dated checks and promissory notes. Folks have been showing them to me all the way up the valley from Duckweed Flats. *I* could write you a check right now for any amount you wanted, if you didn't insist on me having cash in some bank to back it up."

"That's dumb, Longarm. You can't buy land and such with rubber checks. Folks tend to take things back when a check bounces."

"Sure they do. But you see, the so-called railroad outfit don't *want* the land, the coal, the lumber, and the other supplies they've contracted for. The worthless paper they've been spreading is the honey on the fly-paper."

"Then what are we getting stuck in, son?"

"Greed. Everybody's heard all the tales of railroad robber barons. The papers have been educating hell out of us as to their roughshod business methods, and the awesome profits to be made in Western railroading. Harriman and Hill have been fighting for the Northwest rail traffic with dynamite and worse. Down South, C. P. Huntington and Jay Gould have just gone to war over the Southern Pacific, with lots of gambling men making money just betting on the winner."

Longarm let that sink in before he added, "I'd bet on Huntington if I could get decent odds. The point is that everybody expects a railroad outfit to cut legal corners. So that gets us to the embarrassing part. T. J. Porter isn't up here selling watered railroad stock. He's up here collecting bribes and kickbacks."

The old postmaster frowned and nodded thoughtfully as Longarm elaborated, "Everybody knows that a railroad brings prosperity to a town. Everybody knows about towns that died when the railroad passed them by in favor of another, friendlier town. It only stands to reason that a politician bribed with free rail shares would want to protect his holdings by making it worth a surveyor's while to run his tracks one way rather than another. What the hell, it's only the taxpayers' money."

"I see how that meeting tonight was meant to vote. The kickbacks from coal and lumber merchants would be cold cash, eh?"

"Sure. A man with a peckerwood sawmill or a small coal shaft wouldn't try to bribe the railroad direct. He'd be too smart. He'd just skin the bloated plutocrats by paying off the railroad agents who could see that he got a fat contract from the boss. T. J. likely asked for five percent of the first year's purchase orders, cash in advance. We'll sweat such details out of him after I arrest him."

The old man rose and took a holstered pistol and gunbelt from another drawer. As he strapped the rig on with a grim expression, he said, "You've convinced the hell out of me, son. I've got some friends we can call on. I'll have to rustle up someone to watch my store while I round them up."

"I'll mind the counter for you," Longarm said. "It might be more discreet if nobody saw me paying social calls with you. They already know I'm the law. They don't know I'm onto them. But if they spotted me calling together a posse . . ."

"Say no more, son. This is sort of fun, now that it's coming back to me. I'll line the old boys up. But then I'll tell 'em to lay low until the sun goes down and the meeting down the way is called to order and we just naturally drift in."

They went out into the main store and the old man showed Longarm his price list and told him not to give anyone credit before he got back.

He left, and Longarm found a stool by the cash register. He put his hat and rifle aside and sat down, feeling sort of foolish, like a kid selling lemonade.

Two housewives came in and looked startled, but let him sell them the ball of yarn and paper of needles one of them wanted. He decided storekeeping wasn't such a hard task, after all.

Then, of all people, Miss Sue Ellen Brooks from the steamboat trip came in. She looked surprised too, and asked him what on earth he was doing behind the counter.

"Needed a job," he smiled. "How are you and your coal dealer getting along, Miss Sue Ellen?"

She sniffed and said, "If you must know, it's all over between me and Gower Powers. I came here to buy a card of buttons for my travel duster. Do you have any?"

Longarm shrugged. "Beats me. Let's look. I think the buttons are over here with the other sewing notions. Yep. Here's some button cards. You just pick out the one you want, Miss Sue Ellen."

The girl chose a card of imitation horn buttons and unsnapped her purse. Longarm said, "Heck, your money's no good here, Miss Sue Ellen."

"I assure you I can pay, sir. Praise the Lord, I still have money to get home on."

"Buy yourself an orange or something on the train to remember me by."

She hesitated, then said, "Well, I am terribly budgeted. You really are a very nice man, Mr. Lansford."

"My real name's Long. Custis Long. I'm a U.S. deputy marshal in disguise."

"I know. Gower mentioned the fight down the river. Before we had our *own* row, of course. What I meant about you being nice is not that you're a lawman, and not that you do favors for ladies. You're the first person I've met since I broke up with Gower who hasn't asked me about it."

"It ain't my business. I know for a fact that your intended is a mean but honest businessman. That's all they pay me to look into. It ain't a federal offense to upset a pretty gal, as unjust as that may seem to you."

Sue Ellen laughed and said, "You're cute. If you must know, I think it's my fault that I can't get along with Gower. Lord knows, we both tried. But, coming up on the stage, I just realized I couldn't love a man who sucked his teeth and whistled the same tune over and over half the night. You must think I'm being unreasonable, but—"

He interrupted, "I'd say it was more reasonable to decide such things before you marry up with a gent than after! I ain't much for gossip, Miss Sue Ellen. I don't aim to arrest Gower Powers and you don't aim to marry up with him, so let's say no more about it."

She nodded and said quietly, "You're right. How are we to get down the river now that the steamboat's gone?"

Frowning down at her, Longarm said, "I disremember us making plans to go anywhere together, ma'am."

"Oh, are you aiming to stay here in Kimaho, then?"

"Not if I can help it. You're right about the steamboat being gone for a spell now. I figure on riding some and rafting some until I can meet up with the rails again at Milk River."

"Rafting?"

"Sure. The water's still eight or ten inches deep, even up here. After I get my business finished here, I aim to lash together some timbers, climb aboard with my possibles, and just ride free down the river with the current. It's the fastest comfortable way I know."

"My," she said, "it sounds so . . . so *piratical!* I wish *I* was a boy. But of course it would hardly be proper for me to even dream of such an adventure, wouldn't it?"

He didn't answer. "Well, wouldn't it?" She repeated.

"Yeah," he admitted. "Most folks would be sort of shocked at the notion of a couple floating down the river all alone for days and nights and such. On the other hand, who'd know about it?"

She blushed and blurted, "Good heavens, *we* would!" Then she put her buttons away and went outside, still flustered. Longarm stared after her sort of wistfully.

Then he grinned, turned to the cash register, and rang up "No SALE."

Later that evening, as the sun was setting, Longarm stood near the town hall with the postmaster and a dozen mean-looking old men. The meeting had already started inside, and the chamber of commerce had posted a man at the door who told everyone who asked that it was a private meeting.

"Let's wait till they break up and take the skunk as he comes out with his carpetbag full of money," the ex-Ranger suggested.

Longarm fumbled a cheroot from his pocket as he said, "Risky, two ways. I don't like shootouts in the dark on crowded streets, and your friends and neighbors have enough embarrassment on their plates *before* they bribe the bastard."

He looked around at the grim-faced, elderly posse and added, "You gents understand how vital it is to take the skunk and any sidekicks backing him in there *alive,* don't you?"

The postmaster spat, wiped his mouth with a sleeve, and said, "Hell, it don't matter if he lives or dies. If this was Texas in the old days, we wouldn't shilly-shally with no fool trial."

"I know," Longarm said as he took out a match, struck it on his thumbnail, and ignited his cigar. "But I have my orders and the Post Office will want to question everyone connected with the plot, too. So don't any of you shoot nobody you don't have to."

He started around to the door, his cheroot clamped firmly between his front teeth. The postmaster fell in at his side and started to ask how they aimed to get past the doorman. Then he saw that Longarm was pinning his federal badge to his lapel and nodded, saying, "Yep, that ought to do her."

Longarm clumped up the steps and tried the knob. When it wouldn't turn, he drew his gun and hammered on a door panel with it. The door opened and a heavy-set man said, "You can't come in here."

Then he recognized Longarm and said, "Oh, it's you."

Longarm recognized him, too. It was Dobbs, the man who'd been sitting next to him during the gunfight over cards. Longarm said, "Howdy, Dobbs. This is official, so you'd best stand aside."

Dobbs did, and Longarm walked in and down the center aisle. T. J. Porter was on the speaker's dais, facing him. As he saw Longarm coming, he looked sort of green and stopped in the middle of the speech he'd been making. The men seated on either side of the aisle buzzed and muttered as he passed them. T. J. said, "We was discussing the coming prosperity of the valley, but you're welcome to sit in, Deputy Long."

Longarm stopped a few paces away, gun in hand, but held down at his side politely. He said, "I don't need to hear your pitch, old son. I hereby place you under arrest for the federal crime of interfering with the mails of these United States. Anything you say can and will be used against you, and I advise you to keep both hands in plain view at all times until you've been searched and cuffed."

T. J. stood frozen in place with his mouth open. But Longarm moved fast when he heard the postmaster yell, "Longarm, duck!"

Shots rang out behind him while he was diving head-first for cover!

Longarm crashed among some men seated beside the aisle, and they all hit the floor together in a cussing tangle of bodies and folding chairs. The tall deputy shoved a fat man off him, crawled clear, and spun on his behind to face the general noise and confusion.

There was a lot of it. The air was blue with gun-smoke, and guns were popping like it was the Fourth of July again. Somebody called his name, and when Long-arm answered, the postmaster yelled, "Dobbs threw down on you from behind. I think he's down. I can't tell for sure."

Longarm crabbed along the baseboard toward the speaker's dais. One lamp was still lit, but it was hard to see anything in all the gunsmoke. He slid over the edge of the platform and spotted T. J. Porter. The flashy con man was on his back, behind the speaker's stand, dead as a turd in a milk bucket.

Longarm spied an eddy in the smoke and knew a door had opened. He nodded grimly to himself and rose to run across to the side door beyond the dead man. As he charged out the door and crabbed to one side, a bullet whipped through the space he'd just been silhouetted in the doorway. Longarm had spotted the flash. The gun was behind a woodpile near the corner of the building farthest from the street. His unseen enemy fired again as Longarm dashed across the narrow side yard and dropped behind some ash barrels. A bullet thunked into the barrel he was hunkered behind, sending up a cloud of ash. Longarm found a chink between the barrels to peer through. But there wasn't much to see. The other was forted good. Worse yet, he had a whole damned town hall to work his way behind.

Longarm studied the standoff, chewing the end of his cheroot. And when another shot dusted him with ash, he swore as he realized for the first time that he was still holding a lit smoke in his fool teeth!

Sheepishly he started to snuff it. Then his eyes narrowed and he reconsidered. His problem was that he was pinned down and the other wasn't. If the invisible shooter chose to, he could work his way unseen from the woodpile, rise behind the hall, and just run like hell into the darkness. But if Longarm moved in before the unknown assailant decided to pull stakes, he'd catch a bullet for sure.

A figure came to the side door and started to look out. Longarm yelled, "Get back inside, goddamnit!" and the fellow did.

The man hiding behind the woodpile hadn't fired. Was he still there? Longarm felt in his coat pocket. Sure enough, he still had the torpedo he'd taken off that fool kid in Denver.

Grinning like a kid himself, Longarm touched the fuse to the lit end of his cheroot and lobbed it beyond the woodpile.

Nothing happened for a few seconds. Then the tiny bomb went off with a godawful roar and the already wounded Dobbs jumped up from behind the woodpile to fire a volley into whoever had fired from behind him.

Longarm put a bullet through Dobbs' spine, of course, and got to his feet. As the echoes and gun-smoke drifted away and the postmaster came to the side door again, Longarm said, "You can come out now. You only winged Dobbs, but I thank you just the same."

The postmaster joined him near the woodpile as Longarm reloaded. He said, "There's another three in there, besides the one called T. J. They was supposed to be his surveyors or something. How come Dobbs tried to gun you, son? I thought he was one of us."

Longarm said, "They had to have someone who was known in the valley working with them. You might say he was their intelligence service. A local boy would know who could be approached and who'd be best to steer clear of. More important, Dobbs would be privy to any suspicions voiced around the potbellied stoves."

The postmaster nodded and said, "It's all so simple, once you study on it. I'm sure sorry the old boys got so excited and started shooting, though. How are you going to clear up all the petty details now?"

"I won't have to," Longarm replied simply. "You're my witness that I tried to take them alive, should anyone raise a fuss."

The old man cocked an eyebrow and asked, "Who do you think you're shitting, son?"

Longarm just smiled. The old ex-Ranger laughed and said, "Yeah, I was wondering how in hell you'd ever prove some of them wild charges if the gang hung tough. All you really had on them was that the railroad was a fake. You'd have played hell proving murder without a confession, and men don't tend to confess to murder much."

Longarm said innocently, "Well, an arresting officer is allowed to shoot in self-defense. Is it my fault some of your old sidekicks might have decided to wash the local linen the old-fashioned way?"

"You sneaky rascal. You knew it would turn out this way, didn't you?"

"You ought to know better than to ask," Longarm replied. "You were just saying how few men confess to such matters, remember?"

A rancher who'd be going down the valley in a few days said he'd be proud to deliver the borrowed bay to the army at Fort Benton, and Gloria had said he could keep the rifle for now. He'd leave it for her at Milk River, when and if he got there.

It only took him a couple of hours to knock together the timber raft in the shallows downstream from town. It was well before noon when he satisfied himself that it would hold together and started putting his possibles and some supplies from the general store aboard.

He was sitting crosslegged on the raft, cutting himself an aspen sapling for such poling as might be called for on a gentle downstream drift, when Miss Sue Ellen Brooks came along the bank and said, "Oh, there you are. I thought you might have left."

Longarm noticed she had on her travel duster and was carrying her bags. He said, "I was figuring on shoving off as soon as I finish peeling this pole. It's setting up to be a fine day, and I mean to eat my dinner out on the river."

"How can you cook on a wooden raft?" she asked.

He pointed with his chin at the box of sand near his spread-out bedroll and said, "I don't need a big fire.

I've got plenty of jerked beef and beans. Might catch some fish along the way."

She said, "It sounds sort of lazy and shiftless, but I guess every kid has wanted to float down a river on a raft at least once. Is that one bedroll . . . it?"

Longarm said, "Man only needs one bedroll if he's rafting down the Big Muddy alone."

"What would he do if he had, well, a passenger?"

"Ain't sure. Have to study on it some before bedtime, but as you can see, it's early yet. I reckon a passenger could always get off, if she got spooked."

He finished the pole and folded his penknife to put it away before he stood up. He placed one end of the pole in the mud and said, "I don't know about you, but I'm off to seek adventure and maybe a catfish for supper. Are you coming or not?"

She said, "Oh, I've always wanted to do something as romantic as this, but I don't think I can."

"Sure you can," he told her. "Just hand me your bags and take yourself a seat. I'll do such poling as is needed."

She shook her head. "I don't think it would be proper."

"You're right. It even sounds improper to me, and I'm a boy." Then he winked at her and started to pole himself away from the bank.

Sue Ellen sobbed, "Wait, I want to play too!"

So he steadied the raft and waited while she splashed shin-deep out to him and threw her things aboard. Then he helped her onto the raft and she sat there laughing up at him and said, "I don't know what on earth's come over me. Look at my feet. They're all wet."

He said, "Take your shoes and socks off if you like. They'll dry long before we come to the next landing."

"Oh, are you going to put me off at the next landing?"

"Not if you don't want me to, Sue Ellen. You're welcome to go as far as you like with me."

She blushed and laughed again. Then she asked severely, "Are you talking dirty to me, Custis?"

Longarm poled them farther out into the current as he shook his head and replied, "Hell, no, it's early yet."

SPECIAL PREVIEW

Here are some scenes
from

LONGARM SOUTH OF THE GILA

thirtieth in the bold
LONGARM series from Jove

Chapter 1

With a ringing "yay-hoo" that rivaled the war-whoop of any Indian Longarm had ever heard, Patches slapped the reins sharply on the necks of the four-horse team, and the stagecoach lurched forward. A sudden glare set Longarm's eyes to blinking as the stage rolled slowly into the cone of light from the locomotive's headlight. The glare grew dimmer as the horses settled into their harness and the stage moved faster. The headlight became a yellow disc that disappeared as they mounted a rolling rise and dropped behind it. Then the light was completely gone and the night closed around them.

Temporarily blinded by the headlight's glare, Longarm could see very little except the white, blurred faces of his companions on the seat and the rumps of the horses ahead. Gradually his night vision returned and he could see Patches' rough-cut features and Billy's youthful face, and when he looked over the bobbing ears of the lead horses, he could also see the ruts that marked the road to Tucson. He hadn't needed to see the road to know it was mostly ruts; the lurching of the stagecoach had already told him that was the case. He turned to Patches.

"Ever hear of a place west of Tucson, a little town called Mina Cobre?" he asked the driver.

Patches shot a stream of tobacco juice off to the side of the rattling stagecoach before shaking his head. "Nope. Not much wonder if I ain't, though. There's new places popping up in the territory every day."

"It's just beyond a town called Quijotoa, down close to the border with Mexico," Longarm persisted.

"Never heard of Qui-whatever-it-is, neither. Sounds like a Papago town to me. Or maybe Mex, left over from when that part of the territory belonged to Mexico."

"Don't this stageline go on west from Tucson?"

"Sure. Clear on out to San Diego, in Californy. But the road follows what there is of the Gila River going on west. I'd guess this Mina Cobre place is a good piece south of the Gila."

"I never heard of it neither, mister," Billy volunteered. "But I ain't been in the territory very long. Never even been to Tucson, come right down to it. Keep telling myself I oughta see what it's like there, instead of going back to El Paso for a spree when I get some time off, but Texas is more home to me than Tucson'd be."

Just then the ruts got deeper and rougher as they crossed an alkali flat, and Patches gave his full attention to the straining team. After they'd rolled on a mile or so past the rough stretch, Billy's eyelids began to droop. His head sagged forward and he began to snore gently, swaying in the seat.

After a short while, the young hand's snores and the swaying of the stage began to make Longarm sleepy. He let himself slip into a light doze that lasted until he felt the driver's elbow nudging him in the ribs. His eyes snapped open and he looked around. The moon had come up, showing a starkly bare landscape, its baked soil cut by the ruts of the road, with here and there a towering saguaro cactus or a rock outcrop. Patches started sawing on the reins. Longarm hadn't seen any kind of landmark, and saw none when the team came to a halt.

Patches said, "Poke the youngster awake, will you, friend? This is where he wants to git off."

Longarm nudged Billy with his elbow. The young

cowhand opened his eyes, yawning. He asked, "We there already?"

"Yep," the driver replied. "You say hello to Tom and his missus when you git to the ranch. Tell 'em I'll be looking for 'em to flag me down, next time they head for the bright lights."

"Sure will."

Billy dropped off the seat. Patches geed up the team. The young cowhand waved, and started walking at right angles to the road. Longarm's professional curiosity made him glance back now and then. The desert moonlight was new to him and he kept testing its quality against a time when his life might depend on gauging the range of a rifle shot in the night. He watched Billy until the youth was lost to sight in the darkness, then took out a cheroot and lighted it. He was conscious of the stage driver's curious gaze flicking over him now and again, but did not show that he noticed the scrutiny.

Finally, Patches could hold back his curiosity no longer. "You mind me askin' what your line of work is, friend?"

"Not a bit. Ask away," Longarm replied.

"Dagnabbit, I *am* askin'!" The driver paused long enough to send a squirt of tobacco juice over his shoulder before adding, "You got the look of a lawman or a bounty hunter, but I'm damned if I can tell which one."

Longarm saw no reason for an evasive reply. "Deputy U.S. marshal. Out of the Denver office."

"You're a hell of a long way from home, ain't you?"

"A piece."

"I guess you got a name," Patches suggested. "You know what mine is, from Billy."

"Long," Longarm replied.

"Wait a minute! You ain't the one they call Longarm, by any stretch of the imagination, are you?"

"My friends call me that. Other folks too, I guess."

"I heard about you from Cy Ewing! Me and him was hacking down in Galveston when you busted up

Kester's gang! Cy drove you around town there, one night."

"That was a while back," Longarm said. "I guess I disremember your friend."

"Well, Cy never claimed he knowed you, but he sure did know he'd drove you that night." Patches shook his head. "Well, it's a little bitty world, I guess. I'm real proud to have you on my stage, Longarm."

"Thanks. But I'd appreciate it if you'd just sort of keep quiet about me being a marshal. For now, at least."

"Why, sure." Patches was silent for a moment, then he asked, "Headin' for this place you was askin' me about, Mina Cobre?" When Longarm nodded, the driver said, "Guess I give you a right short answer before. Tell you what, you ask the men in the stage station when we git to Tucson. Likely they can tell you how to git there."

"Thanks. I'll remember to ask." Longarm tossed the butt of the cheroot away, and it landed in a tiny flare of sparks on the hard soil. He asked, "How much further before we stop? I could do with a bite of grub and some hot coffee."

"Just a little ways up ahead now. You can see the station when we top the next rise."

As they reached the crest of the rise, Patches began yelling "yay-hoo" even before Longarm saw lights ahead. His wild calls brought results quickly; lights showed ahead, and as the stage careened down the slope and drew closer to the station, the black, shadowy figures of men showed against the glowing lanterns. They were soon close enough for Longarm to see the stage station, a raw wood shanty that stood beside a pole corral in which several horses were standing. Patches hauled back on the reins. The stage slowed to a halt and he set the brake and swung to the ground. Longarm dropped from the seat on his side of the stage.

"You folks can git coffee and hot biscuits inside,"

Patches announced. "Conveniences behind the station. The lady goes first, you men can wait. We won't be pulling out for ten or fifteen minutes, so there ain't no hurry."

Two men were leading a fresh team from the corral to replace the horses that had drawn the stage from the railhead. Longarm watched them for a moment, then walked leisurely to the station. Inside the low-ceilinged shanty, the air was hot and laden with the odors of stale bacon grease, sweat, and horse manure. A hollow-faced woman with graying, straggly hair, and dressed in a wrinkled, shapeless wrapper, was handing out cups of coffee and molasses-smeared biscuits from a rickety, unpainted table at the back of the room.

Longarm took his place in line and waited his turn to be served, paid the dime the woman requested for his coffee and biscuit, and went back outside where he could breathe more freely. The fresh team had already been hitched up, but he saw Patches busy doing something to the stage and walked over to look. The driver was removing the back of the middle seat and fitting the two pieces to span the gap between the front and rear seats. He looked up and saw Longarm.

"Give ever'body but you and me a chance to stretch out and grab a little shut-eye," he explained. "These Celerity Wagons don't quite come up to a feather bed, but a fellow can doze where the road ain't too damn rough."

"I guess it's better'n sitting up," Longarm said, eyeing the bare, uneven boards dubiously. "But I'll keep on riding up by you, if it's all the same."

"If you change your mind, you can git down and nap after we leave the Tombstone Junction stop. There'll be a lot of 'em get off there to wait for the local stage south."

Longarm nodded. "Sure. We'll see how I feel then."

"Excuse me," a woman's voice said. Both Longarm and Patches turned around. The woman in widow's weeds had come up behind them. They could not see her face through the dark veil that shrouded it, but her voice sounded troubled. She said, "Can I talk with you a minute, driver?"

"Name's Patches, ma'am. Talk away."

She looked at Longarm and said, "I mean, in private."

"He's a law officer, ma'am," Patches explained. "I don't guess it'd hurt for him to stay, if you don't mind. If you got some kind of trouble, maybe he can even help you."

"Well . . ." She hesitated for a moment, then blurted, "It's that man sitting by me, Mr. Patches! He keeps . . . well, it's awfully dark in there, and he keeps trying to get his hand up under my dress. And he says things, ugly things, whispers to me so soft the others can't hear him. I thought if you talked to him, or maybe changed my seat or something . . ."

"Just a minute, ma'am," Longarm said. "First off, you mind telling me your name?"

"Moore. Sarah Moore."

"My name's Long, Mrs. Moore. Now, excuse me if I ask you this, but you didn't lead this fellow on any, did you?"

"I most certainly did not!" she snapped. "I kept pushing him away. I . . . I didn't want to stir up trouble in the coach."

"It'd only have been trouble for him, most likely," Longarm told her. "But I can see it would've put you in a sort of embarrassing position." He thought for a moment, then said, "I'll tell you what. Let's you and me walk back to the station and stand outside the door till he comes out. I'll have a talk with him, and I don't imagine he'll bother you the rest of the trip when I get through with him."

"You want me to call the passengers out about the time you get to the door?" Patches asked. "Maybe you can nab him easier if ever'body comes through the door in a hurry."

"Good idea," Longarm said. He took the woman's

223

arm. "You just come along now, and let's see what happens."

Two or three of the passengers had already come out of the station by the time Longarm escorted the woman back to the door. Patches waited until they stopped, then yelled, "Board up now! We'll pull out soon as ever'body's on the coach!"

Standing in front of his companion so that she would not be seen at once by those coming through the door, Longarm waited for the tinhorn to appear. He grabbed the man by the collar as he passed and swung him around. The fellow's pale face was twisted angrily when he saw the woman standing behind Longarm. He said, "Whatever this woman's told you about me is a lie!"

"How'd you know she told me anything about you?" Longarm asked him. "Seems to me you just convicted yourself of what she's accusing you of doing."

"She invited me to feel her!"

"I did not!" she snapped. "I kept trying to push you away!"

"She's lying!" the tinhorn insisted.

"Shut up!" Longarm commanded. "Now, just so you won't think I'm just butting in, I'm a deputy U.S. marshal, and I'm—"

Before Longarm could finish, the man twisted around, and his sudden move took Longarm by surprise. He'd had only a loose grip on the tinhorn's collar, and he felt the cloth sliding through his fingers before he could tighten them.

Just in time, Longarm saw the man stretching his left hand across his body, reaching for his right forearm as he completed his turn. With a quick, sharp kick, Longarm booted the tinhorn's right arm upward. There was a flat-sounding explosion, and the slug from the tinhorn's sleeve gun cut the air above Longarm's head and thudded harmlessly into the wall of the stage station. Behind him, Longarm heard the woman's belated scream as he immobilized the man by twisting an arm behind his back.